FEAST
OF THE
SIN
EATER

AN EZEKIEL CRANE NOVEL

J. KENT HOLLOWAY

CHARADE
MEDIA

Feast of the Sin Eater

Copyright © 2023 by J. Kent Holloway

ISBN: 978-1-0882-9192-4

Charade Media, LLC
www.charadebooks.com

To Granny Morrow, whose use of mountain medicine (and tobacco juice) on me as a young boy inspired Ezekiel Crane and the mysteries he solves.

CHAPTER
ONE

The Koep Farm
June 19
2:34 AM

The wage of sin is death and no one in Boone Creek, Kentucky knew that better than the Sin-Eater. In fact, as he lay there in his bed, coughing up chunks of his own tar-stained lungs and blood, gasping for even the slightest trace of breathable air, he knew it was finally time to pay up himself. It was also time to pass on the torch to someone else, while simultaneously absolving him of the countless sins he'd consumed for the last fifty-two years.

With tired, weary eyes, he looked over at the one he'd chosen to replace him, now standing at his bedside.

"Do you understand what I've told you, boy?" the Sin-Eater asked.

His apprentice nodded.

He was young, but no younger than the Sin-Eater when he'd first taken up the sacred task. At the time, he'd simply been Isaac

Koep, son of Joseph Koep, and heir to a long line of Sin-Eaters dating back to the Old Country.

The day he'd taken up the mantle had been a trying day for Koep. The imminent loss of his father, lying on his own deathbed —one quite similar to the hand-crafted oak bed Isaac now lay upon. His father had called to him, ignoring his four older brothers, and had told him of his mission. The mission of the Sin-Eater. Since Isaac and his wife, Gladys, had not been able to have children of their own, he'd spent the last few months—since being diagnosed with Black Lung—searching for a suitable replacement. And he was quite proud of the choice he'd made.

"The mantle of the Sin-Eater has been passed down in my family from father to son for goin' on nine generations...from back when we lived in Germany." The Sin-Eater, Isaac Koep, coughed. More unrecognizable chunks of tissue mixed with rust-colored goo spewed from his mouth to coat the wool blankets that worked to keep his fever down. He should have known this was how his life wound end. Thirty years of working in the dust-filled recesses of the Tegalta coal mines would do this to anyone. "I ain't got no young 'uns. But I've watched you from a very, very young age. I couldn't imagine anyone better suited to take over my duties as the Sin-Eater than you."

"Thank you, sir," the apprentice said with a tilt of his head. "I won't let you down."

The bedroom door opened, and the Sin-Eater's wife entered, carrying a tray of food and drink. Steam swirled from a bowl of soup, rising up to the ceiling and permeating the room in a rich aroma of chicken broth and herbs. Tears ran down her cheeks as she dutifully brought the victuals over to his bedside, and laid them on the edge of the mattress. Once she was satisfied that the tray was stable, she stood, and walked over to the other side of the bed while wiping away the tears with the hem of her apron.

"Oh, no need for that, Gladys," the Sin-Eater said, taking her hands into his and giving them a reassuring squeeze. "All will be well soon. Now, get." He motioned for the door. "I love you, and am thankful for the years we've had together. But this here's for the men only." More coughing. "Still have to charge the boy here with his mission. The ritual's the key. Without it, I'm doomed to walk the earth—a mindless shade—forever. Can't do the ritual with women folk muckin' about."

He pulled her hand to his lips and kissed it gently, before offering her one last squeeze. She squeezed back, bent down and kissed him on the forehead, then turned around and walked out the door without another word.

"You wouldn't prefer her to be with you…I mean, here at the last?" the apprentice asked, stroking the light stubble of his sprouting beard. "She's your wife after all and…"

"Never you mind about that, boy. We're runnin' out of time." He wheezed for breath, a sensation that felt like salt grinding against sandpaper. "The ritual. Gotta complete the ritual. Fast."

Without another word, the old Sin-Eater reached into his covers and produced a tattered burlap sack before handing it to his young charge. "Put this on."

The man took the sack and slipped it over his head. He then swiveled the sack around on his head until he found the eye and mouth holes cut into it, and looked down at the old man for further instructions.

"Good," Isaac said. "From now on, you wear that whenever you're called. Whenever you are carryin' out yer duties. No one must know who you are. Guard your name tightly, son. Guard it tight."

"How come? Why don't no one around here know who the Sin-Eater is? Ain't it an honor to be chosen? Shouldn't the Sin-Eater be lauded as a hero?"

The Sin-Eater tried to laugh, but nearly choked on the effort. "You'd think, wouldn't you, boy? After all, we are tasked with eatin' the sins of the dead. Absolving them of their transgressions, and keepin' their spirits from runnin' amok in the streets of the Living. A heroic charge if ever there was one, I'd say." He reached over to his nightstand, and withdrew the oxygen mask hanging on its corner. Bringing the mask to his face, he took three deep breaths before lowering it and speaking again. "But think about what it is we're doin'. We're physically takin' other people's sins—many of them too horrible to name out loud—into ourselves. We're heapin' their condemnation onto ourselves. Not only their sins, but those who came long before and were absolved from Sin-Eaters in the past. Nah. To the people out there, we're unclean. Not evil, mind you. But unclean and wicked by our very nature."

"So the mask makes sure no one out there will treat me bad just because of my callin'."

The old man smiled. "Exactly. Everyone wants the Sin-Eater when the time comes, but no one wants to admit they want us. And no one definitely wants to be associated with us. So, we keep our identities hidden by the scarecrow mask you're wearin' now."

The youth nodded. "Okay. Now what? What do I do now?"

Isaac Koep took another puff from the oxygen tank and nodded toward the food tray. "Lay that here on my chest."

He did as the older man told him, and waited.

"Now, repeat these words," the Sin-Eater whispered. His throat was raw, making it difficult to speak now. "I give easement and rest now to thee, dear man."

"I give easement and rest now to thee, dear man."

"Come not down the lanes or in our meadows."

His protégé continued. "Come not down the lanes or in our meadows."

Isaac nodded, smiling. "And for thy peace, I pawn my own soul. Amen."

"And for thy peace, I pawn my own soul." The younger man looked down at his mentor; his face grave. "Amen."

"Good," the Sin-Eater said before gesturing to the bowl of

soup and bread resting on his chest. "Now, eat of the bread and soup. Drink of the wine. Consume it all, and with it, you will be drawing my own sin, as well as those I've consumed over the years, into yourself."

The apprentice grasped the wooden spoon from the now-cooling soup, and lifted it to his lips before stopping. A tremor—almost a seizure—seemed to course down the young man's limbs for a moment, then a strange gleam shimmered in his eyes from beneath the hood.

"Mr. Koep," he said. His voice seemed different somehow, as if coming from a great distance. It was colder too. Ice cold. Like the voice of the dead.

The old man glanced up. His eyes were weakening. Already, his protege's face was growing dim. Harder to see. Time was running short.

"What happens if I don't eat of the food? I mean, before the person dies?"

The question stopped Koep cold. He'd all but predicted the answer to that very question about a month ago at Esther Crane's home when she was attending to the needs of those struck down by the Leechers.

He cleared his throat, focusing his drifting mind to give the best answer he could think of. "All would not be lost," he said. "You can still absolve their sins within three days of the person's death."

"And if I don't get to them within three days?"

The Sin-Eater shivered. He wasn't sure if it was from the icy fingers of Death fast approaching, or fear of the direction the young man's questions were taking.

"Legend says, boy, that after three days, a person's spirit departs." His body was now trembling underneath his sheets. "Forced to wander the earth aimlessly 'til the trumpets sound."

The apprentice seemed to mull that over for a moment. He blew on the cooling soup, then raised the spoon once more, but stopped unexpectedly. "Since you started teachin' me...since you chose me to be the next Sin-Eater...I've been studyin' hard."

"Good." Isaac eyed the still uneaten food resting on his chest; his eyes silently pleading for the boy to complete his sacred task. Time was, indeed, running out.

"And among my studyin', I talked to my Mother-Bride about it all. And she told me a story I found a might interestin'."

Mother-Bride? What's he talking about?

The protege placed the spoon back into the soup and leaned in to stare the older man in the eyes. "Seems if a Sin-Eater forgoes his callin'...lets these ingrate people die without absolution...that he, if'n he knows what he's doin', can actually feed on those wanderin' spirits instead of their sins."

Isaac's blood went cold. He opened his mouth to protest, but the young man's hand came down fast across his lips, preventing him from crying out.

"From what I was told, they call it the Ghostfeast. And it can make a Sin-Eater mighty powerful."

The Sin-Eater grabbed hold of his apprentice's wrists, struggling to throw him off. To cry out to his wife for assistance, but his grip held firm. The young man smiled at him from underneath the mouth hole of his mask. A chilling, maniacal smile. Then, he tipped the tray off the bed with a flip of his wrist. The bowl clattered to the hardwood floor, its contents splashing out across the man's leather boots.

"I don't think I'm hungry right now." He kicked at the pooling soup on the floor. "Think I'll save mine for later. Maybe in about four days or so."

Isaac tried to scream under the boy's strong hand, but he no longer had any air left in which to use. As he struggled, his apprentice reached around the old man's head, and slowly withdrew one of the pillows.

"I do appreciate your trust in me though." The apprentice raised the pillow above Isaac's head. "Not many people in this world believed in me. Not many ever gave me a chance to make anythin' of my life…ya know, 'cause of who my kin is and all. But you did. You believed in me." He laughed. "Of course, I suppose, you don't really know the 'real' me though. Can't trust who you can't see. But I'll take what I can get. So, I'll forever be grateful to you for that."

Then, without another word, the Sin-Eater lowered the pillow across Isaac Koep's face and held it in place. Two minutes later, the man's struggles were over. A minute and a half after that, the Sin-Eater walked out of the bedroom, met Gladys Koep at the foot of the stairs and sent her quickly to catch up with her husband in the spirit world.

CHAPTER
TWO

Mel Jackson Residence
Boone Creek, Kentucky
December 18
3:45 PM

The moment Ezekiel Crane stepped through the front door of Melvin Jackson's rundown mobile home, he knew they had another murder on their hands. Without even seeing the body, he knew exactly what he'd find once he made his way to the back bedroom. Blood. Lots and lots of blood. The floor and walls would be coated with it. He'd also see the same cryptic German phrase scrawled with a finger in the canvas of blood. They did, indeed, have a serial killer running rampant in Boone Creek, and if he wasn't mistaken, that wasn't even the bad news.

"Crane! Glad you're here. Thank you for comin' so quickly!"

Crane's train of thought now broken, he looked up to see the near-emaciated figure of Sheriff Gerald Slate coming toward him from the back of the house. The normally sour-faced sheriff gave an appreciative smile as he extended a hand to him.

Crane accepted the hand and gave it a firm shake. "I must

admit, Sheriff, I'm still not quite used to being treated so cordially at these scenes." He gave a slight nod of appreciation, then began slipping on a pair of latex gloves.

"Well, you don't have to worry none about that superstitious garbage from me. You're the duly elected coroner of Jasper County now..."

"Not a difficult feat when no one had the courage to run against me."

"That's their own fault. You know I ain't from around these parts," Slate said. "Never fell for all that 'cursed' mumbo jumbo they spew about you. Far as I'm concerned, yer the most qualified coroner I've ever worked with, and I'll tell that to anyone who asks."

Crane offered a smile at that, but pondered just how different the sheriff's attitude toward him was back in April during his investigation into the Kindred, and the appearance of the Leechers. At the time, Slate was under the thumb of a doctor claiming to be from the Centers for Disease Control investigating the strange resurrections of seven of Boone Creek's citizens. Turned out, Dr. Maher was not actually from the CDC, and Slate had failed to check her credentials. When Crane had found out the truth, he'd confronted Slate about it, and the sheriff's tune had changed almost immediately. From that moment forward, he treated Crane like a long lost chum.

"Thank you for that, Sheriff." He nodded toward the back of the house. "Now if you'd please show me to the body so I can get to work?"

"Oh. Oh, yeah." The sheriff pulled down the rim of his Smokey Bear hat, turned around, and started ushering Crane to the back. "Call came in from Alice Granger. She came by to bring old man Jackson supper, as is her custom since his wife, Martha, passed away back in October. Mel's been pretty ill lately. End stage liver disease. Wasn't expected to live but a few more days —a week at the most—according to Alice, so she's been making sure he eats proper, and gets enough fluids other than moonshine.

"When she got here, the house was secure, but Alice has a pass key. When Mel didn't come to the door when she knocked, she figured he was sleepin' one off. Used the key to let herself in, then searched the house for him."

Crane followed close behind, taking in the sheriff's narrative, then paused at the sound of a raven cawing. He glanced up to find the source of the noise perched on the door leading into the back bedroom. A raven as black as pitch; its gleaming eyes glaring accusingly at him. In response, he rolled his eyes, and waved his hand—forcing the ephemeral bird to disappear in a haze of smoke and brimstone. Of course, no one else at the crime scene had seen it. They couldn't. The Raven was Crane's own burden to bear. A harbinger of the dead. And it told him of something else he would find when he entered the actual crime scene.

The shade of Mel Jackson.

"As you'll see, this one is pretty much the same as the others." Slate was still talking when he stopped at the bedroom door, and gestured for Crane to enter the murder room. "Maybe even messier than the rest. Definitely more violent." The sheriff shook his head. "Crane, I don't know how much longer I can keep this quiet. The Feds need to be called for murders like this."

"And as I've already stated, the Federal Bureau of Investigation is sadly unprepared for what we're dealing with."

He reached into the messenger bag hanging at his waist, and withdrew a camera before walking past Slate and stepping into the room. He'd been right. The first thing he saw upon entering was the haggard, weary specter of Mel Jackson, standing directly over his own body. His mouth was twisted in a grimace of abject sorrow, and Crane imagined that if he was able to hear such things, his ears would be overcome by the gut-wrenching wail of the dead man's own grief. He counted it a blessing that the curse that allowed him to see the lingering dead had been kind enough to forego such auditory torment.

After a few seconds, the shade turned to look at Crane—his mouth still pantomiming the silent cries of the recently deceased —and pointed down at his body.

Crane made no attempt to communicate back. Shades, after all, had only minimal comprehension. They were not, as many people mistakenly believed, ghosts of the departed. They only retained a very small portion of their former personalities, and any attempt they might make to 'communicate' was merely a product of habit from their former lives and nothing else.

There was, in Crane's experience, no such thing as 'ghosts' in the conventional sense. As the Good Book says, "Absence from the body is presence with the Lord." Once a person died, their spirit immediately moved on to their final destination. But every once in a while—as in the case of extremely violent deaths—an echo of their former selves might still linger. Typically, they were like ghost images on a TV with bad reception, mindlessly going through the mundane routine of their day to day former lives.

Mel's obvious distress over seeing his mutilated corpse on the floor of his bedroom would soon fade, and he would join the hundred and ninety-four other shades that continuously haunted Ezekiel Crane.

"What do ya think?" Slate asked, breaking his train of thought. The sheriff remained outside the bedroom, a handkerchief covering his nose and mouth. He obviously had no desire to endure the carnage again.

For the first time since entering the room, Crane looked down at the body. The man's once chocolate-colored skin now seemed gray and mottled, drained of most of his blood. Dark webs of green-hued veins tattooed his entire body where he was beginning to decompose. His face was swollen; his eyes clenched shut with his expanding cheeks and his engorged tongue now protruding from his lips.

Crane paused, feeling the air around him. "Is the heater on?"

Slate grunted an affirmative. "Thermostat's down the hall. It's set at seventy-eight degrees."

"Looks like he's been dead about three days then." He looked up at the ceiling to find a vent almost directly overhead. "Maybe two. The heat's blowing directly on top of him." Snapping a series of photos first, Crane walked through the still-screaming shade of the dead man, and crouched down to the left of his torso. With his gloved hands, he nudged open Mel Jackson's pajama shirt, and took in the multitude of stab wounds that perforated his chest and abdomen. "Yep. Looks like the same suspect. Extremely aggressive. Overkill, really. But looks also as if he's intentionally trying to be more violent than he needs."

"Maybe he's just hopped up on meth or somethin'."

Crane shook his head. "I don't think so." He leaned in for a closer look at the wounds. Though there were one or two that appeared chaotic and haphazardly placed, the majority of the stabs seemed uniform. Evenly spaced. Parallel and perpendicular to one another. "This seems almost ritualistic. He gets precise in his stabbing, probably once his victim is unconscious." Crane stood, and moved over to the bed. A pool of crimson spattered the pillow and sheets, spraying out in all directions. "Mel was sleeping. The suspect entered without waking him, and struck him over the head with something heavy." He glanced around the room, but couldn't locate the cudgel. Satisfied it wasn't in the room, he continued surveying the blood patterns, and continued his scene reconstruction for the sheriff's benefit. "The impact awakened the old man, but he was dazed. Slipped out of the bed, and that's when the killer began stabbing him. He dropped to the floor, incapacitated, and then his attacker began to take his sweet time."

Crane took several more photographs of the bed, the blood patterns, and the entire room in relation to the body. He then turned his attention to the walls. It was what he dreaded the most upon entering. The bedroom itself was tiny. No more than ten foot squared, and the walls—just as all the other scenes before it—looked as though the killer had used a paint roller to spread the victim's blood in a thick even coat that covered four feet across on each surface. And in the middle of each blood-stained canvas, the all too familiar words were scrawled in thin, thorny letters: *Vorsicht, die Geistesser*.

German for 'Beware the Eaters of Ghosts'.

Crane sighed as he studied the words.

The Eaters of Ghosts.

A not-so-subtle reference to the Ghostfeast.

The Willow Hag had warned him it was coming, back in April, but he'd never imagined it would arrive so soon. And truth be told, he was still uncertain as to its meaning. The lore of the Ghostfeast was shrouded in the shadows of his people. Granny had referred to it a few times when she was alive, but she'd never bothered to teach him what she knew about it. All he knew was that it was a horror that occurred every so many generations, and that those who fall prey to it were doomed—their souls lost forever in a never ending abyss.

The Ghostfeast, legend said, was a sacrifice to feed the devil in order to keep him from strutting back into a town he'd once had a firm grip on. That was the extent of Ezekiel Crane's knowledge of the legend, and that unnerved him more than anything the carnage in this current murder room could ever do.

"Crane?" He turned to see Sheriff Slate glancing around the corner of the hallway. "You okay? Ya kinda spaced out there for a minute."

Crane gave a polite nod, and began walking toward the door. "I've seen all I need to at the moment." He stepped into the hallway and drew in a deep breath. The shade of Mel Jackson stood next to him now. "My body removal crew is outside. They'll remove Mr. Jackson, and take him to the office, and I'll conduct the autopsy first thing tomorrow."

"And what should we do until you've done that?"

Before Crane could answer, there was a commotion outside among the deputies guarding the scene. He looked out the screened front door to see a blood-soaked young man with a shaved head and wearing an EMT uniform struggling with the police to get into the scene.

"Let me in, you pigs! I wanna give that S.O.B. a piece of my mind!" When the two cops finally managed to push the man back, he glanced up to see Crane staring at him from the doorway. "You! This is your fault! All of this is your freakin' fault! You're to blame for all of this...everything bad that happens in this town can all be traced back to you!" He pointed at Crane. "I swear to God, you'll get what's comin' to you, Crane. I swear it!"

Three more deputies appeared from the crowd and managed to lead the irate man away from the crime scene. The paramedic cursed incessantly as they led him to his rescue unit.

"Who was that?" Crane asked.

"You don't know?"

"Should I?"

"From the way he was cussin' you, I figured he was a friend of yours."

"As I said, it's par for the course in this town. So, who is he? Why was he covered in blood?"

Sheriff Slate pulled out his notepad from his pocket and flipped through the pages. "According to my notes, he's Eugene Coleman. An EMT with Fire-Rescue and the first responding medic to the scene."

Crane nodded. "What's his relationship to Melvin?"

"None, that I know of. As far as I know, he's just the paramedic who showed up to render aid to him. I guess he just really really doesn't like you very much." The sheriff cleared his throat. "But you never answered my question."

"And that was?"

"What should we do now until you finish the autopsy?"

"You a religious man, Sheriff?"

"From time to time."

Crane turned to look the man square in the eyes. "Then I suggest you use your time to pray." He moved toward the front door, opened it, and turned back to the sheriff. "Because before this is over, we'll need all the help we can get."

He strode out of the door with the shade of Melvin Jackson and his Raven shadow tailing close behind.

CHAPTER
THREE

Mel Jackson Residence
December 18
4:25 PM

A crowd had gathered outside the property of Mel Jackson once news of the murder had spread. Concerned citizens, insatiable gossips, and town busybodies lined themselves along the crime scene tape, wrapped up in their winter coats while hugging their chests tight to fend off the crisp December air. Many stood on tiptoes to catch even the slightest glimpse of the action most only saw on overly dramatic forensic crime shows.

A handful of the less tactful onlookers had backed their pickups as close to the yellow tape as possible—their oversized tires churning up Mel Jackson's already unkempt yard—and set up lawn chairs in the beds, along with Styrofoam coolers filled with beer to enjoy the spectacle. More than a handful of them sported bright red Santa hats and elf-ear muffs, unconcerned over their macabre disrespectful display of Christmas cheer at such a somber occasion.

Of course, there were actual mourners for the deceased as

well. A small cadre of Jackson's family huddled on the other side of the property, offering comfort and support to one another, while simultaneously cursing the gawkers who'd been drawn to the crime scene like vultures circling a decomposing meal.

The Sin-Eater watched all this in fascination. Standing unnoticed within the crowd of onlookers, he studied all those around him with careful, detailed precision. The grievers had caught his attention first. The mournful wails of the women had captivated him. The way they screamed up at the heavens on wobbly rubbery legs; arms splayed into the air with warbling cries of anguish. Cries obviously designed to draw attention to themselves in their woeful time of grief.

The Sin-Eater would have laughed at the sight if it wouldn't have threatened to reveal his presence there. Such thinly veiled attempts to garner sympathy were indeed laughable, and the men by their sides were eating it up. Wrapping their arms around the women so nobly. Patting their shoulders. Silently providing literal shoulders to cry on.

Yes. It was laughable, indeed.

Then, of course, there were the spectators. Emotional carrion feeders drawn to feast on the tragedy of others to make themselves feel strong. Superior. They'd turned the murder of the decrepit old drunk into a sporting event. As deputies flitted back and forth from their cars to the crime scene vans, and then back to the house, the crowd's eyes followed every step. It was like a macabre tennis match to them. Back and forth, back and forth. Their heads would turn with each new trace of movement from the other side of the tape.

That is, until Ezekiel Crane walked out of the murder house, snapping off his latex gloves in an unconscious flourish. The moment he made an appearance, the crowd grew uncharacteristically silent. To each person, eyes instantly were downcast, as if no one dared look the man directly in the face lest they turn to stone.

The Sin-Eater could understand their fear. Of everyone in Boone Creek trying to stop him, Crane was the most formidable of them all. He'd experienced firsthand the harsh magic the man employed, and knew better than to underestimate his capabilities.

He understood the crowd's loathing for the man, as well. No one despised Ezekiel Crane more than the Sin-Eater. No one had more reason to revile him. In part, it was this man that caused him to become the Sin-Eater in the first place. And, despite the admonitions of his *Sponsa-Mater*, he would do all within his power to break the enigmatic Crane before he was finished.

As the tall, powerfully-built man with sandy blond hair and goatee strode across the lawn to his pickup truck, the Sin-Eater followed his every move. Watched each subtle ripple of muscle with every graceful step. His jaws clinched tight at the sight of the man he hated with all his soul. He willed away the visceral growl burning in his throat as Crane opened the door to his pickup and slid into the driver's seat before starting up the engine and driving away.

Crane's day was indeed coming. But first, the Sin-Eater would continue to feast.

CHAPTER
FOUR

County Road 43
Ryder Bluff
December 18
4:38 PM

E zekiel Crane focused on the winding mountain road, as he drove straight for his home on Ryder Bluff. The sun had already dropped below the mountain, casting the road in a miasma of purple and orange-hued shadows. The headlights of his Ford F-450 pickup had come on automatically, but the cool evening air mixed with the warmer air from the valley had already churned up enough fog to make going difficult—especially in his state of mind.

"So, it's the same guy?" The question came from his brother, Josiah Crane, who now sat in the passenger's seat of his truck. "This Eater of Ghosts guy?"

Crane nodded, not wanting to be drawn into a lengthy conversation about the killer or what he represented. He just didn't have enough answers to begin speculating at the moment.

"And you think he's building up for this...this Ghostfeast thing?"

There were times that Ezekiel Crane enthusiastically preferred the company of the Dead to living beings. At least they were silent. Most of the time, anyway.

He nodded again.

"Are you going to talk to me, brother? Or are you just going to sulk until we get home?"

"My apologies." Crane winced when he realized the apology sounded a bit more biting than he'd intended. After all his brother had been through, he certainly didn't deserve such behavior. "I'm afraid I'm just in no mood for any kind of discourse at the moment, Josiah."

It was his brother's turn to nod. "I can understand that. You're worried."

"Indeed I am." He glanced over at Josiah and offered him the slightest trace of a smile. "But not just about the Ghostfeast. A great deal weighs on my mind at the moment, and I'm afraid there's little relief in sight."

The trees rushed past them as Crane continued to negotiate the treacherously narrow road.

"You mean about Ms. Brennan?"

"To start, yes. Ms. Kili shows no signs of overcoming her catatonic state any time soon, and that troubles me. This is not the same type of fit that you've endured all these years. She's not in a coma. She's awake. Alert at times. But remains unable to communicate in any way. Whatever the Willow Hag did to her, it's proving far beyond my skill to remedy."

His brother seemed to consider that for a few minutes, then shrugged. "But that's not the only thing that's bothering you either, is it?"

Crane glanced sideways at him while raising an eyebrow. "You're trying your best to lure me into discussing things I have no desire to talk about, aren't you?"

"I'm your little brother." He beamed. "It's what I do. I also want to help if I can."

"I'm afraid at the moment—with the foe we are facing—that might be a little too dangerous for you. I'm not sure how capable this guy is yet."

"You let me worry about that." He sighed. "Now spill. What else is eating at you, Zeke?"

Crane thought about it for a few moments, then cleared his throat. "The Kindred."

"What about them? Jael's taking care of them. She's got it handled."

"I'm not so sure." He held up his phone so his brother could read the text he'd received earlier that day. "Our sister's concerned. Of the original seven Kindred, three have already died under her care. Their cause of death is undetermined even now. Two others are wasting away—refusing to eat anything other than raw protein. Intravenous feeding doesn't seem to work."

"But they're not human. You said so yourself. Just mutated teratoma tumors supercharged with the One-Eyed Jack spores..."

"...and magic. Let's not forget the Willow Hag's magic."

Josiah nodded at this. "But the point is, these aren't true human beings. They're not the resurrected bodies of the original seven victims of One-Eyed Jack as people first thought. They've been even more catatonic than Ms. Brennan since April. Nothing of their souls hardly left. It's why their families agreed to..."

"Their families still have no idea what they are," Crane interrupted. "They still think they are indeed their loved ones returned to life, and I have no intention of letting them believe differently. It was my hope, however, to somehow find a way to return their souls—their spirits—to these new bodies if possible."

"But they're deteriorating faster than you imagined."

"Yes." Crane gripped the steering wheel tighter as he turned into their driveway. "And according to Jael's text, the two remaining strong Kindred seem to be mutating even more. Growing larger. More feral. From her description it sounds like they're becoming something very similar to what occurred with Cian Brennan last year, and that worries me more than you can possibly imagine." He put the truck in park, turned off the ignition, and slid out of the driver's seat onto the driveway with his brother close on his heels. "And that's why I'm so preoccupied, little brother. For the first time in my life, I'm truly beside myself with doubt. I'm lost...lost without..."

The two strode up the cobblestone walkway to the front porch.

"Without Granny," Josiah said.

Crane nodded.

"Have you given anymore thought to what we talked about? About using the Hag's own recipe...to bring Granny back from..."

"No!" Crane spun around on his brother, his eyes flashing with anger. "We won't even entertain such blasphemy again, do you hear me?"

But his brother was no longer there. Crane stood there, holding the front door open, and forced himself to take several deep breaths as he stared into the space his brother had only occupied seconds before. After a full minute, he let out another sigh, and walked into the house. Taking off his coat and hanging it on the coat rack in the foyer of the home, he began walking toward the back of the house until he came to the guest bedroom. The door was cracked open, and he gave a gentle tap with the knuckle of his index finger.

"Come in," came a soft-spoken feminine voice from the other side.

He nudged the door open, and stepped into the bedroom to

be greeted by a pretty blonde nurse sitting at the bedside of his comatose brother, Josiah.

"Did y'all have a good day today, Ezekiel?" Heather Cole, his brother's nurse and love of his life, asked as he entered the room. "He was gone for an awful long time. I was beginnin' to worry."

Besides Ezekiel Crane, Heather was the only person on earth —as far as he knew—capable of seeing and talking to his brother's astral body. In reality, she'd been the first, having been a nurse working for his sister while she searched for a pharmaceutical cure for his condition. During that time, they'd developed a rather unusual bond, which led to her being able to talk to him. A tragic love affair ensued, and in the desperate passion of two lovers, they'd devised a plan to track down and kill the Willow Hag, thinking it would release Josiah from his unnatural sleep.

Their plan had failed miserably, and a lot of people— including the brothers' grandmother, Esther Crane—had perished because of it. But she'd continued her ministries to the younger Crane even to this day, and Ezekiel was thankful for it.

"I do believe he enjoyed his day out, Ms. Heather," Crane said, with a slight bow. "Now, if you'll excuse me..."

"You want to see to Kili," she said. "She had a good day as well. Her eyes are moving more. Like she's actually lookin' around."

Crane smiled at the news, and turned toward the door. "Thank you, Ms. Heather...I'm not sure what I would do without your services."

He walked out the door, headed toward the other end of the house, and once again, tapped on a semi-closed door. This time, however, there was no response. And while none was expected, Crane would not allow himself to enter the room without announcing his presence first. After a pause, he gently pushed open the door, and looked into Kili Brennan's bedroom.

She sat in Granny's old rocking chair, absently moving back and forth while her eyes stared blankly out the window into sprawling woods behind the house. As usual, she was in a pair of men's silk pajamas with a quilt draped over her legs for warmth. She wore no slippers or socks, and even attempting to put some on her was one of the few actions that could create any emotional response in her catatonic state.

This, of course, unnerved Crane more than he let on. Asherah refused to wear shoes and socks because it hindered her connection to the earth and its magical properties. It was a lesson she'd learned from her mother, but reinforced by the Willow Hag, who also—when in human form—went without shoes. Kili's subconscious desire to follow suit concerned Crane that the Hag's hold on her was stronger than he'd originally believed possible.

"Ms. Kili," Crane said softly, his molasses-like voice as soothing as he could manage. "How are you feeling this evening?"

He moved around in front of her, pulling up a stool on which to sit. Her eyes followed his movements, just as Heather had suggested, which pleased him. He smiled to let her know this, but she simply remained as passive to his charms as she had since falling into her current state back in April.

A product of being marked by the Willow Hag.

Kili had been hexed with the same curse that plagued Ezekiel Crane. A Death curse, and one not easily dealt with by even the strongest of minds. Something had happened in the Dark Hollows on the day that Granny had died. Something that had shattered the pretty young redhead's psyche beyond anything Crane was able to cure. Which, of course, was the Willow Hag's plan all along. The ancient witch needed the sustenance of fractured minds in order to continue her extended existence, and Crane had no doubt this was the fate the Hag had in mind for his friend.

"I'll be hanged before I let that happen to you, Ms. Kili," Crane whispered, leaning forward to pat her hand resting above the quilt. "She'll not lay her gnarled hands upon a single strand of your head. Not again, anyway."

She blinked at him, then looked down at his hand, which still held her own. Then, she looked back up at him, and screamed. It was an ear-piercing shriek that rattled Crane's own teeth. Then, after a moment, she stopped, and for the first time in eight months, spoke.

"They're in agony, Crane. So much pain." She pulled her hand away from his and pointed out the window, toward the woods beyond. "Out there. Surrounded in a world of blue. So much misery. Anguish." Tears streamed down her face as she turned to look him in the eyes. Her face grew fierce. Her eyes blazed. "*Vorsicht*, Crane. *Vorsicht, die Geistesser*."

Beware, Crane. Beware the Eaters of Ghosts. It was perfect German, but to Crane's knowledge, Kili couldn't speak the language. But before he could question her about the strange proclamation, she leaned back in the rocking chair and stared once more off into space.

CHAPTER
FIVE

Bailey's Pub
December 18
8:47 PM

"When's this gonna stop? How many of us have to get cut to ribbons before that no-good sheriff does somethin'?" Eugene Coleman growled as he downed his fourth mug of beer in as many minutes. He was still wearing his blood-soaked EMT uniform, and no one dared to sit near him because of it. His shaking hands slammed the empty mug down on the oak table before he took a series of deep breaths to calm his nerves. "You guys didn't see Mel's body. I did. Ain't never seen nothin' like it in all my life."

"I'm sure he's doin' everythin' he can, Gene," Carl Bailey, the owner of Bailey's Pub said while wiping down the bar with a booze-stained rag. "He's a good man. I hear he was one heckuva law man up in Lexington in his day."

"And he's bein' stymied at every turn by that devil, Crane, the way I hear it." It was now Seth Thompson's turn to pipe into the conversation. As a young black man of only eighteen years of age, Seth was without a doubt one of the most angry and cynical souls Bailey had ever seen. "Refuses to let Slate call in the FBI. Won't let 'im even call the state police for help. Ya ask me, these murders got Crane's name written all over 'em."

The handful of patrons holed up in the town's one and only bar nodded and grunted their agreement over Seth's pronouncement. Bailey just continued to clean, wishing the guy would cool his jets before he caused any real trouble. It wasn't exactly legal to sell the kid alcohol and the bar owner found himself wishing he'd stop calling attention to himself whenever he was there. Then again, it wasn't exactly legal for Bailey to sell alcohol to anyone in Jasper County—it being legally 'dry' and all.

"Ya'll know I hate Crane as much as the next feller, but I don't think *he's* even capable of somethin' like this," Bailey said, hoping to calm his riled-up patrons. "I mean, he's capable, I reckon. But not really his style."

The door to the pub opened, letting a gust of winter chill sweep through the room, and a shapely pair of legs followed right behind. Every head in the place turned to see Candace Staples, dressed to kill with a form fitting silk dress that was just a little too low cut to be considered classy. In the flashing red and green Christmas lights inside the pub, it seemed almost sinful just to gaze on her.

The petite blonde pursed her lips as she took in the bar's occupants like a lioness in a room full of gazelles.

"My, oh, my," she said, walking directly toward the bar with long, luscious strides. How she wasn't freezing to death from the sudden drop in temperature after the sun set, no one knew. Even fewer cared. They only wanted to see her move some more. "What's a girl gotta do to get a drink around here?"

Instantly, nearly every hand in the bar shot up with silent nods to Bailey to indicate they'd happily take care of her tab.

She smiled, leaning back against the bar—her chest heaving

seductively as she giggled at their enthusiasm. "Well, no one can say chivalry's dead here in Boone Creek, now can they?"

Bailey placed a cold glass of beer next to her, and returned her smile. He'd known Candy for a long time. Pretty much all her life. While most of the womenfolk of Boone Creek despised her for her sexually promiscuous ways, the men all pretty much lauded her bravery for bucking the social norms, and embracing her feminine wiles as she had. Bailey proudly counted himself among the red-blooded men who appreciated her generous affections.

Like most, he'd been grieved terribly when she'd died last year. Not because he truly cared about her—he wasn't sure any of the men in town did—but rather, because it put a definite crimp in his otherwise dull 'social life'.

Now, she was considered one of the Kindred—one of a handful of One-Eyed Jack's victims who'd mysteriously returned to life several months after they'd been found dead. And while the others had amounted to little more than living vegetables, Candy seemed more alive—not to mention insatiable—than ever.

No, this was his bar's regulars' favorite time of the week... the moment Candace Staples came in and chose her conquest for the weekend. And everyone was poised to battle any of the others who seemed to be gaining the upper hand until she picked.

Bailey glanced over at Eugene Coleman. His eyes hadn't strayed from her from the moment she'd walked in. His right leg shook almost violently against the table leg and a near deluge of sweat glistened off the poor boy's brow.

Man, that kid's got it bad, Bailey thought, returning his attention to the countertop. *A few weekends as her chosen buck and he's a complete wreck...like a junkie lookin' for a fix*. The bar owner was almost embarrassed for the paramedic. *Was I ever that young and stupid?*

"So…what are you'uns talkin' about on this fine, December evening?" Candace asked, breaking Bailey's train of thought. She glided up onto the barstool, and made a show of taking her seat. "Did I hear somethin' about Ezekiel Crane when I was walkin' in?"

She took a long pull from her glass while eyeing each man over the rim with the slightest hint of a smile. Though no one wanted to take their eyes off her—somehow, she was even more alluring since she returned from the dead—the use of Crane's name seemed to break the testosterone-induced tension by giving them each a common enemy.

"Just talkin' about Mel Jackson's murder, Candy," Eugene Coleman mumbled. "As well as the others."

Candace scowled. "Yes. There was another one today, wasn't there?" She spoke the words so low they were almost inaudible, as if the very taste of them on her tongue disgusted her. "And you'uns think Ezekiel has somethin' to do with them, do you?"

There were a handful of noncommittal shrugs at the question, but Bailey nipped any serious discussion on the subject in the bud. "I think some of 'em are just kinda hopin' it's him, but we all know it ain't." He poured a mug of beer for himself and took a swig. "But somethin' mighty dark is happenin' around here. We've never had murders like these before, Candy. Brutal. Senseless. And even weirder, all five victims were near death's door as it was."

Seth Thompson perked up at this. "Ya know, yer right. I'd never thought about that before. But it all started with Gertrude Sterns. She had cancer of the brain. Doctors even gave up on treatin' her 'cause they said there weren't no hope. Put her in hospice care and gave her a week or two at most to live."

"Same with George Garnes too," Bailey continued. "Different illness, but he wasn't expected to live much longer either. And finally, there's poor Mel. A drunk if there ever was one, with a pickled liver that had all but given up the ghost." The barman shook his head. "Just makes no sense."

Candace seemed to mull this over for a while; her eyes narrowing as she stared into her now empty beer glass. "Given up the ghost, you say? Well, that is an interestin' turn of phrase." She set the glass down, then slipped off the stool like a stream of honey from a comb, twirled around, and laughed. "But I'm bored with talkin' about all this gruesome stuff. Little Jimmy's stayin' with his kin in the Gully for a few nights, so I'm here for some fun! Which one of you fellas are gonna accompany me home tonight?"

There was a flurry of movement the moment the question was spoken, and the entire room scrambled toward her in a sudden rush. Fists were thrown. Faces smashed. Beer bottles knocked across inebriated heads for the slimmest chance of garnering Candace Staples' affections that night.

All of this, of course, was done to the Willow Hag's utter delight.

CHAPTER
SIX

The Crane Homestead
December 18
9:45 PM

E zekiel Crane stepped out onto the back porch with his cell phone to his ear. "I'm not sure what's happening," he said. "You just need to get here as soon as possible. In case she needs you. I'm in the middle of something at the moment, and might not be able to offer the care she needs."

"So it's bad," came the voice on the other end of the line.

"Indeed. But nothing for you to fret over. For now, Ms. Kili should be your number one concern." He stepped off the porch, peering into the fog-shrouded woodline beyond.

"No problem. I'll be there by tomorrow afternoon at the latest."

"Good. Now, I've got something I need to check out. We'll see you tomorrow." He hung up the phone and stuffed it into his jacket pocket, then clicked on the Stinger flashlight he held in his other hand. "Now, let's take a look at what's gotten Ms. Kili so worked up."

As he stalked toward the woods, he pondered Kili's cryptic message. For the first time in ages, she'd seemed so lucid. So much like her old self, until she'd started spouting off in German. That one was new. Granted, it wasn't the first time she'd spoken in an unfamiliar tongue. Her sensitivity to the *Yunwi Tsunsdi*, the fae-folk who still call these mountains home, had caused her to speak ancient Gaelic when infected with the One-Eyed Jack spores last year. A language of her European bloodline, no doubt. But German. That was definitely a new one to Crane.

But her seemingly unearthly knowledge of the pain and suffering of some group of unknown victims wasn't surprising to him in the least. Once again, she was already capable of communicating with the Yunwi Tsunsdi. Probably others from the spirit world as well. And there was no telling what the Willow Hag's hex had done to augment her innate supernatural abilities.

So if she said there was something out in these woods—something causing pain to a great number of people—he had no reservations about searching for whatever dangers lurked there. The real question was where to begin?

Crane strode up to the edge of the woods, and stopped. He flicked off his flashlight and looked down at the ground, reading the roots that jutted up like tentacles of some great subterranean beast. There was only a half moon above, peeping in and out of the clouds, which made seeing anything in much detail problematic.

Normally, when searching for something, sight would hardly be necessary. He'd simply find a good sturdy stick, and use it as a dousing rod to trace whatever he was searching for. But despite what most people thought, divining was not magic. Crane's own theory relied mostly on physics, a strong will, and a hyper-observant mind. Truth was, divining was little more than connecting the electromagnetic field of one object with something akin to it. Want to find a person? Use a piece of the missing person's hair or skin. The hair, being part of the missing person molecularly, is attracted to its host on a subatomic level. Sharing the same electrical field, it simply guides the diviner to the larger source.

One could find water—one of the original purposes of dousing—in a similar fashion. Let a drop of water on the tip of a stick, and the electromagnetic connection will draw the diviner to a larger source of water.

The key to both these examples, however, was that the diviner knew precisely what they were looking for, and utilized an element similar to the original. In this case, Crane had no idea what he was looking for except that it was more than likely something of dark magic and violent toward its victims. A dowsing rod would not work if he didn't know what to look for, so he would need to employ a slightly different approach. One that Granny had used a few times in his life, but had been loath to teach Crane specifically.

Crouching down at the base of one of the trees, he reached into the messenger bag slung over one shoulder, and withdrew a piece of wood about a foot and a half long. He then pulled out a strip of cloth—torn from one of Kili Brennan's shirts—wrapped it around one end of the wood, then tied it with a woven lock of her hair. He placed the object on the ground in front of him, pulled out three old apothecary bottles, and popped them open before dropping dashes of each bottle's contents onto the cloth.

In folk magic, everything was a symbol that led to its own desired effect. The ingredients Crane had used had no magical properties in and of themselves. But combined together, with a focus of will on what he wanted from the talisman, and he should be able to locate the source of Kili's ranting with very little effort. Ground stinkweed, for finding all things putrid and repulsive. Iodine for locating someone injured. And finally, brimstone. Sulfur. For seeking the dead.

He picked up the piece of wood and lit the cloth with his father's old flint-and-naphta lighter. Instantly, the torch began to burn, emitting an otherworldly green and yellow column of smoke into the air. Closing his eyes, Crane muttered a silent prayer. He opened them again, and watched as the smoke began to drift through the woods in a southwest direction.

Without being able to apply pitch to the cloth—an act that would have rendered the 'magic' powerless—Crane knew he had only a short amount of time to find what he was searching for before the flame would go out. So, without looking back, he stepped into the darkness enveloping the forest ahead and began following the column of mystical smoke.

THE SIN-EATER WATCHED as Ezekiel Crane hefted the torch above his head and stepped into the woods. He struggled to contain the fit of laughter threatening to overwhelm him as the vexed seventh son of a seventh son flailed about in his desperate attempt to discover his true identity. An impossible feat, and one that would surely drive Crane mad with grief if the Sin-Eater didn't plan to eventually kill him himself.

He knew it was a risk being out here. Watching the man he hated so much. The location talisman Crane had crafted might easily lead him directly to where the Sin-Eater was hiding at that very moment. Though he doubted Crane would ever believe him to be the source of all the evil that had befallen the five that had been murdered—no, make that seven. No one had ever found the bodies of Koep and his wife.

But he couldn't help himself. He'd become quite the voyeur since taking on the mantel of the Sin-Eater. Watching people had become a way of life. Witnessing them commit the most sensuous delights—sinful vices. He'd watched them do all manner of things to one another, both pleasant and painful, and every once in a while even the latter for the sake of the former. Of course, he'd gotten the most pleasure watching as they grew sick. Weary. Deteriorating close to the point of death. That's when he liked to watch the most. Those final moments. Those days before the Reaper planned to come a'callin'. And that, of course, is precisely when he would switch from mere voyeur to active participant. A thief. That was when he'd steal the Reaper's victims right out from under his noseless face.

But he found the watching the most tantalizing aspect of his mission. There was no doubt about that. So, now, as he followed Ezekiel Crane through the bramble of winter-dead trees, his mouth practically salivated from the experience. He knew what the man would find just a few yards further. Knew how he would react when he put the pieces together. And the thought of it all was simply delicious to him.

In anticipation, he padded quietly through the detritus of dead leaves, sticks, and pine needles. His slight frame made moving with stealth far easier than the tall sandy-blonde man he was following, so he had little worry about announcing his presence to him. The animals—and other, darker things—that called these woods home, however, were another matter. It was better to watch where one stepped around here, and the Sin-Eater knew these woods well enough to avoid anything that would call attention to him.

The strange, eerie smoke wafting up from Crane's torch continued to lead him directly where he'd left the glass shards. Just a few more yards. Now, just a few feet. He watched as Crane stopped, seemed to sniff the air, then turn in his direction. The Sin-Eater stiffened. Refused to take in even a single breath.

Did he hear me? See me?

But no. The human heart, as corrupted as it is, was intuitive. It knew when it was near another such as itself, but the human mind is often at odds with it. The brain cannot always process what the heart knows. Crane sensed his presence, but he couldn't be sure. Couldn't articulate what his instincts were trying to tell him. Which was definitely a relief to the Sin-Eater, who exhaled quietly when he was certain he was safe.

After a brief moment, Crane turned back in the direction the smoke was leading him, and continued his journey deeper into the woods. Seventy-three feet later, he stopped again. Precisely where the Sin-Eater knew he would. He watched as Crane crouched down, examining something on the ground. Tentatively, he picked an object up that shimmered in a light blue glow in the torchlight.

The Sin-Eater smiled. He'd found them. The shards. And best of all, he'd know exactly what it meant. The Sin-Eater definitely enjoyed the act of voyeurism, and he resolved himself to satisfying this new fancy of his at every opportunity.

CHAPTER
SEVEN

Woods behind the Crane Homestead
December 18
10:30 PM

E zekiel Crane picked up the piece of broken glass and held it up to the light. It glowed with a blue radiance, and his heart sank at the very sight. Setting the piece down, he rummaged through the rest of the glass until he found a long slender sliver—a piece that had once been part of the neck of a royal blue bottle. He stroked the inside of the glass with his fore-finger, feeling a thick coat of lard grease along its surface, and confirming what he already knew.

Ghost bottles. Judging from the pile of glass, there'd been at least a half a dozen. He glanced up at the nearby branches to see six strands of twine blowing in the breeze. Twine that had once held the bottles to create a Bottle Tree—a hoodoo talisman designed to capture ghosts and evil spirits. The practitioner would take a number of blue bottles and coat the inside of the bottle necks with lard. They would then hang the bottles from the trees. It was believed that passing spirits, being attracted to the azure hue, would climb inside and become trapped by the lard.

Finding the bottles smashed meant that whoever hung them had set the spirits inside loose—but Crane feared they'd not been allowed to get too far once they'd regained their freedom.

Annoyed, Crane dropped the glass into the pile, and stood with a low growl. The killer had set these traps. Near Crane's own home. That could not be a coincidence, which meant whoever the killer was, they knew of the exact nature of Crane's death curse. Knew his land would be teeming with shades of varying degrees. A virtual buffet for anyone who knew the ancient rites of the Ghostfeast.

And even Crane didn't know those rites—which said something most peculiar about this particular serial killer. The fact that he knew them was one of the most telling clues as to his possible identity, and provided him with a direction in which to pursue come morning.

Digging into his bag again, he withdrew a camp shovel, unfolded it, and set to work digging a small hole near one of the trees. Once completed, he found a handful of smooth pebbles and placed them in a circle inside the hole before pouring a dash of honey and snuff in the center of the stones. He then carefully placed each shard of glass inside the hole, and covered it up once again.

"Spirits of the wood," he muttered while packing the dirt down tight with the flat of the shovel. "I remove these dangers from your presence. Know this. Know that I will find the one doing this, and see to it that his massacres are stopped. Wander not among the lanes and meadows in search of vengeance for the evil done to you. I offer a vow to you. I will end this."

He patted the soil down once more before standing to his full height.

Wander not among the lanes and meadows.

The phrase was familiar to him, but he could not recall where he'd heard them before. The phrase churned in his mind, trying to find purchase...something tangible to hold on to. For some reason, he knew it was important, but for the life of him, he couldn't figure out how.

Easy, Crane. It'll come to you.

Instead of dwelling on it, he packed up his gear, turned back toward home, and began making his way out of the dense woods with a heavy heart.

CHAPTER
EIGHT

Jasper County Sheriff's Office
Morriston, Kentucky
December 19
8:10 AM

Sheriff Gerald Slate had been expecting Kentucky State Trooper Cody Stratton sooner, once word of the murders had begun to spread, so he was a little out of sorts when the five foot five-inch police officer with a massive Napoleon complex strutted through the front door and walked straight back to his office without even waiting to be ushered in.

"Good to see you, Cody," Slate said, standing up from his desk and offering a hand.

The trooper removed his Smokey Bear hat, and placed it on the desk while ignoring the hand. "So when were you planning on letting us in on this little killin' spree you have around here, Sheriff?"

"Beg pardon, son?" Slate was not an overly proud man, but he was well known around the county for expecting the proper respect of others in the community—including other law enforcement officers. He especially didn't appreciate young, brash police officers, hardly old enough to shave, to waltz into his office unannounced and speak to him like some kind of underling. "First of all, I reckon as sheriff of Jasper County, it's pretty much my prerogative to handle my investigations any way I'd like. If that means I want to handle a few murders in house...without troublin' you fine folks on the state level...that's pretty much up to me, now isn't it."

Stratton had pretty much grown up in Jasper County, and unlike most state law enforcement officers, had been graced with being stationed near home. Though no one would dare say it out loud, it was pretty much a well known fact that his daddy—a state justice who hailed from the wrong side of the tracks in Bearsclaw Gully—had pulled some big time strings to ensure his son's choice of station. The kid, hardly old enough to drink legally, had only been out of the academy for two years, and already saw himself as the ultimate law in the area. Slate had no doubt the boy was looking to make a name for himself...with possible aspirations of holding political office one day. The last thing he needed in this murder investigation was a wannabe politician mucking it all up.

"Don't give me that crap, Sheriff. State has legal jurisdiction wherever we want," Stratton said. "And I want in. We can't leave a case this important to the likes of a corrupt Podunk law enforcement office like yours."

Slate gritted his teeth over the trooper's last comment. He considered himself a good cop. An honest cop. And while it was true he'd been persuaded a few times to look the other way by the likes of Noah McGuffin and his lieutenant, Asherah Richardson when it came to their drug operation, he'd never considered himself corrupt. Just a pragmatist. As long as McGuffin held control of the drugs in Jasper County, other crimes were kept naturally low by the criminal hierarchy. It was, in his opinion, an unfortunate truth, but sometimes it was necessary to grease the devil's wheels in towns like this for the greater good of the community. Corrupt or not, he could honestly say he'd never once accepted a bribe from anyone, nor prospered from any illegal activities committed by McGuffin's or Asherah's crew. It was a fact he was proud of, and one that his predecessor, John Tyler, could not say.

"Look here, Stratton," Slate growled. "I don't care about what the state can do. Don't care who your daddy is, either. I ain't about to let you walk into my office and bully me into..."

"I want in, Sheriff. You're gonna let me in." Stratton placed both palms on Slate's desk and leaned in. "This don't have to turn into a pissin' match. I won't even call in my superiors. But I want to be part of this investigation." His face softened, and he arched a single eyebrow. "Please."

Slate eyed him up and down as he leaned back in his chair, kicking his feet up on the desk.

"When you walked in here, I thought you wanted in this for yer own agenda," he said. "But that ain't it, is it? This case... there's somethin' about it for you. Right?"

Stratton remained silent; his Adam's apple undulating up and down his long, thin neck as he contemplated how to answer the question.

"If you want in, you're gonna have to convince me, son."

After another minute of silence, the state trooper glanced over his shoulder as if checking to ensure they were alone, then sat down in one of the chairs opposite the sheriff.

"Okay, fine." Another look behind him, then he turned to look at Slate once more. "But what I'm about to tell you don't leave this office."

The Crane Homestead
December 19
12:20 PM

THE VOICE WAS BACK. Amid the cacophony of the anguished screams filling her mind—cries of the dead all around her—and the wistful chatter and jubilance of the Yunwi Tsunsdi, the Voice had returned.

"*Kkkiiiiiiillllllliiiiiiiiiii Bbbrrrreeennnnaaaannnnn. Iiiiittttt'sss ttttii-iiimmmmeeee tttoooo wwwaaaakkkkeeee uuuupppp!*"

It was such a familiar voice, but it seemed to Kili as if she'd not heard it in centuries. Millennia even. She couldn't quite place where she'd heard it before, but she knew it was familiar to her. Knew it was something important.

But not more important than this. Not more important than what I'm doing at this exact moment.

She wasn't certain where she was, or what exactly she was doing at that moment. For some reason, her mind wouldn't focus. Wouldn't process. Wouldn't function. She knew her eyes were open. She knew she was seeing things with her eyes, but for the life of her, she couldn't understand what it was she was looking at.

And she was perfectly fine with that.

She was fine with that because wherever she was, and whatever she was doing, she was safe. Protected. The Willow Hag—whatever that was—couldn't get to her here. The horrible thing she had done—she had no idea what that was either—couldn't affect her here. She was safe. Content. Happy even.

Or she would be, if the Voice would leave her alone.

"*Iiiiitttt'sss tttiiiiimmmeee tttoooo ccchhhhooooosssseeee, Kkkkiiil-llliiii.*"

No, thank you. I don't have time to choose. I'm busy. Now please, leave me alone.

"*Ccchhhooosssseee.*"

Why was that Voice so familiar? Where had she heard it before? As horrible as the screams of those poor spirits out there in the blue field were, she much preferred them to this Voice. At the same time, there *was* a distinct sense of comfort found in the deep resonance of that Voice. The Voice that sounded, somehow, feline.

Don't be an idiot, Kili. Cats don't talk, so how can it sound feline?

But it did nonetheless. Very feline. Familiar and feline.

Her eyes were still open, so she tried to see the source of the familiar Voice. She looked. She strained to focus, but if she saw it, her mind wasn't about to tell her so. It was locked up tight to keep her safe. Safe from the Dead. Safe from a curse. Safe from…*her*?

Who's her?

An image flashed across her mind's eye. A portly older woman with thick brown hair and glasses. A kind face that always seemed to smile. A bright smile. A warm smile. In this mental picture, the woman was sitting across from her on a picnic table. Enough food to feed an army. People—important people—were talking. Talking about something equally important. Dead people…walking around. They were talking about that.

The scene shifted. Same kindly old woman standing before her in a dark forest. Only this time, she didn't look so kind. Her face was twisted. Seething. Hate-filled. Spittle flew from her mouth. Her eyes were bloodshot with rage.

Nope. No, Kili. Don't look at it. Let's think of something else.

"*Wwwaaaakkkkeeeeee   uuuuppppp,   Kkkkiiiilllliiii   Bbbrrreeennnaaannn. Aaanndd ccchhhooossseee.*"

Her eyes blinked. She'd felt that. Her eyes had actually just blinked.

No, no, no. Not now. I'm not ready yet.

"Kili, it's okay. I'm here now."

Wait. That's not the Voice. The feline voice. That's a different voice altogether, but just as familiar.

"I'm here," the new voice—the voice *not* inside her head—said. "Please wake up. Please just look at me."

She blinked again. She knew it. She'd blinked, and she couldn't stop herself. No matter how much she struggled against it, she was waking up. She was leaving her safe place. She was being spat out of her mind and into the world of Death. Into the world of the Willow Hag.

"Ccchhhoooossseee! Yyyyooouuu mmmuuussssttt."

That Voice. That familiar feline voice.

The Taily-po. It is the Taily-po.

"Kili, can you hear me?"

She felt something touch her hand. Something warm and gentle.

No. Don't touch me! Don't wake me!

She blinked again. And saw a face. It was blurry, but it was there. Bright blonde hair. Chiseled chin. Dashing smile spreading across a tanned face.

She knew that face.

"Kili?" the face asked.

Blink.

The face cleared up a bit more. More details. Green eyes that seemed to sparkle. Gleaming white teeth. The blonde hair was perfectly manicured. Very expensive.

No, I can't wake up. Not yet.

"Wwwaaakkkeeee!"

She did. No matter how much she struggled against it, she blinked one more time, and everything flashed into living, vivid color. Blinding color. Bright lights. Greens of the forest and blue of the sky beyond the window she was currently facing.

And beside her, sitting on a stool next to her rocking chair and grasping her hand for dear life, was Alex Davenport looking overjoyed.

CHAPTER
NINE

The Bookshelf
Boone Creek, Kentucky
December 19
12:30 PM

E zekiel Crane unlocked the door to his bookstore in downtown Boone Creek and stepped inside. After locking it again, he weaved his way through the shelves stacked with musty-smelling paperback romances and men's adventure novels toward the back of the store. His findings in the autopsy of Mel Jackson were weighing heavily on his mind and he found himself in dire need of seclusion to best articulate his thoughts.

Once at the back of the store, he unlocked another door leading to a spiral staircase to his upstairs private library. He took the stairs, two at a time, walked over to a set of bookshelves immediately to the right, and selected five leather-bound tomes on witchcraft, occult symbology, and vodou cosmology before taking a seat in the high-backed reading chair in the center of the room.

Laying four of the books on the table next to the chair, he

leaned back and riffled through the volumes unsuccessfully until he opened the book labeled *Esoteric Iconography of Occult Practices*. He eagerly flipped through its pages, searching for the sigil he was keen on researching.

His phone rang, interrupting his train of thought, but he ignored it. The caller ID told him it was Mr. Davenport, but at the moment, his research was the most important thing and could not allow for any distractions. Lives were at stake, and he'd already been far too lax in his investigation. He would not allow anyone else to die because of his own ignorance, if not incompetence.

He chastised himself again for his blatant oversight. He'd been such a fool not to have seen it before. The stab wounds. They'd not been the random cuts of a deranged mind at all, but something far more sinister. Even worse, the positioning of the wounds was identical on all five bodies. Precise. Intentional. Meticulous. And he'd not seen it. Not until observing them on the skin of a dark-colored black man.

After flipping through the pages for nearly a minute, he came across the image he'd been looking for. Two concentric circles— one much bigger than the other—with a Greek cross intersecting in the center. The cross's lines extended out from the larger circle and were tipped with hollow circles. Around both the circles and the cross were four arrows pointing counterclockwise.

The Kongo Cosmogram. Or, the Yowa Cross, depending on the intent.

It was a symbol employed by any number of African and African-American religions. Vodou. Palo Mayombe. Santeria. And even less structured practices such as hoodoo.

The symbol, according to the book Crane was reading, had multiple meanings and nearly an infinite number of interpretations. The cross first acted like the points of a compass—east, north, west, and south. The circles on the cross's tips also represented the rise and fall of the sun. Everything above the horizontal line represented life. Everything below represented the spirit world.

It was that last bit that meant more to Crane than anything else. He turned the page, scanning its contents for more about the lower half of the cosmogram. It appeared to be a representations of death, spirits, and the energies such spirits could provide a mortal man existing above the horizontal line in the Land of the Living.

The sudden rustle of feathers arrested Crane's attention. His head whipped up to see his black feathered companion perched on top of the bookshelves closest to the staircase, preening its wings with an almost contemptuous indifference. As Crane studied the bird, the sound of someone clearing their throat brought his gaze down from the bookcase and toward the staircase door.

"My, aren't you focused tonight, my love," said the caramel-skinned beauty standing in the doorway of his study. She leaned against the doorframe, allowing the dim lighting from the floor below to shine through her sheer, flower-print sundress, revealing the seductive curves concealed beneath. "So, are you going to offer me a drink or is chivalry really dead?"

Crane's eyes narrowed. "It's funny, Ash. I was just thinking about you, and voila, speak of the devil."

She glided into the study on bare feet—unaffected by the chill of the December evening—and moved over to him. Sidling up to his chair, she got down on her knees, caressed his thighs with her soft, delicate hands, then laid her head down in his lap. Her unusual emerald eyes looking up at him with faux innocence and delight.

"Really? You were thinking about me?"

He shifted his legs, and stood up from the chair. "I'm in no mood for your games, Asherah. I locked the door downstairs, but obviously you're too stubborn to take the hint. What are you doing here?"

Picking herself up off the floor, she pursed her lips in mock hurt. "I've just come to see my beau. Is that so wicked of me?"

She moved closer to him, laying a single hand on his chest. This time, however, he didn't back away. As he looked into her eyes, he saw something there he'd not seen in a long time. The hint of sincerity.

"I'm rather in the middle of something, Ash. I've no time for courting at the moment—whether I might like to or not."

"The killer. You're investigating the ghost killer, aren't you?" Her face was suddenly grave.

Crane cocked his head. "Why do you call him that? What do you know about the murders?"

She put her arms around his waist, and pulled tight against him. He didn't back away. Though he knew the dangers of growing too close to the woman who'd stolen his heart as a youth—dangers for both of them—he was tired of fighting his own attraction to her. Tired of the struggle. He knew the Death curse placed on him by the Willow Hag precluded any true emotional connection with her, but he had to admit, it felt good to be so close to her again after all this time.

"I've seen the signs," she said, resting her head against his chest. "Seen the broken shards—the ghost bottles—all throughout town. In particular, close to each of the victims' houses. Plus, you yourself told me what the *Mater-Matris* said about the coming Ghostfeast. Just put two and two together."

"And you know we can't put stock into anything the Willow Hag tells either of us, Asherah," Crane said, allowing his right hand to stroke through her hair. "And you need to stop calling her that. She's no longer your Matron Mother. She's not deserving of that honor."

"Ah, but she's the only mother I've ever truly known. I don't really remember my own."

They stood there, silently for several moments, savoring each other's embrace, until finally Asherah Richardson pulled away and looked up at him.

"Were you really thinking about me with your nose crammed in that dusty old book of yours?"

He allowed himself the slightest of a smile, and nodded, before moving over to the reading chair and opening the volume up to the image of the Kongo Cosmogram. He then pointed to the page.

"Your mother...your *real* mother...was a vodou mambo, right? Do you recognize this?" he asked.

She shrugged. "I've seen it here and there, but not from anything of my mother's. Basically little more than a diagram of the cosmos by followers of hoodoo." She paused before looking back at him. "I don't think there's any real power in it though. It's more conceptual than anything else."

"You sure about that?"

"Well, certain seers use it in rituals to gain power from the spirits. Insight and visions, as well as to take an oath to their loa, or whatever the equivalent is in their particular practice. But it's not a hex or anything. Nothing of real magic from what I've heard. Just a depiction of the world...the living one and that of spirit."

Crane felt his heart beginning to race as more pieces of the puzzle began to fall in place. "A depiction of the worlds. Like a map, maybe?"

She shrugged. "Maybe, but..."

"Like a map to the Land of the Spirits?"

"I don't..." She paused, an eyebrow raising as she pondered the question.

"Blast! Why didn't I see it sooner? So many deaths could have been prevented if I'd only seen the pattern sooner."

"I don't understand. See what?"

Crane picked up a notepad and pencil resting on the table by the reading chair, and began scribbling on one of the pages. After a minute, he handed the pad over to her. The page depicted a series of dashes forming a semi-circle with the curved portion below the horizontal line. A single vertical line of dashes ran down the center and extended out below the curve.

"At first, I'd speculated it was depicting a bow and arrow, facing down," he said, tracing the image with his finger. "A sign of a hunter or something similar."

Asherah's eyes widened as she studied the image.

"Ah, you see it now too, don't you?"

She nodded.

"These are the wound patterns on each of the bodies."

"It's the lower half of the cosmogram," she said, her voice almost a whisper.

"The spirit world half, yes. Our killer appears to be focusing entirely on the spirit world within his own cosmology. He has no interest in the living portion…or at least, he's not concerned with it in regards to whatever ritual he's practicing."

"Or she," Asherah corrected. "You can't rule out this might be a woman."

With a raised eyebrow, he gave a nod of assent.

"So now what? What will your next step be?"

Crane pondered the question a moment before offering a shrug. "In lieu of tracking the killer him—*or her*—self, I'll do the next best thing." He placed the notebook and pencil back on the table, then shelved the books he'd been studying. "I'll simply track the magic."

CHAPTER
TEN

Tom Thornton's Farm
December 19
10:07 PM

Tom Thornton leaned back in his recliner and downed the remainder of his last bottle of Jack Daniels. His head swam in tumultuous spinning circles. His fingers were numb, and he could barely hold onto the empty bottle as he tried to place it carefully on the floor beside his chair.

He wasn't doing very well, and it had nothing to do with the massive quantities of alcohol he'd been binging on for the last day and a half. It was the tumor in his brain. The inoperable one that the doctors said would kill him within the next six months. He'd already begun to feel its effects in the searing knife-wound-like headaches he'd been getting lately. Headaches that bent him doubled over in agony. The only thing that seemed to help ease his suffering was the liquor, and now he was out of that.

"J-johnny?" he shouted.

No one answered.

"Johnny, you there?"

He waited some more, then yelled, "Bud? Ben? Any of you'uns here?"

A moment later, a hulking three-hundred pound gorilla of a man lumbered into the living room, picking scraps of chicken from his beard.

"You need somethin', Rev?"

Thornton rolled his eyes. Caleb. Of all his flock to be chosen to watch over the ailing minister, it had to be Caleb.

"Yes, my boy. Come over...over here furaminute." Because of his drinking, Thornton was having a difficult time formulating words at the moment, which was dangerous considering how dense the childlike giant helping him could be. "Take a sheet, er I mean, a seat." He waited for the big man to comply before continuing. "I need y-you to run to the shtore-fer-me. Pick up a few...a few things. You'll need to write 'em down th-though, okay?"

Caleb nodded, then pulled out a small notepad and pen from his shirt pocket before nodding a second time for Thornton to continue. Thornton rattled off a list of liquor he thought might come in handy, and told the big man to ask Ellen Hendrix, the grocer, to put it on his tab. Satisfied the list was simple enough for a chimp to follow, he sent the big man on his way, and propped his feet up on the recliner's elevated stool with a sigh.

Before Caleb had been gone more than a minute, the dark thoughts Thornton had been entertaining before his booze ran out returned with a fury. He was going to die. Really really going to die. And soon. It didn't matter how much he'd slaved for the spirits he'd called Masters for the last twenty-three years of his life. Didn't matter that he'd made himself available twenty-four-seven to the Nameless Ones' *majordomo*, the Willow Hag. The works he'd done tirelessly and without complaint—the unholy church he'd established in the heart of the Dark Hollows —none of it mattered a hill of beans to the heathen gods he'd served so faithfully over the decades. He was going to die, and they didn't care.

A stab of sharp pain shot through the lower part of his abdomen, and he winced. His bladder was full. He needed to piss, but when he tried to sit up in the chair, he was unable to find strength enough to push the recliner's stool down, and sit up enough to stand. For two full minutes, he writhed around in the chair, struggling to get out, but to no avail. After two and a half minutes, he could control it no longer and urine streamed down his leg, soaking into his underwear and pants.

Oh, God…I need another drink.

Truly fearful, he reached into the folds of his robes, and withdrew a small, tarnished medallion hanging from a chain around his neck. The medallion—a charm that was supposed to help ward off hexes cast against him—felt light and cheap in his hand. It no longer held the hope of destiny within it as it had when it had been given to him by his former teacher.

So worthless. I've wasted so much of my…

There was a knock at the door, startling him. Then another. And a third. Slow, quiet knocks. Knocks of someone who had all the time in the world. The thought irritated Thornton. He had everything in this world. Money. Power. Respect. And was even feared by many within the community. The only thing he no longer had a surplus of was time. And the deficit angered him more than he would have ever believed possible.

"What?" he shouted from the recliner while tucking the medallion back into his robes.

The person at the door didn't respond, rekindling his irritation. It wasn't Caleb. He hadn't been gone long enough to have made it back from the store. Plus, he wouldn't knock anyway. The buffoon hardly understood anything remotely resembling etiquette like that.

"What in tarnation do you want?" he yelled. "I can't come to the door, so you might as well just let yerself in!"

The door to the kitchen creaked open, followed by the faint sound of footsteps walking across the mildew-covered linoleum floor. Thornton craned his head to see who'd entered, but the chair's headrest was too high and he was still too inebriated to push himself up enough to peer over.

The footsteps moved closer, onto the carpeted floor of the living room. He heard the soft rustle of fabric. Robes. Or a long coat maybe?

"Who's there? W-what do ya want?"

His irritation was escalating to full blown anger now.

He heard someone move up just behind the chair, then lean over near his left ear.

"I give easement and rest now to thee, dear man," the stranger whispered in his ear. "But unlike those who've come before me, I ask that you do come down the lanes and walk within our meadows. Do so as you please, until I come for you again. Until I call you to the Great Feast of the Ghosts. And for this service, I'll own thy soul."

Thornton gasped at the words. Unlike most within Boone Creek, he'd witnessed his share of sin-eating rituals. Knew the prayer that was supposed to be spoken, and understood precisely just what this new variant meant. Now, truly fearful for his life, he struggled to roll out of the recliner, but a strong left hand pulled him back into his seat, just as the figure walked around to face his intended victim.

The once-powerful cult leader grimaced at the sight while emitting a terrified, high-pitched keening. The man before him was slight of frame. He was dressed all in black from head to toe. In his gloved right hand, he held a wooden bowl, a spoon, and one of the most wicked-looking jagged knives Thornton had ever seen.

The dark reverend's eyes moved up to the man's face, which was covered in a sackcloth mask—customary enough for any Sin-Eater. But like the liturgical rites, this one had altered the mask in the most heinous of ways. Black smears of charcoal and paint had been scrawled across the fabric, giving the impression of a vengeful human skull. But that wasn't what sent a horrified chill down Thornton's spine. It was this new Sin-Eater's mouth. The customary hole, used to eat the offering of the dying person's sin, had been completely sewn up with haphazard, jagged stitches. Sewn up so that no sin would ever touch the masked man's lips again. Sewn up for his own hateful purpose.

Thornton moaned as he stared at the stitches, but knew there wasn't anything he could do. The Nameless Ones had abandoned him. So had the Willow Hag. And there would be no redemption for his sins in the afterlife. He was doomed.

"Now," the Sin-Eater said with a high-pitched whisper. "Let us begin."

CHAPTER
ELEVEN

Tom Thornton's Farm
October 19
11:45 PM

Ezekiel Crane eased back the sheet covering the body of Tom Thornton and grimaced. It was the same as all the others, with two exceptions. The first was that Thornton's shade was nowhere to be seen in his home. The second difference was a new addition to the murders no one had seen before, yet Crane himself had begun to suspect. A wooden bowl and spoon rested casually on the dead man's blood soaked chest. A stew, now cold and untouched, filled the bowl.

"What do ya think it means?" Sheriff Slate asked, gesturing at the bowl.

Crane sighed. "It's part of the Sin-Eater ritual. Only, it looks as if the ritual's been altered. The Sin-Eater is supposed to eat the food inside the bowl, representing the ingestion of the dying man's sin. The fact that it's uneaten indicates Thornton's sins were not taken away."

"Which means?" This last question came from Corporal Cody Stratton.

Crane turned to the state trooper and glared. How he'd managed to ingratiate himself into this investigation, Crane could only guess, but his participation was a problem. There weren't too many people in this world that had truly earned Ezekiel Crane's ire and distrust. Most of the slights that had been done to him, he'd been able to easily forgive...or at least, to develop a facsimile of understanding. But Stratton and the Crane family had gone back for years—since Cody's childhood and his unhealthy infatuation with Crane's sister, Jael. The childhood crush, however, wasn't the issue. It was the direction in which Cody's obsession had taken that was unforgivable.

"It means, Corporal, that Thornton's shade is now free to wander the earth for all eternity, unless..." Crane stopped mid-thought and turned to Slate. "Sheriff, send a couple of your men out to do a search of the property. Have them look for any blue bottles that might be hanging from nearby trees."

"Bottles?"

"I'll explain later, just please have them search for any signs of bottles...even glass fragments." The sheriff walked over to his nearest deputies to relay the instructions while Crane continued with his examination of the body.

"So, Corporal, who found the body?" Crane said, grinding his teeth with every syllable. He'd not spoken to Stratton since the 'incident'. Hadn't even laid eyes on him since Crane had nearly killed the trooper's father for his role in covering up the horrific crime that had befallen his sister. He was well aware that Stratton's feelings toward Crane were quite mutual.

"One of the reverend's disciples," Stratton said, rifling through his notepad. "Some retard named Caleb..."

"I'll thank you not to use such a pejorative label for Mr. Caleb Thatch, Mr. Stratton," Crane said, scanning the body for any more clues. "I'm familiar with Caleb. He's not 'retarded', to use your vernacular. He's not even mentally challenged. He's quite bright when he needs to be and strives to be helpful to anyone in need. And though he was, sadly, an acolyte for Thornton's blasphemous religion, he's a good kid." Crane turned a warning eye to the trooper. "So watch your mouth when you talk about him."

The state trooper swallowed, his face reddening with Crane's withering stare.

"Now, please recount Mr. Thatch's narrative leading up to discovering the body."

Stratton explained how Tom Thornton had recently been diagnosed with a tumor in the brain and had been given very little time in which to live. His church members had taken turns taking care of the convalescent reverend. Tonight had been Caleb's turn, and Thornton had sent him out to buy more liquor.

"He returned maybe forty-five minutes later," Stratton continued. "He doesn't have a license, so he had to walk to Hendrix Grocery Store. He said when he got home, he noticed the kitchen door standing wide open, but just thought he'd forgotten to close it like he often does. He proceeded to store the liquor away, then carried a bottle of vodka out into the living room. That's when he found him." The trooper paused. "He swears he didn't touch him, though I'm not sure I believe that. The guy had blood all over the cuffs of his shirt sleeves."

Crane nodded. "Besides the body, did he say if he saw anything strange?"

"Like what?"

"Like anything strange, Corporal. It's not a difficult question."

Stratton's face tightened. "Look, Zeke, you and I need to get somethin' straight here and now…"

Crane turned, towering over the smaller man, and held up a finger. "No, you need to understand something, Mr. Stratton. I'm not sure what strings you pulled to be here, but I do not answer to you. As the county coroner, this is my investigation. If

I ask a question, there's a reason. No matter what our differences in the past may be—no matter how much we might not like each other—I have a job to do. Part of that job is taking my investigation in any direction I think is pertinent, which means, I don't need to explain my questions to anyone. Do you understand?"

The trooper opened his mouth to speak, closed it, then let out a sigh. "Caleb didn't mention anything strange, but then, I didn't exactly ask him that question."

Crane raised an eyebrow, then looked toward the kitchen where Caleb Thatch sat nervously at the table.

"Fine. I'll go ask."

"Good man," Crane said as Stratton limped away to carry out his orders.

With the distraction taken care of for the moment, Crane returned his attention to the exsanguinated corpse still laying in the recliner. After snapping a few photographs, he carefully removed the wooden bowl from the chest and picked through its contents. Though tests would need to be run, the stew looked to be of the standard beef variety with nothing unusual about it at all. The spoon, still resting on top of the stew, looked clean and unused. Satisfied, he set the bowl aside and took a closer look at the dead man's chest. With great care, he lifted the shirt up to expose the man's shredded abdomen. Though he'd have to wait until he cleaned him up for autopsy, Crane could just make out the telltale sign of the lower portion of the Kongo Cosmogram carved into the muscle.

So, it is indeed the work of our killer. Even more disconcerting, he seems to be playing a perverted role of the Sin-Eater.

"Sheriff," Crane said, drawing Slate's attention from across the room. "Has anyone seen or heard from Isaac Koep or his wife lately?"

The sheriff squinted, as if trying to recall an important fact. "No one's mentioned them lately, no. But then, they've always pretty much kept to themselves. Don't really have friends and rarely ever leave their farm. Why?"

Of course, Crane knew the reason the Koeps stayed out of the social limelight around Boone Creek. He was one of only a handful of people in the area that knew Isaac's role as the Sin-Eater.

"Maybe you should send a deputy out to their farm. Check on them."

"You think Isaac is involved?"

Crane shrugged. "Not sure. I'd just feel better if we checked in on them. I haven't seen Mr. Koep in months. His wife often visited the bookstore and I haven't seen her in a while either. I'd just like one of your deputies to perform a well-being check if that's okay."

Slate nodded, then turned to his nearest deputy and directed him to the Koep farm. When the deputy left, the sheriff returned to Crane.

"So what are you thinking?" he asked. "I know that brain of yours is workin' on something and the Koeps are a part of it."

"Too soon to tell," Crane replied while lowering Thornton's shirt back and stepping away from the corpse. "All I know is that whoever is committing these murders is connected with the Sin-Eater tradition and Isaac..."

A sudden eruption of loud angry voices outside Thornton's house interrupted Crane's train of thought. Something hard struck the side of the house, followed by the sound of shattering glass.

"Sheriff, I think you need to come out here," Cody Stratton said, poking his head through the kitchen door.

Slate and Crane rushed out to investigate the commotion and were greeted by a mob of locals, shouting obscenities at Crane and all but accusing him of being responsible for the murders. At the forefront of the crowd stood the paramedic from the day before, Eugene Coleman.

"I don't care what you say, Sheriff! Your coroner there's behind these killings!" Coleman shouted. "You need to do somethin' about him or we will!"

With his eyes fixed on the EMT, Slate whispered over to Crane. "This guy definitely doesn't like you very much."

"Apparently."

"And you've really got no idea why?"

Crane shook his head. "I've never personally encountered him in my entire life, as far as I know."

Sheriff Slate took in a breath, then looked at the crowd. "Ya'll are currently trespassing on an active crime scene," he shouted. "If you don't back up and leave this property immediately, I'll be forced to have my deputies place you under arrest! Do I make myself clear?"

There were more shouts. Then, from out of the crowd flew a bottle, aimed directly at Crane's head. As if in slow motion, the tall mountain man stepped to the side of the missile, lashed his arm through the air, and snagged the bottle before it struck the house.

"That's it," Slate growled. "Jenkins? Rausch? I want every single one of these people placed under arrest until we discover who assaulted Mr. Crane."

"Wait, Sheriff."

Slate turned to look at Crane, who was holding a cobalt blue bottle in his hand. "I'm more concerned with where this came from." Crane held the neck of the bottle up to his eye, and carefully placed his pinky around the rim. Like those he found near his home, this bottle was also lined with fatty lard to capture whatever shade happened to wander inside it. "Yes, take them all to the station, but don't charge them with assault. I need to talk to each one of them as soon as possible."

CHAPTER
TWELVE

Jasper County Sheriff's Office
Morriston, Kentucky
December 20
3:30 AM

C rane stifled a yawn as he poured the last remaining drops of the burned coffee into his styrofoam cup and turned to Sheriff Slate.

"That's all of them, except for Eugene Coleman, I believe," Slate said. "And we still have no clue where that ghost bottle came from."

Crane took a tentative sip of the steaming liquid and nodded, but didn't say a word in response.

"So either someone is lying to us or Coleman may just be the one who threw it," the sheriff continued.

"Or there was someone else in that crowd that hasn't been accounted for."

Crane's eyes glanced past the sheriff's shoulder, following the path of Corporal Stratton as he strutted from the file room over to his desk. Slate followed his gaze and shook his head.

"Look, I know you ain't happy about me includin' him in this investigation. Know you two have some pretty nasty history with each other."

Crane turned back to the sheriff, an eyebrow raised. "I'm not one to hold petty grudges. I can assure you, my dislike for the man would be justified by anyone's standards."

"Way I hear it, he has plenty of reason to dislike you too. From what I was told, you started stalkin' the boy when he was younger. Makin' threats. Then, when his daddy got involved… well, the next part I don't rightly believe you had anything to do with, but he sure does."

Crane chuckled. "What? That I caused his father to have a stroke? Nearly killed him with my 'death curse'?"

Slate nodded. "That's how he tells it. What's more, I think he believes it. And that's how he got himself invited to our little party. He threatened to go to the governor—with his dad's help —and force an investigation into you as the coroner of Jasper County if I didn't let him in. I was honestly tryin' to protect you."

Crane smiled, placing a hand on the sheriff's shoulder. "I know. And I thank you. But there's very little need for concern regarding a state investigation into my office. The Strattons would not do well to have their own lives scrutinized too closely in regards to that incident. It wouldn't bode well with the corporal's own ambitions. However, what's done is done. He's part of this now and I will endeavor to make the most of it." He took another sip of coffee. "Now, before I go interview Mr. Coleman, has there been any word on the Koeps?"

The sheriff shook his head. "No sign of 'em." His eyes narrowed. "But there were some signs of a struggle. Some overturned furniture at the base of the stairs, and…" The sheriff hesitated.

"Let me guess…a bowl of rancid stew."

Slate nodded. "My boys could hardly tell it was stew it was molded so bad."

"It is as I feared. I'm afraid, Sheriff, that the Koeps are dead. Long dead. Perhaps the very first of these killings. We'll need to begin a search for their bodies as soon as possible. The first kill often provides the best evidence since the murderer isn't quite as experienced. Their bodies will yield a feast of clues, I believe."

"If this is going to be a search, I may need to…"

"Yes, exactly. You'll need to bring in some help from the state." Crane glanced over at Stratton, who busied himself at a computer screen. "Fortunately, we have the perfect liaison to help coordinate the search on a state level."

————

EUGENE COLEMAN SAT BACK in the uncomfortable metal chair in the interrogation room and stared up at the ceiling. His body shook, fueled by anger, frustration, and not a little fear. If the cops dug too deep into his life, it could prove disastrous. If he accidentally said too much during the interrogation, everything would be ruined. He couldn't afford that. Too much was at stake. Worse, his life, as he knew it, would be over.

At first, he had decided to just keep his mouth shut and not say a single word. But he knew that would be impossible. Knew that Ezekiel Crane himself would be the one conducting the interview. There was no way he could let that smug ass of a man get by without giving him a piece of his mind. When it came to Crane, he didn't care what he discovered. Didn't care if he found out too much. He was tired of being patient. Tired of playing the waiting game for that devil to just go about his life like the king of the world.

No, if Crane walked through that door, he was going to let him have it.

Who cares what she wants? I'm tired of playing these stupid games.

"Tired of playin' what kind of games?" The soft silky voice came from somewhere behind him. Eugene craned his head around, trying to see who'd spoken, but in the shadowy corners of the room, there was nothing to be seen.

"Who's there?"

"You know who, my sweet Genie-boy."

Eugene tried to swallow at the use of that particular nickname, but couldn't find enough saliva.

"C-Candy?"

He heard a trickle of a laugh, now on the other side of the room...in front of him. Just below the camera mounted high near the ceiling. Suddenly, the flashing red light blinked out. The camera was no longer recording.

"Is that you, Candy?" Attempting to formulate words was more difficult than they should have been. His mouth was so dry. His throat felt swollen. Hot. His cheeks flushed with a similar heat. He wasn't sure whether it was from the lust stirring in his loins or abject terror. He knew what Candace Staples was. Knew *who* she was. For those few bliss-filled weekends in which he'd been chosen to be her consort, he hadn't cared. Even when she began to ignore him...to choose others over him...he'd found himself enthralled by her. Willing to do whatever she asked, just for the off chance of pleasing her enough to garner her affections once more.

But despite that, there was something deep in the pit of his soul that screamed in holy terror whenever he was within her presence. Nothing ever seemed right with the world when he breathed the same air as her. It was as if his entire world was shrouded in shadow whenever he was in the same room with her. Yet even now, he found himself unconcerned in the least. All he knew was that he had to make her happy.

"You didn't answer my question, Gene," she said, still invisible to him. "What are you planning to do, Honeybear?"

"Well...I..."

"Yes?" The voice was directly behind him now, though it had changed. It was no longer the silky molasses-dipped sound of Candace Staples, but something far older. Grandmotherly, yet with a hint of decay.

Eugene whirled around to look, but the shackles securing his wrists caught against the iron loop bolted to the table top and jerked him to a sudden stop.

"Don't you try to lie to me, dearie. I know the thoughts in that small little brain of yers."

"But...but I just thought..."

"I don't keep you 'round to think." Eugene felt icy cold fingers slide across his neck. He looked down to see the gnarled, desiccated hands of a human corpse caressing his shoulders. "Tonight ain't the night to challenge me, dearie. I ain't pleased about the death of Tom Thornton. Didn't like him none, but he had a purpose and was a priest of the Masters. Nothin' good will come from 'is death."

"I d-don't understand...what do you think...?"

"Shhhhhhh, boy. Yer elder is a'talkin'. It's impolite to interrupt." He felt those bony, mummified fingers tighten on his shoulder, sending a white hot streak of pain down his spine. "I'll say this once and only once...leave Ezekiel Crane alone. For now. I'll let ya know when it's time to reel him in...but for now, you best just let him go on his merry way. Understood?"

Tears streaked Eugene's face by now, wrought from the immense pain, as well as the horror of her very presence.

"Yes! Yes! I promise. I'll do whatever you say...just don't..."

But before he could finish the sentence, the hands were gone and the door to the interrogation room was opening to reveal that arrogant face of Ezekiel Crane coming to interrogate him.

CHAPTER
THIRTEEN

The Crane Homestead
October 20
5:30 AM

K ili jumped up from the couch and ran straight to Ezekiel Crane the moment he stepped through the door. Elated to see him, she wrapped her arms around his neck and squeezed as tight as she could.

"Crane! You're back!"

He returned the hug with just as much vigor. "So are you, I see," he said with a weary, but genuine smile. Still allowing the embrace, he glanced past her shoulder at Davenport, and gave him a brief nod of recognition. He'd received the reporter's phone call hours ago, while still at Tom Thornton's crime scene, and had been told of the news of Kili's seemingly miraculous recovery.

Of course, for some reason, her sudden arousal from her catatonic state weighed heavy on Crane's mind, though he couldn't quite figure out why. It was indeed an occasion to celebrate, yet for some reason, he found himself anxious concerning its cause

68

and what it meant for the mark the Willow Hag had placed on her.

"It's delightful to see you up and about again, Ms. Kili," Crane said, squeezing her tight one more time before kissing her forehead, and releasing her from the embrace. "This house has been under quite the shadow since you took ill."

She smiled up at him. She seemed strong. Much stronger than he would have thought possible after lying in a catatonic state for nearly eight months. Of course, Ms. Heather could be credited for that. While she wasn't tending to the needs of Ezekiel's brother, she'd spent a great deal of her free time working Kili's muscles to keep them from atrophying. Her hard work had certainly paid off.

After a moment, Davenport appeared by Kili's side, taking her by the arm, and leading her back to the couch where they'd been sitting when he'd entered.

"All right," the reporter said. "Now that you're here, I've got like a gazillion questions that need some answers."

"As do I," Crane said, moving over to his grandmother's favorite armchair and taking a seat across from them. He looked over at Kili with heavy eyes. "How much do you remember?"

The smile on her face faded and she squeezed her eyelids shut as if the question had struck her physically in the gut. "Enough to know I'd rather not talk about it."

"There's something you need to understand, Ms. Kili," Crane said, leaning forward in his seat and speaking in the calmest of voices. "Whatever you did...no, scratch that...whatever you *think* you did, at the Devil's Teeth that day, it wasn't what it appeared to be to you. You were marked. Hexed by the Willow Hag. An attempt to break your spirit and your mind."

"But I killed her, Crane! I killed Delores McCrary." Tears were now streaming down her cheeks as she spoke. "Don't know why. One minute I was running through the woods after Alex crashed the car. The next, I had a knife in my hand, and was stabbing

Delores over and over again. I couldn't stop. I just kept stabbing."

Crane gave her an understanding nod. "I understand that might be what you perceived to be happening, but trust me...it only appeared that way to you."

Davenport's eyes shot up at Crane; his head cocked to one side in silent question.

"No, Mr. Davenport, that was indeed Mrs. McCrary's body you found Kili standing over in the Hollows that day. And yes, she had stabbed the poor woman dozens of times..." He looked Kili square in the eyes before continuing. "...but she'd been dead for several months before you did so. Her body had been the undead puppet of the Hag. I'm still uncertain for how long. But she wasn't alive when you did what you did."

Kili threw up her hands. "And that's supposed to make me feel better? I had no idea she was dead, and I stabbed her anyway. Hacked her nearly to pieces. And the worst of it is, I have no idea why. I'd blacked out. Only came to my senses when Alex found me." She wiped away a tear with the sleeve of her robe. "Why, Crane? Why did that happen to me?"

"You need to tell her, brother," came a voice from behind Crane's chair. "She needs to understand what's happening. She needs to understand the choice that waits before her."

Kili looked up and past Crane's shoulder. A glimmer of another smile spread across her face before fading just as suddenly. "Josiah? You're awake too?"

Crane went rigid at the question. Davenport, the all-too-familiar expression of confusion painted across his face, looked from Kili to their host. "Um, who are you talking to, Kili?"

She glanced over at Davenport, then back behind Crane, and pointed. "Josiah Crane. That's Ezekiel's brother. I'm not sure if you two have ever met or not..."

"Kili, you haven't met Josiah Crane either," Davenport said. "He's been laid up in a coma since he was a kid. I only learned about him after Ezekiel brought *both* of you here to be taken care of."

Crane stared at the young redhead for several long moments. "You can see him? Josiah?"

"Well, yeah. He's standing right behind you."

Crane looked over his shoulder at his brother. "Care to explain this, Josiah?"

"Crane?" Davenport said, now obviously a little *more* than confused. He appeared to be officially creeped out now.

The younger Crane looked sheepishly at him, and shrugged. "I visited her from time to time. Talked to her. But she never gave any indication that she could see me."

Ezekiel Crane turned back to Kili and the reporter. "This is beyond my wildest imaginings," he said quietly, standing from his seat before pacing the floor. "Mr. Davenport, to ease your consternation...yes, my brother is indeed still comatose. But the same curse that afflicts me also allows me to commune with him from time to time. Not always, mind you, and I'm not entirely sure how since he's not dead. Of course, it isn't without precedent since his nurse, Ms. Heather, was able to communicate with him long before me. It was the reason the Leechers were released upon us back in April, after all." He stopped his pacing, and gestured at Kili. "Ms. Kili, you fell into your fit long before I had a chance to delve too closely into the curse placed upon you by the Hag. I'd not yet been able to discern just how it might affect you..."

His voice trailed off as a myriad of thoughts whirled chaotically through his mind.

"What does he look like?" he suddenly asked.

"Who?" Kili blinked, not quite understanding the question.

"My brother. What does he look like?"

She looked past his shoulder and smiled. "He's cute. About twelve years old, I'd say. Light brown hair. Very tussled, like he's been playing out in the yard and hasn't had a bath in a few days. He's got a wonderful smile. It's very contagious."

Davenport looked at her, then followed her gaze before shaking his head. "I'm still not following this."

Ignoring the comment, Crane shook his head. "Fascinating." He looked over at where his brother was standing. "She sees you precisely how you looked the day the Leechers attacked us when we were kids." He turned back to Kili. "That's not how I see him at all. He's older. In his late twenties. Except for the atrophied muscles, he looks very much the same as his body lying in bed in the back bedroom."

"Ezekiel," Josiah said. "You need to tell her what's happening. You need to talk to her about the choice she'll have to make soon."

Crane shook his head. "I don't even know for sure. This...this curse...it's different. I wasn't able to see the Dead—or supernatural things—for at least two or three years after the Hag marked me. She started seeing it immediately." He paused. "No, that's not true. She was able to see my Raven even before that. Was able to hear and talk to the Yunwi Tsunsdi before the Willow Hag marked her." He narrowed his eyes at her. "And judging by a certain severed tail I found in her pockets after she fell into her fit, I daresay she's been in communion with the Taily-Po as well."

"The tail?" Kili shot up from the couch. "You have it? You found it? Where is it?"

Crane reeled back from the near panic in her voice. Like a junkie in desperate need of a fix. "Ms. Kili, do you crave the talisman so much that..."

A timid knock at the kitchen door interrupted them. They all turned toward the kitchen, tensing with each knock. No one calling this early in the morning could be bringing good news. Despite this, Ezekiel Crane moved to the door with a relaxed grace that disguised his own concern. Something about those knocks did not bode well with him. He sensed an omen in them of something he was not going to like.

He opened the door to find young Jimmy Staples, the ten-year-old son of the late Candace Staples, standing in the doorway, looking up at him with nervous eyes. Something was off about the boy. He looked older somehow. Frown lines marked the corners of his mouth. Crows feet scarred the sides of his face. He was also a full seven or eight inches taller than he'd been the last time he'd seen him. The height and a growth of fine blonde stubble dotting his chin and under his nose made him look more like a young man of fifteen than ten.

He could see the boy was also sporting a 'shiner' under his left eye and a swollen lip, as if someone had struck him several times recently.

"Jimmy? Is that you, boy?"

He nodded, but said nothing. Perhaps the most disturbing change, in Crane's mind, was his overall demeanor. His head hung low, avoiding any eye contact. His entire countenance seemed one of abject sadness. Perhaps even pain.

"Is everything okay? What's wrong? Who hit you?"

Crane's concern for the boy was genuine...not to mention well-deserved.

To the world at large, Jimmy had been a normal happy boy. Normal. Full of love and life. That is, until the death of his mother at the hands of One-Eyed Jack. The child had been so traumatized by the ordeal. Broken and withdrawn. If he'd not been taken in by Granny, he wasn't sure the boy would have survived at all.

But then, his mother had, for all intents and purposes, risen from the grave along with the seven others that became known as the Kindred. Unlike the rest, however, Candace had managed to maintain her personality. Her intelligence. And what most people believed to be her soul. Crane, however, knew better. The creature masquerading around town as Jimmy's mother was merely another puppet whose strings were pulled by the machinations of the Willow Hag. But because no one believed him, social services had allowed the boy to go back to living with Candace, and Crane had spent almost every day worrying about the influence she might have on him. Looking at his haggard and aged appearance, he now felt more than justified for his concern.

Jimmy trembled at the sight of Ezekiel Crane. He wrung his hands while his legs jittered beneath patched-up jeans. "It's...it's my momma, Mr. Crane."

Jimmy's appearance wasn't the only thing to have changed drastically in the last eight months. His voice was much deeper now, as a young man who had already endured puberty. For now, he decided to ignore the issue and focus, instead, on the reason for the visit.

"Go on, son. What about her?"

"She's out yonder." He pointed behind him, beyond the Crane property line. "She wants to meet with you. Alone. Now." Jimmy gulped. "She demands it even."

CHAPTER
FOURTEEN

The Crane Homestead
December 20
5:50 AM

E zekiel Crane stepped out into the darkness, leaving Jimmy
Staples in the care of Kili and Alex Davenport. For her
part, Kili didn't like the idea of Crane going out beyond the
charms that protected the ancestral property from the Willow
Hag and her ilk, especially after Alex had filled her in earlier
about Candace's resurrection, and Crane's insistence that she
was, in reality, the Hag herself. But the stubborn mountain man
had refused to listen to her. He'd simply stated he'd been
expecting this visit from the moment he'd learned that Kili had
awakened. He'd assured her that he'd be fine and encouraged
her to take care of the boy.

The way he'd made the last request, she had the feeling he
meant something more than merely watching over Jimmy,
though she wasn't certain specifically what he'd hoped of her.

"Jimmy, would you like a snack? Something to drink?" she
asked, looking down into the nervous face. She shuddered invol-

untarily at the unnatural changes in the boy. Besides the strange maturing and growth spurt, he seemed gaunt. Bone-thin really. His skin was pale and his complexion was pocked with sores verging on the side of infection. Two of his teeth were blackened with decay and one was chipped. And of course, there was the black eye and busted lip that she suspected was given to him by the creature disguised as his mother.

The boy shook his head, keeping his gaze fixed on his feet, and Kili's heart broke for him. He'd been through so much in the last year and a half. His mother had been brutally killed by the same fungal growth that had killed her own brother. Then, Granny had taken him in. Loved him. Nurtured him. And she'd been killed as well. While living with Granny, he'd grown quite fond of her apprentice, Delores McCrary, who'd turned out to be the Willow Hag in disguise. And she, too, had died a gruesome death. Only to be reunited with his undead mother—possibly the Willow Hag in disguise again, if Crane was to be believed.

"Well, come on," Kili said, holding out a hand for the boy to take. "At least sit down and relax while Crane talks with your mom, okay?"

Jimmy gave her a wary smile and took her hand. When he did, Kili caught sight of something on the inside of his forearm. Something dark and disturbing.

"Oh, what's that?" she asked, lifting his arm up for a better look. It was a three inch, gaping sore. Yellow-green fluid oozed from its edges. The interior wound was dark red and hard to the touch. Kili wasn't certain of what she was looking at, but it looked and smelled infected.

She glanced over at Davenport, and nodded to the bathroom. Understanding the silent request, he darted in that direction without a word.

Jimmy lifted his arm up proudly. "Oh, don't worry. Mama says it's a good omen. A sign of my maturin'. Says it's part of somethin' called the 'Corruption'. I don't rightly know what that means, but she says it's a rite of passage to my manhood, so I reckon that's a good thing." He paused, as if thinking about something. "And she must be right, 'cause I've done grown three inches in the past month! Grown smarter too. I know things now...things I never knew before. It's like knowin' stuff just pops in my head like magic."

Alex came out of the bathroom, holding a bottle of hydrogen peroxide and some clean cloths, then handed them to Kili.

She tried smiling at Jimmy, trying to offer encouragement to him despite her fears. "I'm just going to clean this up a little. It might sting a bit, but it'll keep your arm from getting any more infected. Okay?"

The boy jerked his arm away with a huff. Despite his obvious rapid aging, he still acted very much like a ten year old kid.

"Jimmy, I just need to clean it up a little. It looks bad."

"No! Mama said it's a good thing. The Corruption is good!"

Kili and Alex looked at one another.

"Honey, corruption is never good," Kili said. "Especially when it's an infection."

"Jimmy, why does your mom say it's a good thing?"

He glanced at both of them, biting down on his lower lip as he fidgeted from one foot to another.

"It's okay. You can tell us, can't you?"

He shrugged. "I reckon."

Kili patted him on the shoulder, an attempt to comfort the nervous child.

Jimmy scrunched his nose together as if trying to remember the words. "It's a sign, she told me. A mark to identify me."

Kili and Alex glanced at each other. She then looked over to where Josiah had been standing, but he was no longer there.

"Identify you?" Alex asked. "To who?"

"Oh, that's easy. To the Willow Hag, of course!" He absently rubbed the open, pus-filled sore with his left hand. "I'm going to be her...her concert...con...con-something when I grow up."

"Consort?" Kili asked, her cheeks flushing. *Oh my God! The Willow Hag intends to use the kid to breed.*

Jimmy beamed. "Yeah! That's it! Mommy says originally, the Willow Hag had chosen Mr. Crane. But he hurt her! Lied to her. She says Mr. Crane is an evil man who'll soon get what's comin' to him. That's what she came to talk to him about."

CRANE WALKED down the gravel driveway, marching toward the edge of the property while clutching the rabbit's foot charm around his neck. He didn't need to be told where Candace would be. He just knew, and he strode straight toward her, wary of any magical energies that might be lying in wait for him once he crossed the protective threshold of his estate.

Ten feet outside of its boundaries, he felt her presence lurking in the shadows within a stand of nearby trees.

"You can come out and show yourself, woman."

"You best watch your tone with me, Ezekiel Crane," cooed a silky female voice just before Candace Staples stepped out from hiding in long, sensuous steps. "I have half a mind to turn you over one of my knees. Who knows, you might even enjoy it."

"You've mastered Candace's promiscuous flirtations since you took up residence in her double," Crane said. His voice was little more than an irritated growl. "As if you weren't already dishonoring her memory enough with your blasphemous magic."

She waved a hand dismissively. "Pish posh, my dear Ezekiel. Don't pretend you cared anythin' for the poor woman when she was alive."

It wasn't true. He had cared for Candace once. Even near the end, he'd not given up hope that she'd turn her life around—for the boy if for no other reason. But it would do no good to argue the point. The Willow Hag was simply trying to goad him into a confrontation, and he would not allow that.

"What do you want, Hag? Your time so close to Granny's wards is precious limited. Better speak your peace and leave."

Her eyes narrowed, marring her otherwise lovely features. Candace had indeed been quite the beauty when she was alive— despite a few pock marks dotting her face from teenage acne. She'd been a bit too thin, making her face sharp and angular, but pleasant in its own way. There was nothing pleasant about the face glaring at Crane at that moment.

"These killings, Ezekiel."

That hadn't been what he'd expected from her. With Kili's sudden awakening, he'd fully expected her to appear in order to lay claim to her. He'd assumed the serial murders would have been beyond any interest to her.

"What about them?"

"They've gone too far. You need to stop them."

This was indeed surprising.

"I'm working on it." He eyed her, taking a step toward her. "But I'm curious. Why do you care?"

She laughed. It was almost a cackle, an echo of the thing that dwelt in this fresh, young body. "I didn't. Couldn't 'ave cared less, in fact. But the son of a devil what's doin' this, kilt one of the high priests last night. That, I can't have."

Crane nodded. "Thornton. You're upset over Thornton's death. That's rather touching."

"Ain't got nothin' to do with the man himself, Ezekiel, and you know it."

He nodded at this. The Hag needed to save face now. Someone had disrespectfully killed one of her servants, which was a direct affront to her and her power. She wouldn't be able to abide that.

"And he's got the entire Hollars worked up like a hornet's nest. The haints are walkin' about again, and they're mighty nasty at the moment." She nodded toward Crane's house. "I'm worried about the boy. What they might do to him in their rage."

Now this was new. The last haints that had been conjured up had been the Leechers. They'd been summoned and controlled by Crane's brother and Heather. It had been a nasty business, and one that had ultimately led to Granny's death. But if other haints were rising in the Dark Hollows—enraged and aimless— that was indeed a danger he needed to take seriously.

The fact that the Willow Hag was concerned with Jimmy Staples, however, was not a surprise. It wasn't that she cared for the boy in a way a mother might care for a son. But he was now an investment. She was raising him up for some dark purpose. In the beginning, he'd suspected she planned on using the boy in much the same way she'd intended for Crane himself—as a consort to sire her future offspring.

The boy's unnatural aging had thrown him off balance, but it made a certain kind of sense the more he thought about it. After all, if she wanted him to be her mate and didn't want to waste any more time than necessary, such rapid aging would prove useful.

Then again, the aging might be for some other intent that Crane couldn't even begin to fathom. Either way, it was only in her best interests to keep the boy safe.

"Like I said, I'm working on it," Crane said. "Unless you have anything to offer in way of assistance."

She scowled at him. "You already know who's doin' this, don't ya?"

He nodded. "I know his stolen title, yes. The Sin-Eater. As to his identity, I'm still working on that. Isaac Koep kept his deal- ings pretty close to the vest. He never told me, or anyone else, who he'd taken up to be his apprentice. When he and his wife disappeared, all trace of the Sin-Eater died with him."

"But you know what he's doin', don't ya?"

"I assume you mean that he's preparing for the Ghostfeast.

Just as you predicted back in April." Crane shrugged. "So can you tell me something I don't already know? If not, I'll kindly ask for you to leave."

"Hoodoo," she said with a sly smile.

"What about it?"

"The magic he's a'usin'. It's of the hoodoo variety."

"Once again, you're offering me nothing new. I've already figured that as well."

"And what type o' person uses hoodoo, I wonder?"

Crane rolled his eyes at this. The Willow Hag, as far as the stories go, was supposed to be a spirit of nature. A dark spirit, to be sure, but a spirit nonetheless. Which is why he'd always found it so curious that the Hag could be so racist in her opinion of mortals. She despised any race other than whites, claiming them to be inferior in spirit, mind, and soul. Which was rather odd, in Crane's opinion, if the woman known as the Willow Hag had never been a racist white woman at some point in the past.

Her meaning was crystal clear. Hoodoo was an amalgam of mystic religions of the Congo. A mixture of vodou of Haiti, as well as various other magical practices used by the slaves brought to America during its formative years. In essence, she was implying that the killer, using such magic, was more than likely black.

"Have you talked to Asherah about it, I wonder?" she asked with a sly grin on her face.

"Look," Crane said, "if you have nothing more useful to say, this interview is over. Now, please leave these premises immediately. We'll send Jimmy home in the morning, when it's safer to travel."

He turned to walk back to the house.

"I hear Ms. Brennan done finally woke up."

That stopped him in his tracks. He turned around to face her.

"A might too soon, I think. Reckon she's already seein' the spirits of the dead. These Ghostfeast killin's probably took a toll on her. Woke her up earlier than expected." Her smile stretched unnaturally up her face, reminding Crane of a great white shark's. "She ain't done yet. Not tender enough."

"Her soul is still hers, witch." Crane clinched his fists together, prepared for a fight if necessary. "And she's under my protection here. Until she chooses, she's still in control."

The Candace Hag cackled. "Oh, her soul is hers still, sure. But her body?" She pursed her lips together in mock sadness, and shook her head. "Seems to me you need a little help catchin' this killer. Some bait, maybe?"

A lump began to form in Crane's throat. He took a step toward her, and pointed a finger at her. "Don't you dare, Hag."

She allowed herself a tinkling of a giggle. "Too late," she said, stepping back into the woodline's shadows. "It's already done." Then, she disappeared completely from view just as Crane bolted as fast as he could up the driveway to the house.

CHAPTER
FIFTEEN

The Crane Homestead
December 20
6:10 AM

B efore Ezekiel Crane could reach the porch to his house, the front door burst open with Davenport running outside and shouting.

"Crane! Something's happening to Kili!"

Without acknowledging the reporter, Crane dashed inside, sprinted across the foyer, and slid across the hardwood floor of the living room to Kili's side. She lay there, gasping for breath. Her face was blue; a swelling, purple tongue protruded from her lips.

"Ms. Kili, listen to me," he said, cradling her head in his right arm. With his left, he reached into his shirt, and withdrew a small medicine pouch attached to a leather strap around his neck. He was mildly aware of incessant cawing from somewhere above him, but he paid it no heed. "I know it's going to be difficult to do, but I need you to relax for a bit. I need you to calm yourself long enough for me to do a working on you. Can you do that for me?"

Every muscle in her body seemed to be as tense as steel, but she managed to look up at him through her bulging eyes, and nod.

"Good." He smiled at her before reaching into the pouch, and producing a pinch of a white powdery substance. Carefully, he sprinkled the powder onto her tongue while muttering the ancient words taught to him by Granny years before. Once the words were spoken, he glanced back at the reporter. "Mr. Davenport, call 911. I'm afraid I can do little for her at the moment. She needs medicines that we simply do not have here."

He then returned his attention to Kili's treatment, and prayed the paramedics would be able to get here on time. Though he'd studied medicine during his time away from Boone Creek, and knew a great deal more about the medicine used by his kin, Crane was well aware of his own limitations. He could do nothing more for his friend at the moment. The concoction he'd given her—a mixture of ginger, arnica root, turmeric, and a number of other herbs, roots, and extracts used for a variety of ailments—would help decrease the swelling of her tongue, but other than that, her fate was up in the air.

"What's happenin' to her?" Jimmy Staples asked, as he sidled up to her with a wet towel in hand. He'd spent enough time with Granny to know how to help in a medical emergency, and Crane was most thankful for that. "Why's she sick all of a sudden?"

The boy placed the towel across Kili's forehead, and pressed down gently. A stream of cool water ran from the cloth, down her cheeks.

"I'm not sure at the moment," Crane replied, struggling to keep from hurling a string of curses at the boy's 'mother'. "Yes, just like that. Keep the towel there. Excellent job, Jimmy."

The youth nodded, and kept doing what he could for the sick woman. "Was she hexed? Did my momma hex her?"

The question startled Crane. "Why do you ask?"

Jimmy shrugged. "I dunno." He pressed down on the towel again, forcing more water to squeeze from the fabric. "Sometimes, I don't think she's always my momma. Sometimes, she is. But sometimes, she isn't. I can't explain it. But sometimes, she's scary. I get the feelin' she's workin' magic on me."

"Ezekiel!"

Crane turned to see Heather running into the living room in her pajamas and a bathrobe. Her hair was disheveled, and eyes heavy from sleep.

"It's Josiah! He's gone!" she cried, before looking down at Kili with a gasp. "What's wrong with Kili?"

Crane stood, grabbing the nurse at the shoulders. "What do you mean Josiah is gone? You mean, he's awake?"

She shook her head while tears ran down her cheeks. "No, he's still there. In bed. Vitals are normal too. It's just that I can't...you know...can't find him. Can't talk to him. His spirit's gone."

The room suddenly lit up with the flare of flashing red and white lights coming from the front entrance windows and doors.

"They're here!" Davenport shouted. A few minutes later, the reporter led a duo of volunteer firefighters—paramedics, by the insignia on their uniforms—into the living room, who set immediately to work trying to stabilize Kili.

Crane found himself thankful that Eugene Coleman wasn't among them, though that was probably because he was still in lockup at the county jail.

He turned his attention back to the paramedics that were there. He watched as they applied oxygen, and EKG pads to her, then placed her on a stretcher, and carted her from the house as fast as they could.

Crane turned to Heather. "Stay here. Wait to see if Josiah

returns. Keep me posted." Then to Jimmy. "Make yourself at home, Jimmy. We'll be back in the morning to take you home."

The boy nodded his understanding, and Ezekiel Crane and Alex Davenport rushed out of the house to follow their friend to the hospital.

CHAPTER
SIXTEEN

Old Tegalta Mining Barracks
December 20
5:35 PM

The Sin-Eater smiled as he reached into his rucksack, withdrew thirteen bottles, and set them in a semi-circle on the rickety wooden floor of the abandoned housing unit for the miners of Tegalta Mining Company. The bottles, laid with the semi-circle's curve in a southern direction, seemed to glow with a dull blue light in the dim miasma of dusk shining through the grime-covered windows. He looked down at his handiwork, satisfied the bottles were laid out perfectly in the pattern of the Kongo Cosmogram, just as he'd been instructed by his *Sponsa-Mater*. He then moved over to the nearest cot—the thin mattress rotting from the inside out from years of exposure to the elements—and plopped down on its edge.

Things were going better than he'd ever thought possible. His traps were working like a charm, catching his prey in droves. He'd always known the hills around Jasper County had been chock full of ghosts from years gone by. Knew there'd be more than enough of them to achieve his plan without even bothering with killing anyone; although violent deaths were more apt to produce a shade on which he could prey. Truth be told, if pressed, he'd admit to anyone who asked that he killed because he simply enjoyed the act of taking another person's life. It was the best part of his mission.

"Bet you never seen this comin' when you chose me as your apprentice, did ya Isaac?" he said while pulling off his shoes and socks before laying them down next to the cot's legs. He looked up at the former Sin-Eater's shade, who had appeared the moment he'd stepped through the barrack's doors. The Sin-Eater had gotten used to Isaac Koep's presence in the last few months. In fact, he'd even become somewhat of a comfort to him during stressful times. It was the reason he'd not eaten him after the three day interval was up. He wanted the old Sin-Eater to ripen up for a tastier treat. But for now, it was just nice to have someone to talk to from time to time. "Of course, I reckon I ain't the one you actually thought you were choosin', eh? I kinda fooled ya, didn't I, old man?"

The shade of the old man opened its mouth to speak, but no words came out with the effort. Another blessing. Though the Sin-Eater was capable of using Koep's shade as a sounding board to work out his thoughts, the foul spirit couldn't return the favor. There were no judgmental retorts to worry about. No accusations. No expressions of disappointment. It was, he thought, the perfect kind of partnership.

Not worrying about missing out on what Koep might say, the Sin-Eater slipped out of his shirt and pants, then stood up to pull off his underwear. Soon, he was completely nude. His skin swelled with gooseflesh as the winter air inside the barracks embraced him. It was, of course, all part of the ritual, and something he'd learned to savor. An involuntary biological reaction that proved he was very much alive in a world filled with death.

He stood there, next to the cot, taking deep slow breaths. He focused his attention on the cold air all around him...on the goosebumps...on the hairs standing on end over his whole body. After a few silent moments, he reached into his bag, withdrew a hairbrush, and began to scrape the bristles across the bare skin of his body several times.

Once he felt raw, he strode over to the array of bottles, got down on his hands and knees, and began examining each one with a practiced eye. He searched for cracks. He felt along the necks, exploring the lard that sealed the bottle's interior. He inspected the design of each bottle, looking for any irregularities that might have crept in during the manufacturing process.

He needn't have bothered. He performed a much more painstaking inspection of the bottles before he'd hung them from the trees throughout Jasper County. He knew that the bottles would do their part well. That they were without blemish, and perfect for harvesting the shades he desperately needed for the Feast. But the Sin-Eater prided himself on his thoroughness. The Devil, after all, was in the detail, which meant that the Detail was his own personal act of worship.

Of course, the Sin-Eater hadn't always been this way. In fact, until recently, he'd been just your typical Kentucky ne'er-do-well. Just a regular guy who hunted or fished with his buddies on the weekends. Or just wandered the backwoods for adventure and fun.

Then, came the change. It wasn't a single moment in time that changed him. No. It was gradual. He couldn't quite place when it all started. First, came One-Eyed Jack. Then the Kindred and those damnable Leechers. It was around that time that his *Sponsa-Mater* came to him in the night. Had promised him such incredible things. Had shown him such love when no one else even cared.

She'd shown him so much more as well. She'd shown him who his true enemies were. Enemies like Ezekiel Crane and his precious family. She'd taught him about the Ghostfeast. About how to catch and feed on the shades that wander these lands like so many cockroaches. And she'd given him purpose, as well. She'd directed him to those most worthy to die by his hands.

Until recently, their relationship had been perfection itself. Everything he'd ever hoped for. Which is why he couldn't understand why'd she'd been so upset with him over the death of that wretched Tom Thornton. The man had been nothing but a nuisance to her for years. He would have stabbed her in the back at the first opportunity. He'd been doing her a favor. It had been a show of his devotion.

And yet, she'd gone to see Ezekiel Crane in the middle of the night, begging him to put a stop to these crimes. It was as if she was scared. Scared of the Sin-Eater.

He savored that thought for a moment. The more he reflected on it, a smile began to spread across his deformed face. Imagine that. The *Sponsa-Mater*...scared of him. He rather liked that idea. If he could scare her, then his power must be formidable indeed.

The dying light from outside began to fade even more, wrenching him back to the present. He needed to return his focus to the ritual before he lost all his light.

The Sin-Eater climbed to his feet, walked over to the southeast corner of the room, and picked up a small wire cage containing an overfed and equally sedated rooster. He returned to the semi-circle, removed the bird from its prison, and laid it outside the perpendicular line at the northern half. It struggled to move. Fought to regain enough wits to run away from the danger it knew itself to be in. But the sedatives placed in its food were far too powerful. In fact, the Sin-Eater suspected that if he decided to spare the rooster of the blade that awaited it, it would more than likely die of an overdose in minutes.

That, however, was not going to happen. The Working he planned tonight required living blood.

Blood. Life in liquid form. The great conduit. The quintessential ingredient for transference.

He pondered this for several seconds, while retrieving the guitar he'd packed along with his other supplies, then returned to the southern border of the cosmogram.

It's time.

He wasn't quite strong enough to perform the full Ghostfeast ritual. Besides, it could only be performed on a specific date, every seventy-five years. No, this was something else. To some degree, he supposed, it was practice…a means of perfecting the ritual for the official feast. It was also, in a manner of speaking, more of a snack than anything else. It was a necessary evil. A little intake of spectral energy to hold off the debilitating effects of the disease currently ravaging his body. A mini-ritual to slow down the process and sustain him long enough to see his mission fulfilled. To some, it might seem like a waste of thirteen perfectly good shades, but with each mini-feast he imbibed in, he also grew more powerful.

Slinging the guitar over his shoulder, he stepped into the semi-circle, crouched down, and drew the blade of his knife across the rooster's throat. With pitiful shrieks of pain, the blood spilled out from the bird's neck, trailing into the cosmogram, and soaking into the soles of the Sin-Eater's bare feet. He then stood up, and began playing his own rendition of *Stairway to Heaven* to his complete delight.

The actual choice of song he played for the ritual was unimportant. It was merely the hook to his trap. Shades, and spirits of all kinds, were compulsively drawn to music. They couldn't resist. Therefore, with *Stairway* playing, should any of them try to flee during the transference, the music would draw them back into the cosmogram, and ultimately back into his control.

Plucking the strings of the guitar, he raised up his voice, reciting the words handed down for generations by his own kin. The ancient incantation of the Bakongo people. Words not spoken in civilized conversation for hundreds of years. A language long dead, even from those who lived there to this day.

He'd found it ironic when he'd first learned of it—a descendent of a long line of card-carrying members of the Ku Klux Klan, who despised the black race with every fiber of their being —using Bakongonese heathen magic for his mission. But the driving force that compelled him to his harvest had given him no choice in the matter. *"This is the way,"* she had told him. *"The only way to perform the Ghostfeast."* So, dutifully, he'd committed the words to memory, just as he'd committed the ritualistic prayer of the Sin-Eater's mantle.

"Etu onga nyenego!" he shouted above the sound of the guitar strings. *"Nyenego, nashi gnan. Henehna nashi ga bakongenoh nyenego non!"*

He repeated the incantation. A third time. A fourth.

An old lantern, hanging from the wooden rafters, began to shake. Then, the rows of cots trembled; their metal legs tapping against the concrete floor. To the casual observer, it was little more than a mild earthquake. But the Sin-Eater knew better.

After several more recitations, the very walls of the barracks began to shake, making it difficult to keep focused on the music he was playing. But he managed to keep the tune going as best he could, and when he failed to make a chord, he made up for it with sheer noise. After all, the music itself wasn't what attracted the spirits, but rather the noise being produced. He could have lit an entire barrel full of fireworks and produced the same effect. Of course, there was something quite poetic about playing *Stairway to Heaven* that he liked, so he did the best he could.

Soon, the bottles themselves began to glow with a bright blue sheen. It wasn't light seeping through the tattered old blinds of the windows anymore. The sun was almost entirely set now. No, the luminescence from the bottles was something altogether different. It was his prey…being released from their prisons.

He watched in fascination as the bottles in the half cosmogram pattern grew blazingly bright. Almost blinding him. The excitement of it all fueled his fingertips, and the twang of the guitar played even louder. Frenzied. They were about to arise. They were about to fill him up with their power…their energy. They were about to…

He pulled his hand away from the guitar. The last chord echoed away from him like a fleeting dream. The glow of the bottles dimmed and he once more was standing in nothing more than the light of a single lantern.

Someone was here with him. Someone was watching.

He turned around and instantly spotted the intruder. Josiah Crane. Or at least, his spirit form.

"You," Josiah said, his eyes widening. "Dear lord! What happened to you?"

The Sin-Eater cursed. It was too soon. Much too soon, but Ezekiel Crane's invalid brother was forcing his hand. Without a word, the Sin-Eater bolted across the room to the cot where his rucksack lay. He reached in and withdrew a single blue bottle, then wheeled around and glared at the living specter. Before Josiah could flee, the Sin-Eater muttered a few indecipherable syllables. The bottle began to glow. Josiah lurched forward in pain, then shot for the bottle. There was a blinding flare of light, then dimness once more.

Josiah Crane was now nowhere to be seen, but the bottle was warm and thrummed in the Sin-Eater's quivering hand. The nosy spirit wouldn't be telling anyone what he'd seen here any time soon.

CHAPTER
SEVENTEEN

Jasper Community Hospital
December 20
7:45 PM

Snoring, Alex Davenport jerked himself awake, nearly sliding out of the uncomfortable wooden chair next to Kili's hospital bed. Groggy, he glanced over at the clock on the opposite wall. He'd been watching over his sick friend now for nearly twelve hours, and there'd been no change in her condition other than a plague of boils and open sores now covering her entire body. The doctors had been avoiding her—obviously bewildered by her condition to the point of embarrassment. Heck, even that hatchet-faced Nurse Rollins hadn't been by to check on her in about three hours herself.

He looked over at Kili, the ventilator making a gentle hum with each intake of breath she made. From what he'd been told, it was the only thing keeping her alive at that moment.

"How's she doin'?" a voice asked from the doorway.

Davenport jumped at the sudden intrusion, straightened himself when he realized it was only Crane, then shrugged.

"About the same. They're not telling me much of anything though. But just look for yourself." He gestured toward her bed. "Those sores are getting worse."

Crane strode over to the bed, then leaned forward, examining the splotches along her neck and arms with a detached air.

"Any idea what they are?" Davenport asked. "What's causing it?"

Crane lifted Kili's right arm and brought it closer to his face. "The cause is easy. It's the Willow Hag. But identifying the specific malady, that's an entirely different matter." The tall mountain man turned to look at Davenport. "And you say that Jimmy had sores very similar to these?"

He nodded. "Well, just one that we saw. On his arm. It wasn't anything as severe as this though."

Crane let out a low sigh, then lowered Kili's hand back into the bed, and took a seat. "The Corruption."

"Yeah. That's what Jimmy called it. Said his mom had said it was a good thing. Said that it would…"

"…it would lead him to his future mate?"

Davenport eyed Crane silently for several long moments, then glanced over at Kili. "No."

Crane nodded. "Exactly. There's much more to her scheme than even I know, but I believe the Willow Hag intends to use Kili as her vessel. Wants to procreate too and Jimmy will be the sire when he's matured enough."

"But you said the Willow Hag was a spirit. A nature spirit. How? I mean, how would that even work? Why would she even want it?" Alex fidgeted in his chair as he thought more about it. "I mean, procreation is a biological imperative. That's Biological with a capital 'B'. I know I'm new to all this magical stuff, but I'm pretty sure there's nothing biological about spirits."

"And you'd be right. Only, the Willow Hag's existed, for the most part, inside a living host for the last few centuries. Maybe even longer. It's possible some of that humanity's rubbed off on her. But the most likely scenario is she's looking to find a more permanent vessel in which to inhabit. That was the point of her experiments with the Kindred after all. She was looking to find a host that wouldn't die. Wouldn't deteriorate. The experiment failed miserably. An offspring might provide a more suitable body for her needs."

Alex shook his head. "But why Kili? Why Jimmy?"

Crane offered a sad smile. "In a nutshell? Because of me. She chose Kili because I care for her. She chose Jimmy because I reneged on my deal with her to become her consort and I feel a certain responsibility for Candace's son. There's no great scheming behind it. It's vindictive and nothing else." He sighed, then stood up from the chair. "But as for the Corruption that's occurring now in Ms. Kili, there's another reason it's escalated as quickly as it has. The Willow Hag is trying to lure out the Sin-Eater. At the moment, the illness is killing her. Unless it's reversed or at least slowed, I guess she'll be dead within the week. And given his hunting patterns, I think the Willow Hag is hoping she'll be a temptation the killer won't be able to pass up."

"You think he'll come here?" Alex stood from his chair to meet Crane in the eyes. "In such a public place?"

"Possibly. I believe he thinks he can't be stopped. Hospital security and a handful of overworked nurses wouldn't be much of a deterrent for him." He walked over to Davenport, and placed a firm hand on his shoulder. "That's why I need you to stay here and keep watch over her. I'll set up a few protection charms and wards around the room and the hospital, but I trust only you to keep her safe, Mr. Davenport."

"Where—where are you going to be?"

"To see the only man I can think of who might know more about the Ghostfeast than the Sin-Eater." Crane began moving to the door. "I've got to find a way to stop him before he kills anyone else and the more I know about the ritual, the better prepared I'll be. And, in doing so, hopefully, I'll find a way to undo what's being done to Ms. Kili." Then, without waiting for a response from the tabloid reporter, he walked out of the room and closed the door behind him.

With a sigh, Alex sat back into his chair and resumed his watch over his friend. Her chest rose and fell in a rhythmic cadence with each pump of the ventilator. It just wasn't fair. She'd overcome so much—more than eight months of living in a catatonic state—only to fall into this just hours after waking up.

He became oddly aware that his hands had balled into tight fists as he thought about it. As he thought about the Willow Hag and the evils she'd cast upon this amazing redheaded beauty. And if he was confronted about it...if he was forced to be absolutely truthful...he even found some of his anger turning on Ezekiel Crane as well. He knew it wasn't fair. Knew it wasn't Crane's fault that the Hag had such a beef with him. Still though, there was that curse of his. Alex hadn't really believed it when they'd first met, but as he got to know Crane more, he began to see the truth of it. Anyone who got too close to the man suffered. Many died.

So why does he let anyone get close to him?

Once again, an unfair question. Crane didn't deserve a life without the companionship of anyone. Didn't deserve to live his life utterly alone. But there was a part of Davenport that seethed that the man had allowed—no, encouraged—his relationship with Kili to grow despite the dangers he knew were there. It was completely irresponsible.

Alex leaned back in the uncomfortable hospital chair, keeping his eyes fixed on Kili while his thoughts whirled haphazardly through his mind. Soon, his eyelids grew heavy once more, and he found himself drifting off into a unsettling, dream-filled slumber.

CHAPTER
EIGHTEEN

Grady Falls Pass
Thirty Miles Northeast of Boone Creek
December 20
11:05 PM

E zekiel Crane crested the ridge leading into what locals called the Grady Falls Pass and stopped to catch his breath. The woods around him were thick and treacherous. The ominous clouds above—foreshadowing the snow Crane knew was coming—blocked out any light from the moon, making the hike to Jim Lorrie's cabin in the dead of night more difficult than he would have liked. But Lorrie, who everyone just called the Preacher, was the only person other than Granny who'd know the most about the Ghostfeast and the supernatural happenings going on around Jasper County.

Granted, the Preacher wasn't the most hospitable of hosts in most circumstances, but he'd always treated Crane with a modicum of respect and had never cowed to the rumors of his alleged 'pact with the Devil'. Still, the old reverend would not likely be pleased by such a late night visit to his home from even Crane.

Nor would his two pets. Crane would have to get past them before he could even approach the old man's cabin and that would be challenge enough.

However, he had no choice at the moment. With Kili laid up in a hospital bed with accelerated symptoms of the Corruption, he just didn't have time to honor the codes of etiquette for even a man as respected and, he'd readily admit, feared as Jim Lorrie.

Crane looked down into the narrow valley beneath the pass. A small wood house could be seen in a clearing at the foot of the hills, smoke spiraling from its chimney. A single light burned through one of the windows; the only indication that anyone was awake.

Well, Crane, there's no other way around it. Whether he likes it or not, you have to pay the Preacher a visit.

Cautiously, Crane turned his flashlight back on, then began descending the ridge, navigating the downward slope by grasping at tree limbs one after another, like a child on a set of monkey bars. Five minutes later, he found himself on mostly level ground and heaving for breath.

After a moment, he straightened and looked around. The Preacher's cabin was about two hundred yards ahead and to his left, but the old man's pets weren't the only dangers that lurked along the path. Jim Lorrie was also a long time moonshiner and bootlegger, with an even longer history of feuds with the federal government, as well as other shiners. Because of that, he'd rigged much of the woods around his property with booby traps of the most ingenious kinds. Few would be considered lethal if tripped, but the possibility of mortal injury was indeed likely with some. Crane would have to watch his step from this point forward.

As he approached the wood's clearing, he stopped—freezing in place—and listened. Something had just raised his hackles.

Something was out there…watching him. He clicked off his flashlight, then turned slowly around while peering through the dark recesses of the forest. He sniffed at the air. And listened again.

That's when one of Lorrie's pets began growling at him, just off to his right. With great care, he turned to the source of the growl and stared directly into the narrowed eyes of the hundred and ten pound Rottweiler named Cagney. The monstrous dog's lips curled upwards, revealing enormous canines glistening with drool as it pulled its ears back and hunched down as if preparing to lunge.

As strange as it might sound, the beast of a dog in front of him was the least of Crane's concerns at that moment. For wherever one happened to see Cagney, Lacey was sure to be nearby and that was the pet an unwanted guest really needed to watch out for.

Crouching down to eye level with the dog, he held out his hand, palm up. He then turned his eyes toward the trees above. He scanned the sparse branches overhead, searching for what he knew was there. Soon, he saw what he was looking for…two glowing orbs staring malevolently back at him from a branch nearly twenty feet in the air.

"There you are, Lacey," Crane hissed, remaining perfectly still.

Understanding that she had been spotted, Lacey rose from her perch and within three bounds was down on the ground and padding toward him with slow, languid strides. Soon, she sidled up to her sister and stopped while keeping a wary eye on the intruder.

To say the two animals were siblings would be a misnomer, for Lacey was not of any canine species. Rather, she was a three year old cougar that the Preacher had rescued when she was little more than a kitten and being sized up for a coyote pack's meal. The dog had taken to the cougar instantly and they had become inseparable ever since.

"It's okay," Crane said to them with his hands stretched out in peace. "You two know me. I'm no stranger to these woods."

The cat purred enigmatically while Cagney continued with her low, threatening growl.

"But it's been a while," said a voice hidden by the shadows of the woods. "And lots of mighty evil things been lurkin' around here as of late. Got 'em spooked somethin' fierce."

Crane turned to the voice and watched as Reverend Jim Lorrie melted into view. Though he'd aged a bit since Crane had seen him last, he was still as strong and formidable-looking as he remembered. He stood nearly six feet tall with broad shoulders and chest. A bit heavier in the gut in his older years. His shaved head gleamed in the light of Crane's flashlight. He sported a bushy salt-and-pepper goatee and mustache that did a remarkable job of concealing the man's hair lip and soft pallet. Despite the cold, he wore only a pair of jeans and a flannel shirt with the sleeves rolled up to reveal powerful forearms of a man who'd spent the majority of his sixty-odd years living by the sweat of his brow.

"Fortunately for you, I've been expecting ya," the Preacher said while moving over to his pets and laying both of his large, calloused hands upon their heads. "Though it would've been a bit more polite to come a'callin' durin' the light of day."

Crane nodded. He wasn't even remotely surprised Lorrie had anticipated his visit. "My apologies, Preacher. But as you can imagine, my attention has been pulled in as many directions as possible in recent days. This truly is the first respite I've had to come see you."

"Ah, come on then." With a grunt, Lorrie turned toward the cabin and began moving as lithely over the forest floor as a mountain cat. Cagney and Lacey padded off on their own, leaving Crane to follow the elder man toward his home.

Lorrie's cabin was old; built in the late nineteenth century by the Preacher's grandfather when they first moved to Kentucky from New England. Despite its years of harsh weathering, it was well-maintained and cozy, and had enjoyed the 'luxuries', as Lorrie called them, of electricity and internal plumbing since he added them back in the 1980s.

It had been a few years since Crane had been inside the Preacher's place, but it looked exactly the same. Meticulously well kept. Orderly. The furnishings all handcrafted and polished. The only thing inside the place that was remotely modern was the old vacuum-tube color television with crooked rabbit ears sitting on a log table in the corner of the living room. A VCR sat on top of it with a cassette of The Rockford Files jutting out from the opening.

"Take a seat." The Preacher gestured toward the roughly hewed rocking chair in the center of the room. Crane complied as his host hobbled off into the kitchen where a kettle rested on top of a wood burning stove. "Want some coffee?"

"No, thank you." Though he had little time for the pleasantries of mountain hospitality, he knew better than to rush the older man. Everything the Preacher did was a test of sorts. A lesson to be learned. In this case, he was being shown that patience in the face of adversity was essential to overcoming it.

Lorrie poured a cup for himself, then helped himself to a box of chocolate chip cookies, before moving back into the living room and plopping down in the rocker across from Crane. He took a sip, placed the mug down on an end table next to his chair, then took a bite from one of the cookies before looking over at his guest.

"Now. I suppose you're here to ask me about the Ghostfeast."

Crane smiled. "I shouldn't be surprised. But I'm going to ask anyway," he said. "How did you know?"

The Preacher rarely ventured away from his property deep in the woods near Boone Creek. It was even rarer, since being ousted from his church, for him to busy himself with the idle gossip or concerns of the community. He'd rather spend his time in the wilderness, communing with the Almighty, than muddle about in the affairs of his neighbors. A sinful vice of pride for a minister of the Gospel, by his own admission, but one difficult to break.

"Oh, the Yunwi Tsunsdi have been mighty chatty lately," the old man said, taking another sip from his coffee. "They've been in a bit of a panic since this ghost-eatin' fella reared his nasty lil' head."

Crane took a moment to catch his breath. "You can speak to the Little People?"

The Preacher laughed. "Well, of course, I can. Are you tellin' me you can't?"

Only a very select few had the gift of communicating with the Yunwi Tsunsdi. In Crane's life, he knew of only four—Granny, the Willow Hag, Asherah Richardson, and Kili. And while Granny had been a devout Christian, she'd also been a witch of sorts, making her much more accessible to their kind. But a Hellfire and Brimstone Baptist preacher? That was something Crane had never even considered.

Though the Little People weren't evil, per se, they also weren't heavenly beings either. They were spirits of the earth. Though they readily acknowledged the Almighty, they also weren't exactly His servants either. In fact, they tended to avoid anyone of the Christian faith altogether as a matter of principle. The fact that they openly communicated with Jim Lorrie intrigued him.

"As a matter of fact, they've only felt compelled to communicate with me on one particular occasion...during the One-Eyed Jack affair." Crane leaned back in the rocker. "They've never particularly trusted me."

"Hmmmm...maybe it's the other way 'round?" Lorrie squinted back at him. "Needless to say, they've been keepin' me pretty much in the loop as to what's goin' on. I knew you'd be investigatin' and with Esther gone, I figured I'd be your one hope of learnin' more about the Ghostfeast."

"Was I right?"

The Preacher seemed to consider that for a moment before giving a terse nod. "I reckon I know more about the subject than anyone outside of Bearsclaw Gully anyway."

"Bearsclaw? What do they have to do with the Ghostfeast?"

The old man chuckled. "Pretty much everythin', boy. It was that pack of inbred jackals what first made the deal with those heathen gods, the Nameless Ones, and started the entire ordeal."

Crane pondered the news for a moment. Everything he'd seen so far in his investigation indicated that the Ghostfeast workings were of hoodoo origins. Hoodoo magic was primarily an African-American tradition, and the people of Bearsclaw Gully had a long, bloody history of racial hatred for anyone of African descent.

"That doesn't make any sense," he said, describing the markings of the Yowa Cross he'd found on the victims and its connection with Kongonese magic. "Everyone in Bearsclaw are ardent racists. Almost all of them are members of the KKK."

Lorrie shrugged. "Don't mean they won't use whatever magic is available to 'em to get what they want." The old man got up out of his chair and carried his empty coffee mug and cookie box back to the kitchen. "Besides, back in the days of the pact, there were more slaves there—black, white, and even injun —than free whites. That, after all, was the whole point." He strode back into the living room, lit a pipe, and sat back down. "See, back in the day, Bearsclaw Gully was used as a slavers' trading post of sorts. Lots of people comin' and goin'. Lots of cultures minglin' together. Lots of babies bein' born of mixed races. Heck, I'd say over half the population there now is a mixture of just about everything. More than that are pretty much inbred." He coughed. "Inbreedin' is a definite problem in Bearsclaw. Has been for generations."

Crane raised a finger. The old man was starting to chase a different set of rabbits and Crane wanted to get the conversation back on course. "So what you're saying is that with the interracial breeding, some of the cultural aspects of their descendants were adopted...such as Bakongo magical practices and the like."

"Precisely."

"But why the Ghostfeast? Why do you think the people of Bearsclaw made this pact with the Nameless Ones?" Crane sighed. "Trust me. I know what it's like to be accused of such a thing unfairly. Yes, I might have attempted to strike a deal with the Willow Hag, but as evil as she is, she's not Satan incarnate. Are you sure this isn't just one of the typical old wives' tales about something the people around here don't understand?"

The Preacher chuckled. "This is nothing like your 'pact', Ezekiel. Despite your own youthful indiscretion of trying to manipulate that ol' hag, your heart was in the right place. You were a child who missed his family." He took a pull from his pipe, exhaled, then continued. "The people of Bearsclaw Gully had far less noble intentions when they struck their bargain. They..."

A string of ferocious barks from outside interrupted Lorrie, followed by the sound of metal crashing against the ground. Before Crane could react, the old man was out of his chair, grabbed a shotgun from a nearby rack, and was dashing out the door. Crane followed close behind, slipping through the door before its springed hinges swung it back in place. The sound of Cagney's barks grew more distant and Crane knew whatever had disturbed the Rottweiler was most certainly being chased by two dangerous animals.

A moment later, Crane followed the Preacher around the southwest facade of the cabin to see two old fashioned metal garbage cans laying on their side near the window. Empty cereal boxes, crushed cans, and various other kitchen refuse lay scattered along the ground.

At first glance, it would appear the man's pets had interrupted a raccoon or some other foraging animal in the midst of obtaining its evening meal, but Crane knew that was not the case. Something else among the garbage had already caught his troubled eyes.

"Is that a...?"

The Preacher nodded as he bent down to pick up the dark blue bottle lying on the ground near the cans. "A ghost bottle." The old man turned it over in his hands, examining it carefully, before letting out a sigh. "And I think it's meant for you."

He turned around and handed the bottle to Crane. There, scrawled in black Sharpie over several strips of masking tape, were the words that turned Crane's blood to ice: JOSIAH CRANE.

CHAPTER
NINETEEN

Jasper Community Hospital
December 21
2:14 AM

Alex Davenport slammed his fist against the plexiglass facade of the snack machine with a curse. The darned thing had stolen yet another dollar twenty-five and again, had refused to give up its bounty of Cheeze-It crackers he'd been eyeing for the last few hours. He glanced around, embarrassed by his sudden outburst, but no one was around to level disapproving glares at him.

Not that he should be surprised. Things had not improved in regard to the attention hospital staff had given Kili since Crane had left earlier in the evening. The single nurse on the floor—Nurse Rollins—had all but remained invisible, as if she was hiding from the friends of 'that devil, Crane'.

Frustrated, Alex lowered his forehead against the glass and sighed. He was tired. And hungry. And enraged at his inability to help his friend with whatever weird curse the Willow Hag had placed on her. But mostly, he was just tired, despite having napped undisturbed in Kili's room for the better part of the evening.

They didn't even come in to check her blood pressure. Alex couldn't help but grind his teeth at the thought. *A woman as sick as she and they don't even seem to care.*

With another sigh, he pushed away from the vending machine, strode over to the coffee machine, and poured himself a steaming cup. After a few cautious sips, he turned to head back to Kili's room, then halted the moment he rounded the corner to her hallway.

The door was ajar. He was certain he'd closed it completely when sneaking away just moments earlier. Though rationally, he knew the most likely explanation was that the good for nothing excuse for a nurse had finally decided to check on Kili's vitals; Crane's warning of a possible attack by a serial killer echoed mercilessly in his mind. The mountain man had left Alex at the hospital for the sole purpose of watching over her...to protect her should the killer attack. And what had he done? He'd taken his eyes off her for less than five minutes and possibly let a madman free to do whatever he wanted to her.

Balling his hands into fists, he crept toward the door, straining to listen for the slightest sound of a struggle. Though there was no noise, the hairs on the back of Alex's arms and neck stretched out from their follicles, as stiff as boards. After a moment, he came to the door, took a deep breath, then nudged it open enough to peek inside.

A man stood at Kili's bedside, bent over, and whispering something in her ear. He was short and stocky with sandy blonde hair cropped close to his head, and wore a light blue shirt and dark navy slacks with an even darker stripe down the sides of the legs. A gun was holstered against his right hip, sending a wave of panic down Alex's spine.

Mustering his courage, he cleared his throat and stepped into the room. "Can I help you with something?" The sound of his own voice against the absolute quiet of the hospital echoed inside his skull like a freight train through a tunnel.

The intruder gasped, then wheeled around. An odd expression—not quite fear or surprise, but more annoyance than anything else—stretched across his face. For the first time, Alex was able to get a better look at the stranger. He was in the uniform of a Kentucky State Trooper, silver shield gleaming on his left chest and corporal bars stitched on the sides of each sleeve. The half dozen pimples that dotted his face made him look much too young to wear the uniform, much less to be a corporal with the state police.

"Oh, geez," the trooper said, breaking into a wide smile. His voice had the high-pitched quality of youth. "Ya scared the livin' spirits outta me." He placed a hand over his heart and took several deep breaths. "Wasn't expectin' anyone to be around at this hour."

Alex, more relieved than he would have liked to admit that the intruder was a cop, stepped further into the room and crossed his arms.

"Which begs the question," he said. "What *are* you doin' here so late? Do you know Kili?"

The trooper looked back at her comatose form and shook his head. "Never had the pleasure." He turned back to Alex. "But perhaps I should explain. See, I'm Corporal Cody Stratton, Kentucky State Police. I'm in town helpin' the sheriff out with these murders what's got the town all a'buzz."

Alex's Spidey-sense began to tingle. There was something... not-quite-right...about this man, though he couldn't put his finger on it.

"That still doesn't explain what you're doing in Ms. Brennan's room at two-thirty in the morning."

The trooper glanced at his watch. "Oh, right! Yeah. Some-times I kind of think things and forget I didn't actually say the words." He beamed. His teeth were ridiculously white for a mere state police officer. They were much more suitable to a movie star, or better yet, a politician. "See, I heard about Ms. Brennan's sudden illness, and aware as I am about her relation-ship with Ezekiel Crane, I thought I best come and check on her progress. What with this killer attackin' deathly ill people and all…I figured Crane could use a hand."

Alex tensed. Something just wasn't adding up. "And you came at this time of night? To what? What were you doing when I entered the room?"

"Pardon?"

"You were leaning in…like you were whispering something to her." Alex began to make his way over to the bed, placing himself directly between the cop and Kili. Keeping his eyes fixed on the trooper, he reached blindly toward the phone on the nightstand and picked up the receiver. "Now maybe I've just seen so much in this town that I've become majorly paranoid, but I'm not sure I believe you. If you're telling the truth, you won't mind if I call Sheriff Slate."

Corporal Stratton's smile widened as he nodded at the reporter. "Good idea. Give 'im a call. He'll corroborate what I told you." He gestured toward the phone. "As for what I was whispering to her…I was layin' hands on her and liftin' her up in prayer to the Almighty. As a Christian man, I thought it was somethin' that might actually do some good."

Alex eyed him for several moments, then glanced over at Kili before setting the receiver back into the phone's cradle. Though religion was something rather foreign to him, he knew it was a huge part of the lives of Kentucky people. Salt of the earth, and all that. The explanation made sense…except for one thing.

"And the timing of your visit?"

Stratton chuckled. "Been investigatin' the most recent

murder. Nasty business with Reverend Thornton. It's kept me pretty swamped for the last twenty-four hours or so all. Now's the first chance I've had to come visit. Like I said, I had no idea someone else was keepin' watch over her." That's when the cop's own eyes narrowed. "Speakin' of, I think I've been plenty patient with you up 'til now, but I don't recall you ever tellin' me who you are or what you're doin' here."

Alex shrugged. It was a fair enough question, so he answered it truthfully, telling him about Kili's recent bout of catatonia, her miraculous recent recovery, and finally the strange plague-induced coma she slipped into while in his presence.

"So Crane asked you to stay by her side?" the cop asked.

Alex nodded.

"And where exactly did he run off to? Any ideas?"

"Just said he was going off to meet someone who might know something about the Ghostfeast," Alex explained. "He seems to think that these killings have something to do with it, though he really didn't explain what exactly the Ghostfeast is."

Stratton scratched at his chin as he nodded. His smile had faded. "Not many people alive these days rightly knows. Just a legend in these parts...a legend that fewer and fewer people 'round here are even aware of." The trooper glanced over at Kili. "Odd though. I'd have figured if anyone knew about it, Ezekiel Crane would. What with his death curse and all."

"You know about that?" Alex was surprised. Though most people around Jasper County believed Crane had a curse placed upon him in some form or another, very few people he'd encountered seemed to know the particulars. The death curse. Supposedly, it not only gave Crane the gift to see dead people, it also lay claim to anyone who he developed strong feelings for. People the man cared about, he'd been told by Granny, died... which was the primary reason he kept an emotional distance to most people. Until he met Kili, that is.

"Zeke and I go way back," Stratton said, regaining his warm

smile once more. "Not much about that man I don't know, though he'd be loathed to admit it, I reckon."

"Why's that?"

"Oh, long story. Let's just say we had a bit of a fallin' out a few years back...before he left Boone Creek on his Sabbatical, that is."

Alex thought about that for a second. "You don't really look old enough to have known Crane very well from around that time. What would you have been? Five? Six?"

Stratton laughed. "I get that a lot. Seven actually. Ezekiel's about eleven years my senior."

Alex simply stared back at him.

"You're wondering what kind of a falling out an eighteen year old would have with a seven year old."

The reporter gave a silent nod. There was just something about this guy that set his hairs on end.

"Had more to do with my dad, really," the trooper explained. "Daddy is a state judge now, but back then, he was the county's judge executive...essentially, in Kentucky, that's the guy who's basically mayor, but over all the county." Stratton's smile faltered for a millisecond as he wiped a stream of sweat from his brow, then it returned with its customary brilliance. "Anyway, Crane and Daddy had some pretty heated words one day. The argument led to my daddy havin' a stroke. Happened right in front of a whole mess of people. Needless to say, Crane's curse was blamed.

"Now back then, I used to hang out at the Crane homestead a good bit—Granny always had the best honeycomb candies you ever tasted. That's how I got to know Ezekiel and his brother and sister. They looked after me as if I was one of their own. But after the incident with Crane, my dad refused to let me step foot on their property ever again. Soon after the incident, Ezekiel disappeared. Left town with hardly any word about his whereabouts or goin's on. And though he came back home just last year, I ain't had a chance to come visit until now."

There was something in the way Stratton had told the story that made Alex think there was far more to it. And the tone in the trooper's voice, while reciting certain portions of the tale, gave evidence to the fact that he didn't exactly care for the mysterious Crane one bit. Still, Alex couldn't pinpoint any specific falsehoods in the narrative, so he nodded back at him with acceptance.

"I see. Makes sense," he said, deciding it was time to direct the conversation to something more helpful. "So tell me...any news on these murders? Any suspects?"

Stratton's insufferable grin widened, as he pointed a finger gun at him while clucking his teeth. "Oooh, you!" He cackled at some joke Alex hadn't quite understood. "You know I can't divulge nothin' about the case to no reporters...even if yer friends with Ezekiel Crane. But good try, though. Almost had me spillin' the beans."

Alex smiled back. "You got me." He returned the finger gun shootout. "But what you're saying is that there *are* beans that could be spilled."

That indeed was news. Crane had seemed to think that the murders were well beyond the scope of local law enforcement— or any law enforcement, for that matter. But the young trooper seemed to think that there was something noteworthy he couldn't talk about.

Stratton's smile wavered. "I can neither confirm or deny that." The trooper's muscles tensed visibly under his polyester uniform, as if mortified at his verbal blunder. Then, abruptly, he turned and walked over to the corner of the hospital room and retrieved his hat from a hatrack before moving for the door. "Well, Mr. Davenport, I think I've taken up enough of yer time. Looks like Ms. Brennan there's in good hands and I've got a murderer to catch. So, if you'll pardon me..."

Alex nodded with a smile and wave. "Nice to meet you, Corporal. If there's anything I can do to help you in your investigation, please let me know."

Stratton returned the wave as he nervously backed out of the room. "You know I will." His Cheshire smile reappeared just as the hospital room door closed quickly behind him.

CHAPTER
TWENTY

Grady Falls Pass
Reverend Jim Lorrie's Cabin
December 21
2:43 AM

Crane leaned forward in the rocking chair, unable to tear his eyes away from the bright blue bottle standing upright inside the chalk circle on Jim Lorrie's floorboards. For his part, the Preacher busied himself, darting from a cabinet to a chest of drawers and disappearing into the back of the house before reappearing with an assortment of bric-a-brac tucked inside a metal mop bucket.

The older man took a moment to catch his breath, then eased the bucket onto the floor outside of the chalk circle.

"So ya lost him?"

Although Crane heard the question, he couldn't find strength enough to answer. He simply continued to stare at the bottle and the hand-scrawled label with his brother's name on it.

Of course, Lorrie was correct. Though Crane had taken off after the prowler who'd left the bottle near the trash cans, leading him and Cagney and Lacey on a twisted chase through the valley, all signs of their prey had vanished once they came to Pucket's Grove, a few miles southeast of the cabin. No footprints. No broken twigs. No trail of any kind. Even the dog had been unable to reacquire their quarry's scent. It was as if the person had simply dematerialized from the woods.

After a long pause, Crane gave a curt nod in response to the question, but still kept his eyes glued to the bottle.

The Preacher crouched down on the floor and eased himself into a seated position, Indian-style. He then began picking through the contents of the bucket and setting them next to him without a word. After a moment, Crane glanced over at the working Jim Lorrie was preparing.

A single crystal lens, a box of matches, a pair of binoculars, and a bottle of Windex now rested beside him on the floor. Next his beefy hand withdrew an old kerosene lantern, rusted handle barely hanging onto its mounts, a pair of bifocal glasses, a mirror, and five other similar objects.

"And all this will…"

The Preacher shrugged. "It should. If I do it right. This was your Granny's forte. Not exactly somethin' an old Baptist preacher knows much about." He arranged the odd accoutrements around the circle, starting with the single lens at the one o'clock position and concluding with the lantern at twelve. "But if your brother's really in there…" He gestured toward the bottle. "This should tell us."

"And if he is?"

The old man stopped what he was doing and sighed, but didn't remove his gaze from the floor.

"That, I'm afraid, is beyond me." Once more, he reached into the bucket and produced a long Bowie knife. "Hold out a finger. I need some of your blood."

Crane did as he was told without needing an explanation. His blood. The same blood that ran through his brother's veins.

Carefully, the Preacher stabbed at the finger with the tip of the knife and waited until a small bead of crimson swelled up from the puncture. He then scraped some of it away and swiped it across the lens. He repeated the process for all twelve items around the circle, then looked over at Crane. "I'm afraid there aren't but a few in this ol' world that can release a spirit once it's been trapped in one of these bottles. Remember, these things are designed to capture haints and shades, not livin' spirits. Break the bottle and the spirit could dissipate into nothin'. Try tamperin' with the bottle...or openin' it...and, well, who knows?"

Crane leaned forward. "So, who would know?"

"The Sin-eater...or at least, this particular one...naturally. He's the one who set these traps. He's the one who'd know best how to release yer brother."

"And if that's not an option?"

The old man stood, waddled over to the other rocking chair, and sat down with a groan. "More than likely someone in Bearsclaw Gully. Not many people, mind you. Ghost-catchin' is a dying art. But I'd say you kick enough stones, one or two of the older ones will know a thing or two that might help."

A knot was slowly curling violently within Crane's gut. Every muscle throughout his lean frame felt on fire. His head pounded. His pulse raced. He was losing control. It was a feeling he'd not experienced in quite some time...that sense of helplessness that haunts so many others. He was quickly approaching despair and he knew it. Now, there was no Granny on which to lean either. A mad killer roaming the backwoods of Boone Creek. His friend Kili marked by the Willow Hag and witched into this strange state of Corruption that would surely draw the Sin-Eater out for a morsel he could not resist. And now this. His brother, who'd suffered so much during his short life...all because of that accursed deal he'd struck with the Hag years earlier...was now trapped within this inescapable glass prison.

"We don't know he's in there yet," Lorrie said, as if reading his thoughts. "It could just be a threat."

"Yes," Crane said. "We do. But we need to verify." He nodded to the arcane circle at his feet. "The objects. Lantern, glasses, etc. All representative of better sight, correct?"

The Preacher nodded.

"And my blood acts in much the same way as it would with a dousing rod...it homes in on the target. In this case, Josiah."

The old man shifted in his seat with obvious discomfort. The Baptist in him was struggling against the ancient ways of his Appalachian kin.

"Reverend, have no fear. What we're attempting here is not 'magic'. Dousing is more science than most people are aware." Crane slipped from his chair and knelt by the chalk circle. The opportunity to explain something he understood well was already invigorating his glum psyche. "It's more like quantum physics really. The atoms that make up my blood—or rather, the protons and electrons—magnetically seek out their own kind.

"Let's say, for instance, you're searching for a missing little girl lost in the woods. You take a strand of her hair, wrap it around the rod, and wait for that gentle tug. It is my theory that that tug is merely the subatomic particles of one part being pulled toward its greater sum. Nothing magical about it at all."

Lorrie let out a low growl. "Oh, I get *that*. That's not my concern here." He pointed at the bottle. "It's not even my concern about how a material focus such as your blood will pinpoint an ethereal spirit—though I am curious how that plays into yer little physics theory." He didn't allow an opportunity for Crane to respond before pressing on. "No, what I'm concerned about is yer brother's state in general. It ain't natural. His body in a prolonged coma while his spirit walks free. The Good Book says, 'Absence from the body is presence with the Lord.' So what does your brother's current situation mean exactly in terms of everything I believe?"

"Ah!" Crane smiled at this. "I understand completely. As a matter of fact, I shared your very same concerns when I first learned of Josiah's condition." He shifted the single lens slightly to the left to even the artifacts into a more precise circle. "And while we don't have time to go into it at great length, I can assure you that I've been able to reconcile this apparent theological conundrum with this simple difference. Josiah isn't dead. His spirit is still very much tethered to his mortal coil..."

Crane's voice trailed off as a new thought leapt to the forefront of his mind. *His body. Josiah's body is still alive. That means...*

He looked up at the Preacher. "I'm sorry, Reverend. We've no more time to wax philosophic about our current dilemma. Josiah may not have much time and we need to discern first whether he's actually confined to the bottle or not." He reached out his hand. "So please, assist me with this. It is, after all, your working and not my own. Only you can perform it."

The Preacher nodded and slipped down onto his knees at the twelve o'clock position of the circle. "Looks like the blood's had time enough to set." He motioned toward the glasses at the other end. "Position yourself behind those and focus on the lenses."

When Crane had complied, Lorrie took the matches from the eleven o'clock position, struck one, and lit the lantern before setting the matchbox back in place. The room erupted in the warm radiance of lantern light. Shadows danced across the cabin's walls in ghostly pirouettes.

"Now boy, focus on yer brother."

While keeping his finger tips pressed lightly on the bifocals, he concentrated on Josiah. His face. His smile. His laugh. His atrophied limbs in his hospital bed. The spirit body he'd become accustomed to conversing with over the last few months. After several silent moments, the Preacher began to pray in an indecipherable tongue, mumbling just under his breath while weaving his hands over the circle and touching each of the accoutrements in a flurry of movement.

Crane strained with concentration, but his thoughts shifted uncontrollably from his brother to Kili, then to the Hag and the killer, and invariably ending with the gut-wrenching emptiness of losing Granny. No matter how hard he tried, he could not coax his normally disciplined mind into cooperating.

"What's the matter, boy?"

He ignored the question, blocking everything but his brother from his mind. But he could only hold Josiah's mental image for a few seconds before all the other thoughts rushed back through his mind.

He looked up at the Preacher, who was eyeing him with deep concern etched across his brow. "Now ain't the time for ya to start doubting yerself, son. The people of this godless community need you. So does yer brother."

"I know." Crane sighed. "But I can't remember when I've endured so much before. When bad things happen to me, I can muster on...content that I am right where I'm supposed to be in this life. But this curse...those I love...those I'm sworn to protect..."

Lorrie nodded. "They're all dyin' on ya, I know." He allowed himself the faintest of a smile. "I got news for ya, son...that ain't the Willow Hag's curse. That's life. For everybody. These things...these horrible horrible things that keep happenin' to your friends and family? Yeah, that's just the hand they were dealt. Providence working God's will in our lives. Bad things happen. So do lots of good. You can't keep beatin' yerself up over hexes or luck or whatever else you can't control. Ya just gotta keep movin' on. Doin' what's right."

Crane smiled as he thought about what the older man was saying, then nodded. "All right. Let's try this again then."

"Good man!"

The two resumed their positions at the twelve and six o'clock positions and began the ritual once more. This time, Crane managed to strip away the whirlwind of emotions clouding his mind and place full attention on the task at hand. His brother. After several intense seconds, the lantern flared up, nearly blinding the two men and illuminating the blue bottle with a warm radiance. A moment later, the gas-fueled flame died away, leaving them in the dim cabin lighting once more.

They had their answer. Josiah Crane was indeed confined to the ghost bottle and neither of them had any idea how they were going to get him out.

Twenty Minutes Later

EZEKIEL CRANE STOOD from the rocking chair and reached out a hand to the Preacher for all the information he'd provided. With a sad smile, Lorrie took the hand, giving it a firm shake.

The old man then picked up the ghost bottle containing his brother and gently placed it in Crane's hand before saying, "Go to Bearsclaw. Ask around for Judith Greer."

Crane hesitated. "I'm afraid they won't cotton to my presence there much. I'm not exactly well liked in Bearsclaw."

"You ain't much liked anywhere you go, Ezekiel." The Preacher chuckled. "When's that ever stopped you before?" His face grew serious and he continued. "Seek out Judith Greer. She's an old granny woman of the area. If anyone knows about these bottles and the Ghostfeast, it'll be her."

Crane nodded his understanding and walked out the door without another word.

CHAPTER
TWENTY-ONE

The Green Glen Apartment Complex, #236
December 21
10:15 AM

S amantha Reardon leaned back in her tub, trying to relax as the warm water lapped at her skin. She was finally going to do it. How many times had she gone through this same ritual, only to change her mind at the very last second? She'd lost count. But today was the day. She just knew it. She'd be happier for it. The world would be happier as well. After all, it had made itself very clear on so many occasions that it wanted no part of her and for the first time in her life, she was ready to accept that and give the world what it wanted.

Of course, the Sin-eater had helped with that too.

"It's all right, Samantha," the hooded man seated on the edge of the toilet said to her in a soothing tone. "It's going to be all right."

Nervously, she glanced over at him and shrugged a weak smile. Why on earth she'd even let him into her house was beyond her. How she'd let him watch as she stripped down to nothing and climb into the tub was insanity itself. Yet, here they were. A masked stranger was watching her, naked in a bathtub, and she no longer had energy enough to care. There was just something about his voice...very familiar, yet so young sounding and innocent. Mesmerizing, really. It soothed her in a way she couldn't explain even to herself.

"It's time, don't you think?" the Sin-Eater cooed in her ear with his high-pitched voice. "This old world...it's been so cruel to you."

Tears welled at the corners of her eyes. Her lips trembled as she considered his words.

"It's fed on your misery. Feasted on your fears. Glutted itself on the savagery of your tragedies."

She could contain herself no longer and she bubbled over in a keening sob as she picked up the razor blade resting on the side of the tub.

"Then again, you've not been the best of tenants either, have you, Samantha?" His voice lowered to a mere accusatorial growl as he spoke the words. "Oh, you've committed your own atrocities, haven't you? I taste your sins wafting in the humid air of this bathroom even now." He reached up and pantomimed plucking something from a tree and bringing the imaginary fruit to his mouth. "Mmmm. It's so tasty...that adultery." He sat up, cocking his head to one side. "Mr. McGregor? Really? I'd always thought him to be at least somewhat decent. Guess not."

Her sobbing increased. "H-how? How did you know that?"

The Sin-eater chuckled. "If there's one thing I know, dear woman, it's sin." She could hear his lips smack behind the coarse burlap fabric of his mask. "And it ain't just married men, is it? It's all kinds. All varieties. Heck, you seem to have yourself a new man every other day, don't ya? Who's the latest conquest of yours? Oh right, that paramedic guy, Eugene Coleman. Only he's maybe a little more special to you than the others. Matter of fact, you've fallen in love with him, but other than using your body like a disease-ridden whore, he doesn't even know you exist."

"P-please…" She couldn't control the torrent of tears now. Could hardly speak.

"But your sex addiction ain't the worst of things, is it? I seem to taste some other things…much much darker things. Like that time when you were in high school and you and your friends decided to take a little joy ride."

"Stop it." Her plea was almost indecipherable amid her sobs.

"Jake Menefee—that was your sweetheart, wasn't he—was driving. You all had a little too much to drink…"

"Please, stop."

"…Jake's friend Bobby decided they needed to make a pit stop to relieve himself. Now…where was it you guys chose to do your business?"

Samantha couldn't answer as the tears continued to pour. She felt the blunt side of the razor in her left hand and considered how easy it would be. Just a simple swipe to shut him up.

"Oh, yes. Patty Jenner's house." He chuckled. "Boy, did *that* get out of hand. Patty was a fellow student with you, wasn't she? What was that name you all called her?"

"That was a long time ago!" She surprised herself with the volume of her frantic rebuttal. It was true though. Fifteen years was a very long time.

"Fatty Jenner, wasn't it?" The Sin-Eater shuddered. "Not very original. But then, few high school students are, I suppose. But poor Patty lived with that name for years. All through elementary, middle, and high school. Ever wonder what happened to her?"

"Please…"

"She's dead now. Methamphetamines from what I understand. She hated herself. Hated her self image. Hated that night that the five of you paid her an unexpected visit. Decided to change herself. Began dieting. Trying everything she could to lose that disgusting weight until she soon became hooked on a number of pills. In the end, it was the methamphetamines that killed her...but it was you, Samantha Reardon, that did her in."

"Wh-why are you doing this?"

"Why are you just sitting there in the tub holding a razor blade? Why aren't you allowing that blade to fulfill its purpose? Why aren't you fulfilling your own purpose in removing yourself from existence?" He sighed. "I'm sorry. I'm being quite mean. Truth is...I just want to help you. You've been preparing yourself for this for years. Been practicing it for the last few weeks. And frankly, I'm just tired of waiting. So, let's just move this right along, shall we?"

Samantha shifted in her tub to look at her tormentor. Or was he her savior? She wasn't sure. But now, sitting in this particular vantage point, he looked so small. So insignificant. Yet, at the same time, monstrous in his visage. There was something predatory about the man, yet elfish at the same time. He was a dichotomy she could not fathom. And he terrified her because of it.

"I don't want to anymore." She placed her hands on the side of the tub and attempted to stand. But the Sin-eater exploded from his seat, kicking her wrists with his steel-toed boot, and sending her slipping back into the sloshing water.

"I don't think you have much of a choice," he growled. "Like I said, I'm tired of waiting for you to make up your mind. Your sins have been weighed. Your life has been found out of balance. Your solution to this, Samantha Reardon, can be only one thing."

She wiped at her face with her free hand, though she could not restrain the wracking sobs or tears from flowing.

"End your life now," the Sin-eater said. "Or I'll do it for you. It's your choice."

"I...I..." She lifted up the razor blade. Her blurry eyes followed the perfect edge of it. It seemed to go on for infinity. "I don't..."

The Sin-Eater bolted from his perch, snatched the blade from her hand, and whipped it across her throat in one smooth motion. She suddenly felt very warm. Too warm. Uncomfortably warm. Then, just as quickly, frigid, as if walking out into a snow-swept landscape without clothes of any kind. She shivered. The world around the edges of her sight grew dim.

"Shhhhhhh," she heard the Sin-Eater whisper in her ear. "It's for the best. It's for the best." Then, before everything went black, she heard him say one more thing. "I give easement and rest now to thee, dear lady. Come down the lanes and walk within our meadows to your heart's content. Do so as you please, until I come for you again. Until I call you to the Great Feast of the Ghosts. And for this service, I'll own thy soul."

The Sin-Eater sat back on the tile floor of the bathroom, his hands propping him up, as he watched Samantha Reardon bleed to death in her own tub. He allowed himself a satisfied sigh. That had just been so…yummy.

Of course, she'd really had no option at all. He'd never intended to allow herself to take her own life. That would have negated everything. The most potent of shades came from those he'd extinguished himself. But it had been a most gratifying diversion while it lasted and in just a few days more, he would sup on her in the Ghostfeast.

And with every new kill, his strength only continued to grow. He already marveled at how much power he'd gained in only a short few weeks. He'd gone from a simple nobody—a spiritual orphan whom no one loved, respected, or feared—to what he was now. What he was becoming. Already he found himself able to taste the sins of others—savor their tarnished souls—before they were dead, not just after. He'd done it with that false prophet, Thornton. Known his sins' delicious flavors before he'd even drawn blood. It was doubly true of the Reardon woman.

Of course, he'd almost risked everything last night because of his own hubris. Following Crane like he had...sneaking up to that infernal reverend's house to eavesdrop on their conversation. If he hadn't already been empowered by his last meal, the Preacher's cougar would most certainly have torn him to shreds.

He shuddered at the thought. All his carefully planned work...almost wasted in a foolhardy desire for games. Fortunately, it had all worked out in the end. He'd managed to leave his little present to his nemesis and get back to the Reardon girl just when she was getting home from a night of whoring.

No harm, no foul.

The Sin-Eater stood up, dropped the razor blade into the tub, and watched it sink lazily between the dead woman's pallid thighs. Then he smiled underneath his mask. The exquisite beauty of it all was that another set of sins were already beginning to fill his palate. Another set of vices were starting to materialize in his mind's eye. The sins of his ultimate victim.

The sins of Ezekiel Crane.

CHAPTER
TWENTY-TWO

Route 23 to the Green Glen Apartments
December 21
2:45 PM

E zekiel Crane zipped around the sharp curve of the
winding mountain road faster than he'd intended, nearly
skidding his pickup truck off the shoulder and into the abyss
below. He had to slow down. The snow had finally begun to fall
and the roads were dangerously slick. He'd be no good to
anyone if he killed himself in his investigation.

But a shadow was looming over him...pacing his every move
like a winged wraith waiting to swoop in for the kill. Crane
could feel it. Feel the doom just waiting to pounce and it was
shaking his concentration. He wasn't certain why this particular
case was affecting him so. He figured much of it had to do with
Granny's absence, but not all of it. There was just something...
not right...about his adversary. Though he couldn't put his
finger on it, he sensed that these killings were far more sinister
than they appeared to be on the surface.

He had left Jim Lorrie's cabin earlier that day and made it

home for a couple of hours sleep when he'd gotten the call about Samantha Reardon. Sheriff Slate had sounded somewhat relieved on the phone. Despite a woman's untimely death, the sheriff had expressed gratitude that it was at least one not caused by the serial killer who was haunting the county's sick and dying. Though Crane didn't know Ms. Reardon personally, he'd been told that she was a strong, healthy young girl—a recent college dropout—who'd simply had a tough time in life and had decided to end it all. The near elation in which Slate had informed him of this, of course, bordered on extreme insensitivity.

But as Crane barreled around the twisting roads, a light flurry of snow wafting on the frigid mountain air, he found himself unable to be as optimistic as the sheriff. Though he'd not seen the girl yet, there was something about the description given to him over the phone that hadn't quite set right with Crane. So now, instead of heading immediately to Bearsclaw Gully as he had planned, he was making a beeline to the possible suicide of a girl with a reportedly very sad life.

He slowed his truck down as he came to the intersection of Route 23 and Greason's Pond Road, and hung a right. Immediately, he could see the Green Glen Apartment complex off to the left just a few blocks away. Two police cruisers sat at the parking lot entrance, their lights reflecting off the falling snow in bright hues of blue and red. As he pulled his truck up to the entrance, the deputy inside one of the vehicles scowled when he recognized the coroner, and reluctantly backed the car up to allow access to the crime scene.

Crane pulled through and drove around the complex until he saw the sheriff's car and...

He came to a sudden stop.

A county ambulance sat parked near the curb. Eugene Coleman leaned against the rear of the vehicle with his arms folded and his chin resting against his chest. The EMT, hearing

Crane's approaching truck, glanced up and looked at him with an odd expression. He seemed to have lost the hostility he'd demonstrated so often at these scenes and now looked...was it sadness or fearful? Crane couldn't be sure, though it intrigued him that the man was at yet another death scene. Typically, after someone is declared dead, rescue workers immediately leave the scene and head back to the station. For some reason, Mr. Coleman felt the need to stick around. It was an oddity worth investigating later.

Crane passed the parked rescue unit and pulled up alongside Corporal Cody Stratton's state trooper vehicle.

What the blazes is he doing here?

It was bad enough the corporal had ingratiated himself into the murder investigations. But if Slate was correct, this death had nothing to do with the Sin-Eater or the Ghostfeast. Granted, if the Preacher's hunch was right and the Ghostfeast had indeed originated in Bearsclaw, Cody Stratton, who hailed from that very town, might know a lot more about these murders than he was letting on. Perhaps that was why he'd taken such a keen interest in the criminal happenings in his native county. Whatever the reason, Crane knew he would have to keep a close eye on the man through the duration of the investigation, as well as keep a tight reign on the fury that still burned hot within him after so many years.

Oh, Jael. One day, he'll pay. I promise you that. But alas, not today.

Collecting his thoughts, he put his truck in park and climbed out into the cold. The snow was now coming down much harder and was beginning to stick to the grass and shrubs surrounding the complex. Red and green stringed lights flashed along the edges of the buildings, advertising the coming Christmas festivities just a few days away.

Granny's favorite time of year. A twinge of pain shot through his gut as he thought about it. These last few days, he'd been so busy, he'd not even thought about the upcoming holiday. If she was still alive, she would have certainly tanned his hide for not having the Crane decorations up and on display at the homestead.

"Mr. Crane." Someone hissed his name from behind. He turned to see Eugene walking cautiously up to him. His eyes darted, as if afraid of being seen. "Mr. Crane, I need to talk to you."

Interesting. The EMT's attitude toward him seemed to have turned a one-eighty. Gone was his smug accusatorial glare. In its place was something more akin to unadulterated fear.

"Mr. Coleman? Can it wait?" Crane approached him and could see the man was trembling. For some reason, he doubted it had anything to do with the cold. "I'm in the middle of..."

"Th-that's what I wanted to talk to you about. I should have come clean the other night in the police station." He fidgeted. "But I couldn't. I was bein' watched and..."

The sound of the apartment complex's front door swinging open arrested Crane's attention. He glanced over to see Sheriff Slate and Corporal Stratton stepping out of the building. Crane turned back to continue the conversation with Eugene Coleman, but he was already moving quickly toward the ambulance.

Curious indeed.

But he had no time to ponder what the strange encounter meant. Slate and Stratton had already spotted him and were heading his way.

"Crane," Slate said, extending a hand. "Glad you could make it so quickly."

He took the proffered hand and shook it. Crane then glanced at the trooper and offered a curt nod in his direction. For his part, Stratton did the same without bothering to shake hands with him.

"So, like I said over the phone," Sheriff Slate said, obviously avoiding the growing tension between the two men. "We have an apparent suicide here. From the looks of things, the girl—

who's been hospitalized before, by the way, for suicidal ideations —climbed into her bathtub and simply slit her own throat."

"Not her wrists?"

The sheriff shook his head. "Unusual, sure, but not unheard of. But from the old scars on both of her wrists from previous attempts, she might have just decided to do things different this time."

"What makes you think the Sin-Eater didn't have anything to do with it?"

"Lack of blood, for one thing," Cody Stratton stepped in. "Plenty of it in the tub, but the bathroom is near spotless other than that. From the previous victims, looks like our guy likes to play finger painting before he leaves."

Crane kept his eyes fixed on Slate. "And?"

"Well, also…"

Stratton jumped again. "There's no obvious signs of abdominal mutilation. None of that hoodoo mumbo-jumbo. And on top of that, the usual German phrase *Vorsicht, die Geistesser* was nowhere to be found anywhere in the scene. Looks like this has nothing to do with either this Ghostfeast business or the Sin-Eater."

Crane stiffened at this and wheeled around to look the younger man in the face. "Corporal Stratton," he said with a forced smile. "Pray tell…has the Kentucky State Police taken an official position on this case?"

Stratton blinked. "Well, no, but…"

"Then I kindly ask that from now on, you allow the sheriff to continue this briefing without interruption."

The trooper blushed. It was obvious that Slate could hardly contain a beleaguered smile. Crane, on the other hand, instantly rebuked himself for the petty outburst. It was so unlike him to allow his emotions to be so evident. In fact, he had spent the better part of his entire adult life learning to enslave his emotions entirely to his will as a matter of necessity. The death curse the Willow Hag had placed on him did not, after all, only affect those he cared for. It affected *anyone* he cared about… whether positively or negatively. The stronger the emotion, the more likely for the curse to activate. And while Cody Stratton's childhood actions were unforgivable and though he sorely wanted justice to finally be done against the man, Crane had no interest in allowing the curse that had vexed him for so long to lay claim to another victim…even someone as deserving as the state trooper.

"My apologies, Corporal Stratton," Crane immediately said. "I'm having a trying few days. My patience is getting the better of me."

"Understandable, given the pressure you must be…"

"That being said…" Crane turned to Sheriff Slate. "…when we enter the crime scene, I respectfully request that the corporal doesn't accompany us."

"But…I…" Stratton fumbled for a rebuttal, but he was interrupted before he could get anything coherent out.

"That's fine with me," Slate said, grinning. "If you're ready, we'll head in."

With a gesture that indicated the sheriff should proceed, the two turned and headed into the apartment leaving the state trooper standing alone in the parking lot.

"You know, he's really not going to like that," Slate whispered before he closed the apartment's front door.

Crane said nothing, but waited for his guide to show him to the bathroom. When he entered, he stopped abruptly and looked around. Ms. Reardon's shade stood there, completely nude, and pointing down into the tub in front of her exsanguinated body. The water was thick with blood, but well contained within the confines of the tub. Stratton had been correct. He could see no sign of blood anywhere else.

Of course, a single glimpse of the body told Crane everything he needed to know.

"I'm sorry to inform you, Sheriff, but you're incorrect in regards to the manner of this death," he said, moving over to the tub and crouching down for a better look at the corpse. "It was, indeed, murder and not suicide."

"I've been studying this scene for an hour and a half. You've hardly stepped foot in here. What on earth makes you so sure of that?"

Crane leaned in while slipping on a pair of gloves and tilted the girl's head slightly to the left.

"Tell me, who called this in?"

"I...um..." Slate flipped through his notebook frantically. "Well, that's the weird part. He didn't leave his name. Just called 911, said he was a neighbor who hadn't seen the girl in a while, and was concerned. Asked us to come by and perform a welfare check on her." He paused a moment. "I haven't had a chance to canvass the complex to talk to neighbors just yet to see which of them might have made the call."

"It won't do you any good." Crane turned to look at the sheriff. "I have no evidence, but I believe the killer called it in himself."

"That's assuming it's a murder at all."

"Patience, dear Sheriff." Crane stood up and glanced around the bathroom with quick, easy passes. "The reason I'm so certain that this is a murder, Sheriff, is simple. There are no hesitation marks on her neck. Just a single slash from left to right along her jawline and up toward her right ear." He bent down and lifted the girl's right wrist out of the water. From the base of her palm up to the mid-forearm, old and poorly-healed scars criss-crossed each other in a checkerboard pattern. "As you can see, self-inflicted incisions are rarely clean. They are typically coupled with numerous incidental injuries as the victim works up enough courage to truly hurt themselves."

"Yeah, but you said 'typically'. With the practice this girl has had, I'd say she finally just got over the fear and did it clean."

"That might be possible, but for one problem," Crane said, pointing to the slash across her throat. "The cut starts along the left carotid and rises up toward her right ear. It was at a distinct angle. One impossible to accomplish by the victim. Whoever did this was standing...*standing*...outside the tub."

Sheriff Slate stepped forward and took a better look at the gaping wound.

"Couldn't that be from the elasticity of the skin? The incision simply stretching up to the ear?"

Crane shook his head. "The cuts are far too clean. Tears through stretching would leave skin bridges along the rip. This has been cleanly cut all the way through."

"Well, I'll be..." He scratched at his chin, examining the injury in greater detail while Crane stepped around him to take in more of the bathroom. "Okay. Let's say you're right. This is a homicide. It doesn't mean that it's the Sin-Eater. This doesn't match his M.O. at all."

"How so?"

"Her chest isn't mutilated like the others."

"Ah yes, the half Yowa cross." Crane paused. "That is troubling. But it doesn't disprove that the Sin-Eater is our suspect. It merely suggests that, for unknown reasons, he's switched up his *Modus Operandi*."

"Okay. Well, what about the lack of blood all over the crime scene? Are you saying he's changed things up *that* much? I've been around the block a few times, Crane. Seen my share of serial killers. And while they occasionally do switch up from time to time, they typically don't change too many things in a single crime."

"You've taken photographs of the scene?"

Slate looked bewildered at the sudden change of questioning, but nodded. "Yep. Everything's been completely document—"

Before he could finish the sentence, Crane pushed up the sleeve of his coat and shirt, reached his gloved hand into the tub, and pulled the plug. Instantly, the blood-tainted water began to spiral down the drain and within minutes, was completely empty.

Slate gasped.

At the foot of the tub, near the drain, sat a small sculpture of a bird blown from blue glass.

"The bird, of course, is a crane," Ezekiel Crane said as he stooped to pick it up. He then turned the statuette over several times, then stopped. The words *Vorsicht, die Geistesser* were scrawled on one side of the bird in dried blood. It was faint after so much time in the water, but it was still legible enough. He showed the markings to the sheriff.

"Sonuva..."

"Precisely," Crane said, pulling an evidence bag from his pocket and placing the statuette within. "Not a word of this to Stratton, all right?"

Slate's eyes darted left and right, glancing around as if someone unseen might be listening to their conversation.

"Uh, I don't...why? Do you suspect him of something?"

"It's much too early to tell. For now, however, I've got another lead I need to check out." He lifted up the evidence bag. "Do you mind if I borrow this? It was, after all, obviously meant for me."

The sheriff nodded. "And fine. I won't tell that pimply-faced peckerwood either. Truth be told, if it wasn't for his daddy, I'd have shown him the boot the moment he swaggered into my office." He paused, then pointed a finger at Crane. "But you best keep me in the loop. The moment you know something, you tell me. Got it?"

Crane smiled, nodded, and walked toward the door while stuffing the evidence within the inside pocket of his coat.

CHAPTER
TWENTY-THREE

Bearsclaw Gully
December 21
4:15 PM

There was now a thick layer of snow blanketing the region when Crane pulled into Bearsclaw Gully and from the look of things, it wasn't going to be letting up any time soon. The sky above was overcast with dark foreboding clouds that seemed to reflect the very image of his mood.

To call Bearsclaw a 'town' would be, by most standards of the term, a baldfaced lie. Either that, or the one using the word would be greatly advised to invest in a better dictionary. In truth, the settlement was little more than a series of single-wide trailers, campers, and hovels constructed from spare sheets of aluminum siding, plywood, and two-by-fours. Each of these— probably thirty in all—were set along three criss-crossing dirt roads with a large bonfire pit acting as the 'town' center. A large six-foot stone slab rested directly in the center of the pit, but was now almost entirely covered in snow. Hundreds of cobalt blue bottles—ghost bottles—hung from fraying twine along the handful of oaks and maple trees still standing around the settlement.

A large sprawling estate overlooked the impoverished community from the bluff above like Olympus on high. The estate—complete with an elegant twenty-three room mansion—belonged to Judge Nicodemus Stratton, and had been in his family since before the Civil War.

According to the Preacher, it had been the Strattons, after all, who had started the Bearsclaw slave market a hundred and seventy years earlier and they had prospered much from it. Of course, they also had lived above the mostly inbred residents, still enjoying their aristocratic boots on the necks of their inferiors. But for whatever reason, the residents here adored the family and were bitterly loyal to them.

It was for that reason that Crane most dreaded coming here. He had not been exaggerating earlier that morning when he'd told Jim Lorrie that he wouldn't be well-received here. The feud between the Strattons and Ezekiel Crane had been a particularly violent one and the people here had a very long memory.

Putting his doubts aside, Crane found a place to park adjacent to the fire pit and stepped out of his truck into the brutal arctic wind. Fortunately, with such inclement weather, there weren't a lot of people about to see his arrival within their community.

Before closing the door to the pickup truck, he looked over at the padded messenger bag resting so innocuously on the passenger's seat. The bag containing the ghost bottle with his brother trapped inside.

He sighed.

Of all the misery Ezekiel Crane had caused people throughout his life, his brother had suffered far worse than any. All because of him. All because, as a youth, he'd attempted to make a deal with the Willow Hag. And even now, years since

Crane had made his choice during the Corruption, his brother was still paying for his sin.

"I'll find a way to release you, dear brother," he said in a hushed tone, while grabbing the bag's strap, and tossing it over his shoulder. He then closed the pickup's door and turned to face Bearsclaw Gully.

"Now I suppose it's time to find Ms. Greer, find out what I need to know, and leave this abysmal place."

He shuddered as he looked around the dilapidated community. It wasn't just the Strattons that caused him such trepidation. There was something else here too. Something he could never quite put his finger on. Something dark and ancient...more ancient than the Willow Hag even. A shadow that loomed over the place like a ghostly cloud, squeezing the life from those who lived under its wrath. It was, Crane felt, sentient and vile.

Some of the old timers in the area—including Tom Thornton —referred to it as one of the Nameless Ones. Dark nature spirits of great power and fury. Ordinarily, Crane took such talk with a grain of salt. But ordinarily, he wasn't standing in the heart of Bearsclaw Gully.

Even now, he could sense it. It unnerved him more than he'd ever admit.

Taking a deep breath and pulling up the collar of his coat to protect himself from both the frigid air and watchful eyes, he stepped away from his truck and immediately began walking toward the fire pit. The smell of ash and charred wood clung in the air, informing Crane that it had been used recently. Probably the night before. And chances were, despite the increasing snow, it would be used tonight for the townspeople to gather together for whatever festivities they customarily practiced.

Glancing around, he found a single brick jutting up from the snow, picked it up, and dropped it on one of the larger stones surrounding the fire pit. As he'd hoped, the brick broke into several pieces. He crouched down and took a pinch of brick dust with his right index finger and thumb, and dropping it in his coat pocket for good measure.

A makeshift charm against physical threats...the brick dust symbolizing the smallest components of a brick wall.

Once the charm dust was stowed away, he turned from the fire pit and surveyed the terrain. It would have been deathly quiet, if not for the howling wind blowing down from the eastern ridge. Rusted out pickup trucks, two motorcross motorcycles, and a station-wagon lifted up on cinder blocks sat unoccupied in non-existent driveways in front of several of the homes. An enormous seven foot satellite dish occupied the space directly in front of the door of a small travel camper. Plumes of black smoke billowed out from a handful of chimneys.

There were no Christmas lights here. There also were no mailboxes, so no easy way to identify the residence of Mrs. Greer.

Unfortunately, in this situation, dousing wouldn't be of any assistance. He had nothing of Mrs. Greer's to home in on. No hair or any other substance containing her DNA. Even if he had, the amount of snow—carrying with it the same 'magic' cancelling properties as water—would hinder almost any working he attempted.

No, there was only one way to accomplish what he needed to do and it was the one thing he'd been most reluctant to try. He was going to have to draw attention to himself.

Stiffening his shoulders, he began walking to the home closest to the fire pit and readied himself to knock on the front door.

"Ezekiel?" a familiar female voice spoke from behind.

He whirled around to see Asherah Richardson standing beside his truck. As usual, she was clothed only in her floral print, cotton sundress and no shoes. The cold seemed to have no effect on her at all, but then, he knew it wouldn't. The wind tossed her tangle of hair about violently, shielding her face from his gaze. But he could see enough. He could see her widened, nearly panic-stricken eyes, staring at him.

"Ash?"

"What are you doing here, Ezekiel? You need to leave here. Now!"

Crane didn't move. The look on her face chilled him to the core. Something was happening here. Something he wasn't supposed to be part of or see. He could think of no good reason for Asherah to be here in Bearsclaw, unless…

"Well, as I live and breathe," came the last voice he wanted to hear today. "If'n it ain't my two favorite children come for a visit at the same time."

He stiffened before turning around again toward the fire pit. Candace Staples' Kindred body stood grinning from ear to ear. She wore little more than a tank top and skin tight jeans— and of course, no shoes—with little reaction to the severe weather.

Crane looked over at Asherah with a glare, then back at the biological vessel of the Willow Hag.

"I was about to ask Asherah what she was doing here," he said with a gravelly voice. "But the better one to put that question to would be you, witch."

"Oh me?" She placed a hand on her chest, feigning innocence. "Why, I'm here visitin' my kin, is all. You's the one trespassin' on land what don't want ya here, Ezekiel."

"You have no kin, Hag. You're an abomination. An anomaly that should have never existed in our world. You've no more right to be here than…"

"Have you forgotten already, Ezekiel?" the Hag asked with a giggle. "Candace Staples *is* from Bearsclaw Gully. Her ma and pa live here. They've been watchin' lil' Jimmy while I go about my chores and such. Such kindly folk they are…if not a bit dense. But then, generations of inbreedin' will do that to a family, I hear."

"That brings up another question. What have you done to the boy?"

The Hag's grin broadened. "Whatever do ya mean?"

Crane felt his teeth grinding at the witch's smugness. "You know what I mean. The rapid aging. The disfigurement. At first, I thought it was the Corruption, but it's unlike anything I've ever heard of before."

"Oh, that." She laughed. "Nothing but just good ol' fashioned home cooked meals. Some good ol' healthy mushrooms. A little of my own herbs and spices thrown in for good measure."

"One-Eyed Jack. You've been feeding him the One-Eyed Jack fungus."

She gave a noncommittal shrug. "Among other things."

Realizing he wasn't going to get a straight answer from her, Crane turned his attention back to Asherah. "Did you know about this? Did you know she was harvesting the spores again?"

She turned her eyes sadly to the ground.

"Dear Lord, woman. It's you. You've been cultivating the mushrooms for her, haven't you?"

"Ezekiel, I..."

"I don't want to hear excuses, Ash. I'm sick of them. I suppose the witch will always be your *Mater-Matris* after all."

The Caribbean beauty folded her arms, narrowing her eyes at him. "I don't have to explain myself to you or anyone, Ezekiel Crane. My business is my own."

She blinked and the flash that shone in her eyes betrayed a deep-seated horror she would never admit in front of the Willow Hag. She was scared. Truly, frightfully scared. And since there was little on earth that could frighten Asherah Richardson, Crane found himself more anxious than ever.

This visit to the Gully was not going as expected at all.

"So, Ezekiel, how's that hunt for the Sin-Eater going, boy?" Candace held up her arm and pointed to a watch on her wrist.

"Tick-tock. Tick-tock. Your pretty lil' redhead ain't got much time, I'd wager."

Crane took a step forward, clenching his hands into fists. The moment he did, the sound of several guns being cocked and shotguns being pumped filled the air around him. He glanced in the direction of the sounds to see at least twenty-three men and women—many of whom were gnarled and bent over with genetic deformities—surrounding them and armed to the teeth.

"I'd be careful, Ezekiel Crane," Candace cooed. "You ain't particularly liked by my kin 'round here. I'd say you best be gettin' along."

His eyes shot from one gun-toting resident to the next, then back to the Hag. "Not until I finish what I've come here for." Holding up his hands for the crowd to see he was unarmed, he slowly reached into the bag hanging from his shoulder and retrieved the ghost bottle. "The Sin-Eater. He's trapped my brother's spirit."

"Oh, Ezekiel!" Asherah said, raising her hand to her mouth.

"I've come to speak with Judith Greer. I was told she'd know how to release him."

"Can't be done," the Hag said abruptly. "If he was fool enough to get himself trapped in that bottle, there'll be no releasin' him 'til Kingdom come. To attempt to do so will scatter his spirit to the four winds."

"I'll let Mrs. Greer be the judge of that." He glanced over at the crowd. "Please. Whatever ill will you have toward me, don't let my brother suffer for it. Where is she?"

For a moment, no one moved or spoke. They stared at him with angry, unforgiving eyes, then glanced to Candace, who simply gave a nod of approval. After another few seconds, the largest man stepped forward, shifting his shotgun to his left shoulder, and gestured for Crane to follow him deeper into the center of 'town'.

CHAPTER
TWENTY-FOUR

Bearsclaw Gully
December 21
5:01 PM

C rane stood tall as he followed the big man through the ramshackle town. The conditions here were far worse than he'd perceived when he drove up. Rooftops sagged in many of the hovels; their rusted metal roofs no longer able to support their own snow-laden weight. Faces—long, sad, and grotesque—stared at him from film-stained windows. Large emaciated dogs, chained to pikes in the soil of what accounted for their yards, barked and howled at him as he passed.

"I want to thank you for allowing me to see Ms. Greer," Crane told his guide in a quiet, but confident voice. "I would have never disturbed your village like this if it wasn't absolutely necessary."

The larger man turned and glared at Crane. He was, in fact, much larger up close than he'd been when among the crowd. Rippling with muscle, his arms were thick and powerful looking, though he walked with a stoop, burdened as he was with a cantaloupe-sized boil on his back. His clothes—at least three sizes too small for him—were ripped along the seams and were covered in caked-on filth that comes from having never seen the inside of a washing machine or even a washing board and stream.

"Best not talk to me, devil," he said with a sneer. "Might change my mind and twist yer head right off yer neck where we stand. I'm only doin' this to get you out of here quicker. So don't be thankin' me."

Crane considered the warning and gave a polite nod of assent before turning his attention back to the path they were taking. They'd already slipped past the community proper and their feet were now crunching in nearly a foot of snow toward a stand of trees near the edge of town. From his vantage point, he could just make out the glint of sheet metal just beyond the woods and he assumed it was the residence of Judith Greer.

His suspicions were confirmed when the big man stopped just short of the trees and pointed toward the metal. "Mrs. Judith's in there." He let out a low growl. "And git outta here as soon as yer done. Got it?"

"Unmistakably," Crane said, parting a cluster of branches from the path and stepping into the trees. It was odd. Although Greer's home was not deep in the woods, there was no clear path to it either. The vegetation—dead as it was in the winter months—was thick and filled with brambles. The going would have been much easier if he had a machete to hack his way through.

Whoever Judith Greer was to the people of Bearsclaw, they rarely, if ever, visited her. And, it seemed, she rarely left her own home. This elicited a number of questions about the so-called 'granny woman' that he hoped would be answered when they met.

Ten yards in, he broke free of the tree line to see a quaint little cottage of robin's egg blue wood, white trim, and a tin roof—the source of the glint of light he'd seen from the other side of the trees. A porch, floored in varnished hardwood, stretched around the front of the home, and was supported by four wooden posts painted white. Despite the heavy snow, Crane could tell the home, as well as the yard, were well-maintained. A complete dichotomy from the dilapidated huts that comprised most of the village. It wasn't what one would call 'luxurious', by any means, but it looked comfortable enough. Cozy. And utterly out of place considering the evidence of so few visitors in and out of the tiny secluded property.

Anxious to get about his business, Crane took the three porch steps with a single bound and tapped lightly on the front door. After ten seconds had passed with no answer, he knocked again…this time a bit louder.

"I'ma comin'!" he heard from inside. "Not sure where da fire is, but I ain't as spry as I used to be. So keep yer pants on."

Crane smiled. Automatically, he knew he was going to like this lady, despite her choice of neighborhoods.

A squawking from the trees arrested his train of thought. He turned in the direction of the sound to see the Raven perched on a high branch of an elm tree just to the south. He stiffened at the sight.

"Not now," he muttered to the bird. "Not here."

The Raven opened its beak and let loose with a string of caws as if laughing maniacally at him in taunt.

"Seriously. Now is not the time."

"Not da time for what?"

Startled, Crane turned back to the door to see the foyer of the little house. The door was wide open now. It took him a moment to realize his hostess was slightly below eye level to him and he looked down to see a tiny and ancient-looking black woman in a floral print mumu-style dress.

The woman was very dark skinned and emaciated to unhealthy proportions. Her paper-thin skin hung flaccidly from fragile bones. Her eyes, deep set and clouded over with cataracts, stared up at him with a patience as if she had all the time in the world. Her light gray hair was gathered up in a bun at the top of her head with loose strands exploding outward in all directions like a dandelion.

"My apologies, Mrs. Greer," Crane said with a bow. "I was merely thinking to myself."

She grinned up at him with a smile mostly made up of gums. "You sure you weren't talkin' to that vile excuse for a bird up yonder?" She nodded to the elm. Crane stared back at her in disbelief. "Albatrosses are what's good to have follow ya around, son. Dem…" She spat in the bird's direction. "Dem ain't good fer nothin' what wants to live a bit longer in dis life. If'n I was you, I'd get rid of that critter fer good."

Crane laughed at this. "Oh, that I could, sweet lady. Oh, that I could."

The old woman eyed him for a few moments, then waved him inside. "Well, it's colder than a witch's teet out here, boy. Better come inside and get yerself warm. I reckon we have some work needs to be done."

Once again, he was taken aback. "You know why I'm here?"

Her head cocked at a weird judgmental angle. "Well, o' course I knows why yer here, child. Yer here for da Ghostfeast. They's said you was comin'. Didn't say when, mind you…but that's dem all over. Personally, I thought you'd have been here a lot sooner…after all, they told me you was a'comin' more than seventeen years ago now."

"Seventeen years ago?" But that corresponded, more or less, to the era in which the Willow Hag had first marked him with the death curse.

Her lips turned down in an irritated grimace. "You gonna come inside or are you'uns gonna make me dishonor my upbringin' by shuttin' the door in yo face?"

"Oh, pardon me," he said, quickly stepping past her through

147

the threshold of the home. Instantly, a chill washed over his body like an electrical current running through a hot wire. He shuddered at the sensation, then stopped to catch his breath.

The old woman chuckled. "Feels good, don't it?"

"What? What felt good?"

"Da burden of your curse…bein' lifted off those broad shoulders of yours."

Crane wasn't entirely sure he'd heard her correctly.

"What?"

"You ain't dat bright, are you, Mr. Crane?" She chuckled as she waved at him to follow her through the house. The interior of the place was immaculately kept. He could discern not even the slightest trace of dust anywhere within. The home had the smell of cinnamon and apples and the faintest trace of smoke coming from a wood burning stove in the living room.

"I'm sorry," he said. "I just don't understand. You're saying my curse…the death curse…has been lifted?"

She smiled, then nodded as she directed him to an antique settee near the stove. When he took his seat, she sat down in a chair across from him, placed her hands properly on the lap of her dress, and nodded again. "Yes, the curse has been lifted." Her eyes turned sad. "But I'm sorry, child…it's only lifted while you're in dis house. Once you cross dat threshold to the outside world, it'll come right back on ya. Ain't nothin' I can do 'bout that."

He thought about what she'd told him for a moment. He was disappointed, but for the moment, he seemed to be free of the curse. Of the shades that were constantly swarming him. And of the fear of unintentionally causing someone he cared about to die. Right now, for these brief few minutes inside this enigmatic woman's home, he was free and he would enjoy it while it lasted.

Of course, that didn't mean he wouldn't press her later—when the Sin-eater case was wrapped up—how she managed to block the curse within her home. After all, if she could do it here, why couldn't the same working apply in a more mobile approach? It was worth checking out, surely. But for now, there were more pressing matters to deal with.

He looked at the old woman sitting across from him and marveled at her. She was so unlike Granny, and yet similar in so many ways. The fact that she was black was even more amazing to him. Whether Reverend Jim Lorrie's assertion that the majority of the residents of Bearsclaw Gully had African blood in their veins was true or not, there was no denying the tradition of hatred and racism that had run rampant here since the Civil War. The fact that Judith Greer not only lived here, but seemed almost revered, spoke volumes about her. Whether it was her good-natured spirit or some unseen immense power she wielded, the people of Bearsclaw were more than happy to share oxygen with a woman of color they'd ordinarily rather see hanged.

"So, you're correct," Crane said, breaking the uncomfortable silence that had built up since entering the living room. "I am here to discuss the Ghostfeast. I'm assuming…*ahem*…Candace Staples called ahead to let you know I was coming?"

"Ha!" the old woman scoffed. "That's about as much Candace Staples as I am Beyonce. You know full well what vile thing resides in that abomination of a body."

Crane nodded. Yes, he most certainly was beginning to like this woman. Very much, in fact.

"As for callin' ahead…ain't got no phone for no one to call. But you knew dat too, didn't you, Mr. Crane?"

He had suspected. "So, the Yunwi Tsunsdi. You can speak with them too?"

"Unfortunately. Almost every danged day. They's won't never shut up half da time. It's a wonder I ain't gone crazier than a tick on a grizzly with dem chatterin' the way they do." She paused, once again, becoming much more solemn. "Got worse just 'round the time yer dear ol' Granny died too. Guess they's was sad at her passin', so's dey came to see me instead."

"Did you know Esther Crane?" A lump had risen in his throat as he said the words.

She closed her eyes with a nod. "God bless her beautiful soul. Yes, child, I knew her. A stronger, more lovin' woman you ain't likely to meet ever again in dis life, I'll tell you dat right now. It was such a loss when she...well, ya know."

"Thank you."

"Well, Mr. Crane, that snow ain't showin' no signs of lettin' up any time soon, so I say you best get on with your questions so you can get back to Boone Creek while it's still safe. I reckon the folks 'round here aren't too keen on havin' you stay the night in Bearsclaw Gully."

Crane swallowed. His throat seemed dry. Brittle at the unexpected discussion of his grandmother. "Right. The Ghostfeast. Are you aware of what's been happening around Jasper County?"

"You mean da murders?"

"Yes."

She let out another scoffing laugh. "Honey, whatever's goin' on with that ain't da Ghostfeast."

Crane blinked. "What?"

"Just what I said...it might look like da feast. Might smell like it. Might even sound like it. But it ain't da Ghostfeast."

"How can you know for sure?"

She chuckled at this, patting her knees with amusement. "Because right now, as things stand...I'm da only one on earth what can perform it."

CHAPTER
TWENTY-FIVE

Bearsclaw Gully
December 21
5:03 PM

Asherah Richardson watched as the crowd surrounding them dissipated. Ezekiel Crane had wandered off with Jerry Burkett, being led to Judith Greer's house, and was already out of view. When they were finally alone, she turned to face Candace Staple's smug expression.

"Are you sure it's a good idea letting Ezekiel talk to the Greer woman?" she asked. "Aren't you afraid...you know, that she'll say something to give your plans away to Crane?"

"Oh, you know better than that, dearie." It still unnerved Asherah. Though her voice was distinctly Candace, the words themselves were unmistakably the Willow Hag's. "It's a necessary risk. She's got to size him up, after all. Besides, no matter what, she'll abide by the Ghostfeast. She won't let her personal feelings interfere with what needs be done."

The two began walking away from the fire pit, moving toward a small, rusted-out hovel with corrugated metal making up its four walls. It was, Asherah knew, Candace Staples' current residence. She also knew once they entered through the tarpaulin doorway, the interior would be much larger than should be physically possible. Even more unnerving, they'd be just on the edge of the Dark Hollows...in an even darker corner of it known as Briarsnare Marsh.

"It's just that..."

"It's just that you had hoped Ezekiel wouldn't know your involvement in all this until it was all over and done with." The Willow Hag tisked. "Your feelin's for that boy are gonna be the end of you both. You know that, right?"

"And you know, my 'involvement in all this' is all for him. Everything I do..." She hesitated. "...nowadays, anyway...is all for his sake. I don't care what happens to me. I just want him free of you once and for all."

The Hag cackled as they stepped through the doorway of the hovel and into the Willow Grove, some thirty-two miles southeast of Bearsclaw Gully. Instantly, the carcass that was Candace Staple's Kindred body dropped to the ground in a heap and the door to the Willow Hag's little shack nestled within the grove itself slammed shut.

Asherah had witnessed this phenomenon before and knew precisely what had happened. The Hag was unable to maintain control over the Candace vessel for too long. Once a day, she was required to shed it like an old pair of jeans and refresh herself in the magically charged confines of Briarsnare Marsh. More specifically, in the small island located somewhere within the marsh that she called home.

Here, the ravages of winter had not come. Ever. It was a balmy seventy-three degrees here...year round. Mosquitoes and wasps of all sizes zipped through the air around her. Frogs hidden along the shoreline croaked their morose dirges. The frilly fronds of the willow trees waved rhythmically in the warm breeze.

Uncertain whether their conversation was over, Asherah walked over to the Willow Hag's shack—eternally leaning to one side as if a good gust of wind would topple it over—and knocked on the door.

"Come in, daughter-mine," the Willow Hag said as the door opened of its own volition. "We have much to discuss. Much to plan for. The final stages of my plan—and the destiny of Ezekiel Crane—is 'bout to come to fruition."

Nervous, Asherah stepped through and the door slammed shut behind her amid the cackles of the Willow Hag hidden somewhere in the dark shadows of her hut.

Bearsclaw Gully
December 21
5:23 PM

THE OLD WOMAN was surprising Ezekiel Crane at every turn, throwing him off balance. He leaned forward in the settee. "Pardon my ignorance. What exactly do you mean when you say you're the only one who can perform the Ghostfeast?"

Her lips spread into a gummy smile and she cackled. "Just what I said, child. Ain't no one on earth able to perform the feast other than me...and seein' as how my young'uns are long gone to be with da Lord, I don't reckon anyone will ever be able to perform it once I'm dead. That's why this next Ghostfeast is so essential. It's gotta last."

His mind spiraled uncontrollably as he took in this information. In just a few simple words, she'd turned his entire investigation on its head.

"Pray, tell. Why are you the only one who can do it?"

"Ha! 'Cause that's my sole purpose in dis life. It was da sole purpose in my mama's life. And my grandmama's too." She sat back in her chair and coughed. "We's been here since da very beginnin'. Since the first Ghostfeast. Since before da War what set my kin free from slavery. It was my great grannie what made the pact with the Nameless Ones to begin with. Supply them with a single soul every seventy years to feast on over time and they'd leave our world alone. Dat was da deal and I reckon dey kept their end of the bargain for the most part."

"But why you? Why can't just anyone do it if they know how?"

"'Cause they can't know how, child. This ain't some workin' that any old witch can hack together with a little luck and the right pieces of da ritual." Her eyes narrowed as she looked over at him. "You's also gots to have da gift of Sight. Your Granny Esther had the gift of finding lost things. That's been passed down to you, I reckon. Me? I might not be able to see my hand in front of my face, but I can see the shape of a man's soul. As far as I know, ain't no one ever been able to do that 'cept me and my people."

"And why is that important? Seeing the 'shape' of someone's soul?"

She sat a moment as if contemplating the best way to answer his question, then rocked her body in a forward motion that brought her up from her chair. "Come on. I got somethin' to show you dat'll answer that question perfectly."

Obedient, he followed her through the small house to the back hallway that led to a basement door. Fumbling in the pockets of her dress, she retrieved a large ring of keys and flipped through each of them at least twice until she found the one she'd been after. A second later, the door swung open and the two carefully descended the staircase to the cellar below.

It looked, to Crane, like an old bootlegging operation had once occupied the cavernous space below the house. The vestiges of an old distillery leaned, unused and rusted, against the southeastern wall. Coils of tarnished brass tubing lay in a pile near the still.

Most of the rest of the cellar appeared unoccupied, although just as immaculate as the rest of the house. There wasn't a sign of a dust mote anywhere and not a trace of the typical mildew stink that accompanied so many basements he'd been in before.

When they came to the western-most wall, Crane stopped in his tracks. There, built with old stones and mud, was a small wood-burning furnace, a blowpipe, and the other typical accoutrements one would expect to find in a glass blower's workshop. Next to the furnace, mounted to the stone wall, were five shelves filled to almost overflowing with cobalt blue bottles of various shapes and sizes.

"You...you made all these?"

She shrugged. "Many of dem, yes. Some was made by my mama and some by her mama and her mama's mama. It's a long tradition...this glassblowin' for the Ghostfeast."

He considered this for a moment. "So you and your ancestors crafted the ghost bottles yourselves?"

"Had to. No other way to do it."

"Couldn't you just buy the bottles now?"

She shook her head. "Nope. See, each soul that sacrifices themselves to the feast...they's unique. Their bottles have to match da shape of their soul. That's where I come in. I sees the chosen one's soul, then craft a bottle that fits perfectly with them." She paused, looking up at him. "That's why dis Sin-Eater feller could never truly be performin' the Ghostfeast. Oh, he might be catching a few shades now and den, but he ain't doin' nothin' but feedin' his own greedy self. Won't do no good against the Nameless Ones, I can tell you that."

Crane walked over the shelves and examined the bottles carefully. They were, indeed, all unique. Not a one—nearly ninety in all—were alike.

"There's a lot of bottles here," he said, gesturing to the shelves. "But you keep saying, 'soul', singular."

"Dat's right. One soul, every seventy years. Dem's the rules. No more. No less."

"Then why so many bottles?"

"Why did Tennessee Williams write so many plays? Or Mozart, songs? Or Rembrandt..."

Crane nodded. "I understand. You see souls. These bottles are merely your representation of them."

He glanced at the bottles again, his eyes instantly drawn to one made of a much darker blue...nearly black. Its neck was jagged and twisted. Its lip fractured. Sharp. Overall, it was hideous.

"Oh, you know who that one there is for, don't you, Mr. Crane?"

He turned to her. "The Willow Hag?"

Her face grew stern. "The Hag's got no soul. None that I ever was able to see any how." She moved over to the shelf and carefully lifted the gnarled bottle in her frail small hands. "No, this one is a sad one. And a horrifyin' one at the same time." She handed the bottle to Crane. "This one is the soul you seek."

"The Sin-Eater?"

She nodded.

He hefted the bottle in his hand. Something shook from within, but he couldn't make out what it might be through the near-opaque glass.

"You've seen him then? You can tell me who he is?"

She sighed. "Unfortunately, no." She pointed to her eyes. "I'm pretty good at gettin' around in my own home, but these cataracts keep me from seein' the world most people do. When I 'see' souls, I'm drawn inward. Drawn to da world of the spirit. It's like lookin' at a shadow of a person really. Can't get no description other than general size and shape. I must have seen him alright, but wouldn't have known him if he were standing directly in front of me right now."

Her eyes narrowed at him as she spoke the words.

"Is it possible the Sin-Eater has been down here? In your workshop? Could he have used your bottles for what he's doing?

"Ha! Ain't likely. Besides, all my glassware is all accounted for. Not a piece missing."

Crane knew better than to ask her if she was sure about that. The woman might have been ancient, but her mind was as sharp as a razor's edge. Instead, another question sprang to mind and he asked it instead.

"From our talk, you keep referring to the Ghostfeast as using 'souls', not ghosts. You mentioned sacrifice, but it's hard to sacrifice a shade when they have no volition of their own. What am I missing?"

"Oh, I reckon the term 'Ghostfeast' is a bit misleading. It's a translation from an old Bakongo phrase and don't rightly work in English. Better translation would be Soulfeast, but no one's ever bothered to call it anythin' different." She began walking toward the stairs, gesturing for him to follow. "But an important element of the Ghostfeast is that the sacrifice be alive when it happens. Not no ghost or shade roaming the highways and byways of our world...but a live, good-natured feller who's willin' to offer his soul up to keep dem Nameless Ones at bay."

Crane followed close behind her as she ambled up the steps, ready to catch her if she fell.

"So you're saying that it has to be voluntary?"

"Oh, absolutely. Dem's the rules, child. Not only do they got to agree to it, they can't be tricked into it neither. They've got to knowingly volunteer or it won't work."

They reached the top and walked back into the living room.

"And are there any more rules?"

She nodded. "You already know about the bottles. They got

to be perfectly shaped. Unique to the individual." She paused. "And finally, the Ghostfeast has to take place at the time of Yule every seventy years."

"And the last Ghostfeast?"

"Seventy years ago."

Yule. That's less than two days away. The Ghostfeast is happening this year, whether the Sin-Eater is part of it or not. It can't be coincidence that he started this killing spree in the same year as the actual feast.

He closed his eyes, letting all this new information settle into place within his chaotic thoughts. There was so much to process. Preconceived notions completely erroneous.

"I think I have pretty much everything I need from you, Mrs. Greer," he said, opening his eyes and looking over at her. She, too, seemed lost in thought. Her eyes appeared glazed, staring straight at him with her head cocked at an unusual angle. "I was wondering, however, if I might trouble you to look at something for me. I'm interested in your thoughts."

She blinked, as if coming out of a trance, then smiled up at him. "Oh, for sure, child. I've enjoyed our little chat immensely. What do you need to show me?"

"Two things, actually." He reached into his messenger bag and withdrew the glass crane he'd retrieved from Samantha Reardon's bathtub. "Does this look familiar to you?"

She reached out her gnarled old hand. He handed it to her and she brought it up close to one of her eyes for a better look. "Ain't one of mine. Actually, looks manufactured. Mass produced. Probably came from the Amazon dot com or some such."

He'd surmised pretty much the same thing, but wanted to be sure. "And finally, the most important reason for my being here..." He withdrew the ghost bottle containing Josiah Crane. "The Sin-Eater. He trapped my brother's spirit in here...my brother who's not dead."

Her trembling hand came up to her mouth in a gasp. "Oh, child. Dear, sweet, sweet child." He offered her the bottle, but she waved it away. "Ain't nothin' I can do for you about that. As a matter of fact, me touchin' it might do more harm dan good."

"But I don't understand. You said the Ghostfeast ritual only works on live, willing subjects and the bottle must be crafted specifically to them. While my brother is, indeed, alive, I can assure you he was not willing and I'm willing to bet the bottle wasn't blown with his soul in mind either."

"And I told you…this thing da Sin-Eater is doing ain't the Ghostfeast. You can capture an unwilling person's soul easy enough…'specially if they's already uninhibited by their own bodies." She looked up at him, sadness evident on her face. "I'm sorry. As far as I know, only one that can free your brother is da one what put him in there to begin with. No other way to do it."

Crane's shoulders sagged. He'd expected the answer, but had clung to the last vestiges of hope that the old woman knew something that might have helped.

"Well, I appreciate your time, Mrs. Judith. You've been most informative."

She stood and shook his hand before leading him back to the front door. "Any time, Mr. Crane. It's been a rare pleasure chattin' with you. I'm sure I'll be seein' you again before too long."

He stepped out the door to the uncomfortable electric sensation shooting through his limbs, and the weight of his curse—and the heaviness of his soul—returned.

CHAPTER
TWENTY-SIX

Pulaski Hill Road
December 21
6:15 PM

E zekiel Crane gripped the steering wheel of his pickup truck tight as he plowed across the icy mountain road out of Bearsclaw Gully. The snow had picked up since he'd stepped out of Judith Greer's home, as if his curse was having a temper tantrum for being separated from him during his brief respite. Now, large flakes ticked against his windshield as harsh winds swept down from the hills to buffet his truck with their wintery fury.

But Crane's mind wasn't on the weather as he cautiously navigated the highway. It was on other things. Darker things.

He'd learned much in his chat with Mrs. Greer. In fact, he believed he'd learned more from his visit with her than she'd intended. There was no doubt that the old woman had been genuine in her hospitality toward Crane. She truly liked him and held no animosity toward him. But it was equally evident that she had been holding several crucial pieces of information back as well. It was within these omissions that his greatest discoveries had been made and now, he was beginning to have a much clearer picture of just what the Sin-Eater truly was. Even more important…who was behind it all.

He glanced over at the warped monstrosity that was the Sin-Eater's black soul bottle and shuddered. In the gleam of snow-reflected daylight, the bottle appeared much darker than he'd originally observed. Its lines and contours, wickedly more jagged and grotesque. The soul for whom the bottle represented was a fractured creature. Shattered might have been a better word for it.

Yet despite the pain he surmised the Sin-Eater to have endured in his life, Crane had great difficulty mustering up pity for him. The death and misery the Sin-Eater had brought upon the community…the danger he placed Kili in and the capture of his brother's essence…Crane found it near impossible to find compassion enough in his heart for the murderous creature. Instead, he felt nothing but a deep-seated loathing.

He glanced over at the messenger bag containing his brother's ghost bottle. "He is my brother," Crane growled under his breath. "This is an affront I can hardly forgive."

But you're gonna have to, Crane. It was an internal dialogue he'd put himself through more times than he could count. It had become so commonplace over the years since he was first cursed, he knew predictably where it would inevitably lead, though he knew he would hash it out all the way through anyway. *You can't afford to carry such hate in your heart. Love or hate. They both work the same way.*

"Yes, but it's Josiah." He turned the windshield wipers on the highest setting and slowed the truck as it swung around a sharp right hand curve. "Josiah."

Be that as it may, you'll find a way to release him. It's not over for him. Not yet. Don't let your emotions undo what you've worked so hard to avoid for the last seventeen years. Yeah, you could take that

Sin-Eater out with your death curse. Stop him from ever killing again. But at what cost? And what would become of Josiah then, if you did?

"But I'm not sure I will have much of a ch…"

Before he could finish the sentence, a gust of wind swooped down on his truck, blowing a plume of snow and ice down against his windshield like an avalanche. At the same time, something dark and swift flashed across the road, directly in his path. He jerked the steering wheel hard to the right, trying desperately to avoid hitting the thing. His wheels pulled into a skid and the truck began sliding across the road counterclockwise. Before he could regain control, the tires caught traction on a patch of grass on the shoulder and hurled the pickup over on its side and down into a ditch with a crunch.

In a violent rush of air, his airbags burst from the steering wheel, slamming into his face. Heat from the airbag's expelled gas singed his face. His body tumbled in the cab despite being restrained by his seatbelt until his momentum was halted when the truck rolled to a stop.

Seconds ticked by and Ezekiel Crane didn't move. Snow continued pelting down on the undercarriage of the pickup. He opened his eyes to find himself hanging upside down in his seat. Blood trickled down his forehead and past his brow. He was acutely aware of the smell of gasoline in the air and the ticking of the rapidly cooling engine. Mentally, he assessed himself for injuries. From what he could determine, though he had numerous scrapes and bruises, he could feel nothing resembling broken bones or internal injuries. He could not, of course, be sure whether he was suffering from any internal bleeding, but that was a worry that would have to wait for the moment.

Silently, he thanked the lucky stars above for the brick dust he'd placed in his pocket and its protection against more severe injuries.

With a groan, he unfastened the seatbelt and caught himself as he fell to the roof of the truck. A stab of fire shot through his shoulder from the weight of his body, but it wasn't severe enough to cause concern. Merely a superficial injury, he was certain, but enough pain to cause the corners of his vision to dim.

Or do I have a concussion?

Either way, he felt unconsciousness looming only moments away and he knew he'd have to get free of the truck before he passed out. He wasn't certain how long it would take for someone to spot the vehicle, but in weather like this, he couldn't take the chance.

With his vision fading, he had some difficulty finding the door handle. When he pulled up on the latch, however, he found the door stuck—probably wedged against the side of the ditch. He paused, taking a breath. He felt a cold breeze beating down against his cheeks and he followed the flow of air toward the back of the king cab to find the rear window shattered. Summoning his remaining strength, he grabbed the bag containing his brother's ghost bottle, scrambled his way to the back, then climbed out through the window. A moment later, he felt the icy sting of snow against his face as he collapsed to the ground underneath the truck's bed. He tried to push himself up, but the cold wet ground just felt too good. So inviting.

I'll just close my eyes for a bit. Not too long. Wouldn't want to freeze to death. Just enough to regain my strength and...

But everything was going dark before he had completed the thought.

CHAPTER
TWENTY-SEVEN

324 Burnside Road
December 21
4:15 PM

Corporal Cody Stratton sat in his patrol car at the corner of Burnside Road and Lakeshore, watching the rundown house four doors down with harsh, angry eyes. He was getting impatient. It was taking far too long and he knew that the incompetent Sheriff Slate would become suspicious if he had to wait any longer.

Crane, of course, wouldn't be a problem. From what he'd been told, his old foe was knee deep in trouble in Bearsclaw. His own people would keep a close eye on him, so he wasn't worried about that. But Slate. He was another problem entirely. Especially when it came time to share the tip he'd 'anonymously' received earlier in the day.

"Come on, ya creep. Leave."

He glanced at his watch. He'd been sitting there for nearly an hour, but he had no choice. He couldn't give up now or he'd pay for it dearly later. His mission was much too important to the

Ghostfeast. Too important to *her*. If he failed her, she would never choose him to be her consort. Of course, he could imagine far worse punishments for failure than that.

He was just about to check his watch a second time in as many minutes, when movement from the front door at 324 Burnside Road caught his eye. His target stepped out into the waning light, locked the door behind him, and stumbled to his car. The man was obviously intoxicated. In this weather, he had no business on the road, behind the wheel. However, at that moment, Stratton could not care less for public safety.

He had a job to do and it needed to be done with all due haste.

After his target had backed out of the driveway and had driven off, he waited another five minutes before climbing out of his car and walking over to the trunk. He popped it open and carefully retrieved a large gunny sack, then slipped the strap over his shoulder.

The contents of the sack clicked and clacked together, making him cringe. The last thing he needed was for some nosy neighbor to hear a weird disturbance outside and look out their window. After waiting two beats, he let out his breath and glanced around.

The one positive to having to wait as long as he had was that the winter sun had already dipped down past the mountain ridge, shrouding the street in a snow white darkness. His movements should be relatively concealed unless someone happened to drive by at the most inopportune time. But he'd deal with that if the time ever came.

Hitching the bag higher onto his shoulder, Stratton stole across the street, making quick, furtive steps until he reached the porch. He then glanced around, making sure there were no prying eyes looking in his direction, and crept up the porch steps to the front door. Two minutes later, he'd picked the rudimentary lock, and let himself inside, closing the door behind him.

Stratton took a deep breath. So far, everything was going smooth as silk. It wouldn't do to get impatient in this final step, and make a mistake. He took another breath, then glanced around the filth-covered living room. A flag depicting a Nazi swastika hung, ragged and torn in places, on the wall to his right above the second-hand couch. A flat panel TV, with an Xbox game system connected and paused on the screen, sat on the opposite wall. The floor itself was cluttered with moldy pizza boxes, crushed beer cans, and trash of varying states of putridity.

Talk about sins, Stratton grimaced as he took it all in. *Perhaps sloth be thine, punk.*

Carefully, Stratton searched the rest of the house until coming to the basement door.

Fifteen minutes later, he was out of the house, carrying the empty gunny sack, and running toward his car. The only thing left now was to inform Sheriff Slate of what his 'investigation' had uncovered and the last stage of the Ghostfeast would finally - begin.

CHAPTER
TWENTY-EIGHT

Jasper Community Hospital
December 21
6:34 PM

T he door to Kili's hospital room burst open, startling Alex Davenport from his nap. With a jerk, he leapt up from the chair he'd called a bed for the last twenty-seven hours and curled his hands into fists to fend off whatever attack had awakened him.

Only it wasn't an attack at all. It was Sheriff Slate, heaving for breath. His eyes were wild with excitement and his right hand nervously rested on the hilt of his service weapon.

"Where's Crane?" he asked without any preamble.

Davenport fought off the grogginess that still clung to his consciousness like a colony of ticks. Kili had had a rough day. Though still comatose with no signs of responsiveness, her heart rate had become erratic several times throughout the morning—once even going into tachycardia. Worse, the boils and sores infesting her body had grown and spread to nearly three fourths of her small frame. It wasn't but a few hours ago that she'd seemed to stabilize, allowing Davenport to get some much needed rest. Being awakened so brusquely after so little sleep had been a shock to his nerves.

"Huh?" was the only way he knew how to respond.

"Crane…where is he?"

Davenport rubbed at his eyes. "How the heck am I supposed to know? I haven't seen or heard from him since he left here last night." He allowed himself a reluctant yawn. "Why? What's going on?"

"I think we've got 'im. I was hoping Crane would come with me when we make the arrest."

"The Sin-Eater? You know who it is?"

The sheriff nodded. "An anonymous tip put us on his trail, but everything checks out. I've got a warrant and was heading over now to search his place and, God willin', arrest that filthy S.O.B."

Davenport looked over to Kili, sleeping soundly in her hospital bed. The IV bags the doctors had given her during her ordeal seemed to be doing the trick. The boils were finally beginning to fade. The infection had apparently passed. And if the sheriff was right…if he really was about to arrest the suspect… then she was in no immediate danger anymore.

"Like I said, I haven't talked to him. But if it's okay, I'd like to come with you."

Slate eyed the reporter suspiciously.

"Don't worry. This isn't for a story." He nodded to Kili. "It's for her. Crane thinks she was going to be targeted by the creep. If that's true, I want to be there when you catch him. I want nothing more than to put all this in the past."

The sheriff continued to glare at Davenport, then looked over at Kili. His face softened, then he gave a curt nod. "Sure. But ride-along only. You wait in the car while it all goes down. Copy?"

"Loud and clear," Davenport said, grabbing his coat off the

chair and slipping it on before following the sheriff out of the room.

___

324 Burnside Road
December 21
7:04 PM

THE SHERIFF'S cruiser screeched to a stop at the corner of Burnside and Lakeshore Road with two other patrol cars and the state trooper's car racing up behind him. The snowfall had been upgraded to a full-blown blizzard since leaving the hospital and made the residence across the street nearly invisible in the near white-out.

"Remember," Slate said, slipping out of his seatbelt and opening the door. "Stay here. I'll send someone when it's safe."

The sheriff slid out of his car, straightened his gun belt, and jogged over to the other officers who'd congregated near the trunk of the trooper's vehicle. Davenport watched as the group donned their kevlar vests, stocked up on ammunition, and primed their weapons for their assault on their suspect's residence.

Davenport peered through the snow fall as the officers—now black silhouettes against stark white—began creeping toward the house in a V-formation. Two officers flanked around to either side of the house, while the sheriff and the trooper approached the front door.

The reporter, however, had a very bad feeling about this whole affair. Sheriff Slate had explained everything on the way to the residence and just why they were suspecting the person inside of being the Sin-Eater. The suspect was from Bearsclaw Gully, a place where the Ghostfeast ritual had originated, according to Corporal Stratton. Additionally, the guy, a neo-

Nazi, had a grudge against anyone he didn't perceive as pure-blooded white. Although most of the victims had been Caucasian, they all fell far short of the Arian ideals of Nazi teachings. Finally, their suspect had an immense hatred for Ezekiel Crane, who the killer seemed to have taken an unhealthy interest in during their investigation.

To add to the pile of very circumstantial evidence, it appeared the suspect had close ties to the last victim—though the nature of that relationship was still debatable.

From what Davenport had been told, earlier today, Corporal Stratton had been called on his private cell phone. A woman, who wouldn't give her name or how she was privy to her information, had told the trooper all about the suspect. It had been a story of torment and pain since infancy, as well as a classic sociopathic sadism that had led him to torturing small animals since he was old enough to walk. Worse, he'd apparently become very ritualistic in these experiments of death.

By all accounts, the kid they were now slowly making their way to arrest was a perfect candidate for the killer. He certainly met all the psych profile criteria.

The mysterious woman had promised, too, that they would find all the physical evidence they needed within the home's basement.

But something about it just felt wrong to him. Too easy. Then again, Davenport was a writer with a flare for the dramatic. Maybe reality was often far more mundane. Still, there was just something about this not…quite…right.

He tensed as Sheriff Slate stopped at the front door and knocked. A moment later, the door cracked open to reveal a haze of yellow light from inside. Davenport leaned forward, trying to see the man hiding behind the slab of oak barring the front entrance, but could only make out the shape of a small, wiry male whose arms waved wildly at what must have been a lively exchange between him and the police officers. Then, without warning, the sheriff reared back and kicked at the door. Both Slate and the trooper bolted into the house.

Curious, Davenport stepped out of the car, bundled himself up in his wool coat, and ran—snow crunching underfoot the entire way—across the front yard to the side of the house. He strained to listen for any noise inside, but the sound of the central heating unit rumbling next to him made it impossible. Determined, he shimmied along the wall until he came to the nearest window and peered through the frost-covered glass.

Slate had wrestled the suspect to the ground, pinning him to the floor with a knee to the back, while Corporal Stratton withdrew handcuffs from the back of his gun belt, and handed them to the sheriff. Just as the two deputies appeared from the back of the house, their quarry was secured, and placed on a worn-out old couch with his hands behind his back.

For the first time, Alex managed to get a good look at the suspect. His eyes widened as he took in the facial details.

He...he's really just a kid.

Well, not a kid in the technical sense. But young. Probably only around twenty years old or so, he guessed.

The reporter scoured through mental notes filed away in his brain, but from what he could remember, he'd never seen him before. The way the kid's eyes were bulging out—tears streaming down his cheeks—he was freaking out. Uncertain of what was happening.

This can't be our guy. He's just too...

Too what, Alex? Scared? He got caught. Of course, he's going to freak out.

Still, despite the internal debate, something just seemed strange about this whole affair. Flipping up the collar of his coat, he pushed away from the window and began making his way to the front door. As he stepped on the first porch step, the decaying wood screeched under foot. Instantly, the trooper was at the door, his gun drawn and pointed at the reporter.

"Whoa, Tex!" Davenport shouted, throwing his hands up into the air. "It's just me."

Stratton squinted through the screen mesh at the front door, then scowled. "I thought the sheriff told you to wait in the car."

The reporter shrugged. "Do you do everything you're told to do?"

"I do when it's a law enforcement officer making the demand." The trooper paused, then nodded toward the sheriff's cruiser. "Go back to the car. Get warm. I'm sure Slate will call you when he wants you in here."

"It's okay, Stratton." The voice of Sheriff Slate called out from inside the house. "Let him come inside. Crane trusts him, so I will too."

Corporal Stratton scowled, then motioned him to come inside without a word. A wave of intense heat coming from the open fireplace swept past him as he ducked through the door, a welcome greeting on such a cold day. But that was about the only thing welcoming about the home he now stood inside.

Though he'd been unable to see much of the exterior of the house from the white out, he imagined nothing outside could have prepared him for the den of hate that greeted him now. The first thing he noticed as he glanced around the small living room, was the Nazi flag—its black swastika overlaying a circle of white on red—hanging above the couch. A trophy case sat against the wall next to the couch, filled with various bric-a-brac of the Third Reich. A few Iron Eagle medals, a rusted World War II era Luger pistol, and a Nazi soldier's helmet rested securely behind the glass case. To his left, above the television, were various spray-painted symbols of the Neo-Nazi movement and hateful racial slurs.

He looked at the suspect. He was small-framed, wiry, with close-cropped blonde hair. A pair of camouflage BDUs hung loose around his waist. The stained wife-beater tank top appeared almost painted on, accentuating his sickly frame.

"What did you say this guy's name was again?" Davenport asked.

"Eugene Coleman," Slate said, as he rifled through a closet in the other room. "He's an EMT. Just so happens, he's been at every single murder scene. And been a thorn in our side since day one."

Alex looked back at the suspect, whose eyes were now red from tears—and from the smell of the house, probably marijuana as well. He walked closer to Coleman, confident that the handcuffs holding his arms behind his back would keep him docile enough to approach.

"Please, ya gotta help me," Coleman said behind sobs. "I didn't kill them people. I swear! Crane knows! He knows I didn't do it. Ask him. He'll tell ya!"

Alex looked over at the Nazi flag, then down at the tattoo across the suspect's forearm that read 'KKK'.

"I'm pretty sure everybody says that, dude," Davenport said. "And I think it's pretty convenient for you that Crane isn't here and no one seems to know where he is. You wouldn't be able to shed any light on that, would you?"

Coleman followed the reporter's gaze to his tattoo, then shook his head. "Hey man...I might be part of the Arian Brotherhood, but I ain't a killer. At least...not that I know of..."

That's an interesting way of putting it.

"It's why I tried to talk to Crane earlier today...I wanted to tell him about the weird crap goin' on with me lately." He wiped away a tear with a shoulder. "And I could see by the look in his eye...he didn't think I was no killer. I could just tell!" He sniffed. "I'm tellin' you...I ain't done nothing to..."

"Sheriff, I found something!" Corporal Stratton's voice came from further in the back of the house. "You need to take a look in the basement."

CHAPTER
TWENTY-NINE

Pulaski Hill Road
December 21
3:30 PM

The baleful cry of a raven was the first thing Ezekiel Crane was aware of when he began to regain consciousness. That incessant squawking that had plagued him most of his life sliced through his slumber like a serrated knife, ripping and tearing him back into reality. Slowly, he opened his eyes to a world of white. His arms, extended out above his head from where he'd collapsed, were now covered in a film of powdering snow.

CAAAAAAAW! CAAAAAAAW!

The sound sent a spike of pain into his ice-numbed skull and he winced, then shivered, and finally found the strength to lift his head.

"Quiet, bird!" he hissed in a hoarse rebuke.

He blinked, trying to clear his head of the haze swirling within. The snow where his head had lain was tinted with a dash of crimson. Carefully, he reached up to his forehead and withdrew his hand to reveal blood on his fingertips.

With a struggle, he recalled driving down Pulaski Hill Road. The flash of movement that had caused him to jerk the steering wheel and set the truck into an uncontrolled spin. The vehicle overturning into the ditch. He knew instinctively it had been no accident. The 'flash' that surprised him had been all too human. Or, something uncannily similar to human. It had darted out in front of him on purpose. He was sure of it.

Drawing upon more strength than he had any right to, Crane pushed himself off the ground, dusting the snow from his coat and pants. Though the temperature was below freezing, he'd had the presence of mind enough to wear a thick winter coat, along with thermals underneath his clothing. There would be no frostbite to worry about, except for possibly his fingers, which were bare. He then gave himself one more brief check for injuries, before turning his attention back to his more immediate surroundings.

His truck still hissed and ticked behind him in the ditch. A brief examination revealed that the damage was, luckily, quite repairable. It wouldn't have to be totaled. At the same time, he wouldn't be driving it home either.

He glanced around with wary, scrutinizing eyes. He was surrounded on all sides by a vast wilderness of leafless trees and rolling hills and white-covered gullies.

He pulled out his cell phone from his coat pocket and frowned. He wasn't surprised to find he had no bars available to make a call. There would be very limited reception out here and he was, no doubt, probably ten miles from the nearest house. In this weather, he'd need to find shelter soon or he'd freeze to death before ever finding help.

CAAAAAW! CAAAAAAW!

"Quiet, you infernal bir..." he shouted, turning in the direction of the sound and clamped his mouth shut as soon as he saw *her*. The Raven was perched in a tree on the other side of the road, but he ignored it, focusing instead on the ghostly vision that stood looking passively over at him with sad, patient eyes.

Samantha Reardon. The Sin-Eater's last victim.

What is she doing way out here?

Of course, Crane realized a better question was whether or not she'd been the blur of movement that had caused his wreck. And if so, why?

He took a step toward the street, prompting Samantha's shade to back away a single step.

Odd.

He moved forward once more with the same results. She retreated a single space away. And her eyes...those spectral, black pleading eyes...never removed their gaze from him. In all the years of his curse, he'd never seen a shade act this way. It was as if she was aware. Aware of some unseen danger. And even more startling, aware of Ezekiel Crane.

While it was true that many of the shades he'd encountered over the years had looked at him, mouthing inaudible words of woe, he'd been acutely aware that the act had been more akin to a video tape playing on a loop. The shade was simply doing what a shade does. In the case of Ms. Reardon, however, something was inexplicably different. Her actions were not those of an automaton fueled by a memory imprint of the individual. These were more...well, sentient was the only word that fit here.

"Ms. Reardon," Crane called softly. "Can you hear me?"

She stared at him a moment, then cocked her head to one side as if listening to an unfamiliar noise.

"Do you understand what I'm saying?" he asked, while swiping away a fresh stream of blood dripping over his brow.

She looked down at her feet, held her gaze a moment, then looked up at him again.

Was that a nod?

Crane's heart raced in his chest. He'd never seen anything like this before and the novelty of it both excited him and filled him with immense dread. What kind of power could do this? *What devilry can give a mindless shade sentience?*

Or even more terrifying...could he be looking at the disembodied spirit of a dead woman? It was a concept he was loathe to even imagine.

He took another step, this time, onto the icy road, and she scrambled backwards to keep the same distance between them.

The Raven cried from above.

"Don't run," Crane said. "Let me help you."

Instead, she turned around and began walking into the tree line beyond. When she'd reached three or four feet into the woods, she turned her head to look at Crane once more, then resumed walking away from the road. The moment she disappeared from sight, the Raven shook, ruffled its plumage, and took to the air after her.

Seems like they both want me to follow her. Fascinating.

He tightened his coat around him, pulled up the collar for added protection against the elements, and took off after the dead girl and his ever-present totem. After a few hundred yards into the woods, he caught sight of her again, standing by a fallen tree, and apparently waiting for him. Once their eyes met, she turned again, and stalked deeper into the trees.

Pausing his pursuit, Crane pulled out a can of Copenhagen from his back pocket, took out a pinch, and sprinkled the tobacco in a circle at his feet. He then retrieved a packet of sugar from his coat, and poured a tiny pile in the center of the circle... the customary tribute for the Yunwi Tsunsdi as he entered into their domain. Once the offering was complete, he turned in the girl's direction, and once again, began to follow her ethereal trail, using the Raven as a guide whenever he lost sight of her.

A few minutes later, the trail led to a large clearing near the mountainside where a long dilapidated building had slumbered for at least ten years. Crane recognized the building immediately.

The old Tegalta Mining Company barracks.

Though Crane wasn't in Boone Creek at the time, Tegalta—which had been owned by the Reverend Tom Thornton and his family for generations—had shut down this particular site after a cave-in had killed three of their employees. It had made national headlines. Allegations that the company had allowed the disaster to happen for insurance money had never been proven. And so, the old mining camp and its barracks had laid here decaying for the past decade.

A movement from his peripheral vision drew Crane out of his reflections. He looked over to see Samantha Reardon standing patiently at the southeast entrance to the barracks. The Raven perched on the sagging roof, eyeing Crane with an accusing glare. When the shade observed that she'd gained his attention, she ducked through the door and out of sight.

Taking his cue, Crane walked over to the decaying husk of a building and stopped at the door, giving it a careful once-over. Though the rest of the building was falling apart—the roof at the north end had completely collapsed; its timbers jutting into the sky and giving it the impression of a half-eaten carcass on the side of the hill—the southeast doorway appeared to have been well-maintained recently. New hinges had been hung, which was now complete with a shiny new padlock.

Oh, Ms. Reardon. He smiled. *Wherever are you taking me?*

Crane pulled the padlock up for a quick look. *Standard Master lock. A 175 model. Nothing too extravagant, but decent construction. Probably cost $24.99 at the Morriston Walmart. It should be relatively simple to bypass.*

Reaching into his pocket, he withdrew a paperclip he'd stashed away for such an emergency and bent it straight. He then grabbed the clip near the top and began moving it back and forth until a portion broke away, leaving a small hook at the tip. Squeezing down on the shackle of the lock, he inserted the clip in the small gap between the lock's frame and the middle number wheel and swiped the metal back and forth until he felt it catch against the spring-loaded plate inside. A second later, he felt the lock release and the shackle ejected from its slot with ease.

Easier than I expected. He pulled the lock from its hinge, opened the door, and stepped inside. The barracks building—at least, the portion that was still standing under its own dilapidated weight—was a rectangular, one-room structure of about two thousand square feet. Twenty-four rusty old cots sat in two rows on either side of the room with mattresses now resembling rat's nest confetti than anything else. A pungent tang of mildew, algae, and some unseen decomposing animal hung in the air, assaulting Crane's olfactory senses.

He took another step inside, allowing a few more seconds for his eyes to adjust to the gloom. When he regained a better sense of sight, he instantly observed the now all-too-familiar half-Kongo Cosmogram scrawled in fading chalk in the center of the room. Blue shards of glass, obviously crunched under a heavy boot, powdered the floor inside the cross. Dark splotches of crimson stained the wooden floor in several places around the symbol.

His eyes pulled away from the strange tableau toward the dozens of bright blue bottles hanging from twine tied expertly to the rafters. Bottles of various shapes and sizes. Glimmering from the dimming sunlight that cut through the grime-covered windows of the barracks. A handful of the bottles seemed to sway back and forth on their strings, as if jostled by some imperceptible breeze. Crane, however, suspected a more tragic explanation. These were bottles already filled by the shades that had wandered into this gigantic ghost trap.

He growled as he gawked at the swinging bottles; his hands closing into shaking fists. This Sin-Eater was beginning to enrage him more than anyone in recent memory and it required most of his considerable discipline to keep himself under control.

A furtive movement to his left caught his attention and he turned to see Samantha Reardon shuffling toward a squat empty bottle on the other side of the room.

"Ms. Reardon, no."

But if the shade heard him this time, she didn't show it. Instead, she continued her slow march toward her doom with a haggard and hopeless face.

"Samantha, please," Crane spoke with a quiet, yet determined voice. "Don't do it. Let me help you."

This time, the young, pretty face turned to him and gave him a weak smile. She then turned back to the bottle, took one more step toward it, and disappeared. The bottle shook almost imperceptibly for a moment, flared up briefly with an azure glow, then hung still. Whether she'd been just a shade or something altogether different, she was now gone forever. Lost in the silicon prison of the ghost bottle. Food for the Sin-Eater inside his own personal larder.

"Nooooo." The word was hardly a hoarse whisper that slipped between his grinding jaw and tight lips. "No. No. No."

He imagined a similar scene a day earlier with his brother. Mentally pictured Josiah's own bewildered face as he found himself bonded to the blue glass of the ghost bottle. He could almost hear his screams as he found himself ripped from reality and imprisoned in whatever purgatory the ghost bottles provided. And a lump swelled up in his throat as the rage continued to boil from within.

He thought of Granny and what would have happened if her own spirit had remained long enough to fall victim to the Sin-Eater. Worse, how disappointed she would have been in him for not being able to capture the vile killer sooner. Of course, she would have never expressed that disappointment verbally, but Crane would have known nonetheless. The old woman would have known exactly what to do to stop all of this. And all he'd been able to do was flounder about like a blind man in a razor blade factory.

Finally, he thought of Kili, lying in her hospital bed and enduring some unknown hex placed on her by the Willow Hag. An offering wrapped up in a big red bow for the Sin-Eater. She was helpless to protect herself. And as long as the murderer was at large, she was in constant danger of being his next victim. Worse, no matter how this case turned out, she was still unequivocally marked by the Hag herself to endure the Corruption.

It was all because of him. Josiah. Granny. Kili. All of it. He and that damnable deal he'd struck with the Hag almost two decades earlier. He was the cause of all of this pain and death and sorrow and he wasn't entirely sure how much more guilt he could possibly endure.

"Nooooooo!" he shouted, this time, at the top of his lungs.

Instantly, the barracks room exploded in a shower of glass and prismatic light as the ghost bottles all shattered simultaneously in a reflection of his grief. Glass shards sprinkled the floor, half-covering the Yowa cross and blood stains. The Raven, unseen by even Crane, screeched violently at the silicon tempest. And Crane fell to his knees in rage-induced exhaustion.

His cell phone vibrated inside his coat pocket, making him jump. In his curiosity to enter the barracks, he'd forgotten to check if there'd been any cell phone reception. Still shaking from anger, he reached into his pocket and pulled out the phone. The display read: UNKNOWN CALLER. Concerned that it could be someone from the hospital, he pressed the answer button, and spoke into the phone with a stilted, hoarse voice. "Hello?"

Someone breathed on the other end, as if the caller was attempting to restrain some laughter.

"May I help you?" Crane was beginning to lose his patience and his finger hovered over the END button.

"You owe me some bottles," giggled a voice on the other end. It was high-pitched. Familiar, though Crane couldn't place it. But he knew one thing for certain. The caller was the Sin-Eater.

CHAPTER
THIRTY

C rane tensed as he glanced down at the display of his phone and silently cursed the mocking letters that shone back at him.

UNKNOWN CALLER.

He took a breath, calming himself, then turned his eyes to the shattered blue glass all over the floor.

'You owe me some bottles.' How did he know?

He began scanning the contours of the room, paying careful attention to the dark corners near the ceiling. After a moment, he found the security camera that seemed focused on him.

The psychopath had been watching him the whole time.

"Where are you?" Crane's voice was low...seething. Most residents of Boone Creek would have instantly cowed to such a tone. In the past, under different circumstances or another target, it would have been little more than an act—a tool to get information he needed. Today, it was one hundred percent sincere.

"I ain't stupid, *Ezekiel*." The Sin-Eater's tone when saying Crane's first name was mocking, as if it gave him a great satisfaction to use it. Crane strained to recognize the voice. So familiar, yet equally foreign. He was certain he'd heard it very recently.

183

"Of course, the way you carry on, you'd think you was the only one on earth who was clever. But I reckon, I'm teachin' you a lesson or two. Showin' you there's someone always smarter."

The language and syntax. Definitely local. Not well-educated either. Keep him talking, Crane. Learn all you can from…

"But school ain't over just yet, Ezekiel. We still got some more lessons to teach you."

"We?"

There was a pause. "Figure of speech. Point is, with every soul I feed on, the stronger I get. The stronger I get, the more I know. Know about people. Their private things. Those little tidbits what people like to keep hidden from the rest of the world."

He evaded my question. As I feared, there's someone else involved. And I've a feeling I know exactly who it is.

"I'm talkin' 'bout sins, Ezekiel. I can sense 'em. Taste 'em on the air. They draw me to my dinner, ya might say."

"What kind of sins?" Crane was still fuming over the loss of Samantha Reardon's shade, as well as the other failures he'd suffered since this case had begun, but for now, he'd managed to keep a calm head in hopes of tripping the killer up with his own words.

"Sins like yers, Ezekiel. Sins like that pretty red-headed whore whats been shackin' up with you for the last few months."

Crane's throat tightened. "Leave her out of this, boy." The words were barely audible.

"Or what? What you gonna do to me? Use that death curse of yours to send yer shades out for me? It'd be a right pleasurable buffet, I think."

"There's more to that curse than you obviously know. I'm giving you fair warning. You do not want to see what it can do."

"And you don't want to see what I can do!" The Sin-Eater screamed. "All my life I've lived with the fear of Ezekiel Crane.

It was driven into me by my momma since I was a kid. It's been harped into my brain from every sniveling weakling in this ridiculous hick town! And I'm sick of it. Sick of you. Ain't no one gonna be afraid of you after I'm done with you, Crane!"

So I hit a nerve. Interesting. Whoever this is, he feels slighted by me personally for something. Keep it up.

"The one thing I regret is I wasn't ready in time to take that witch of a Granny away from you before the Willow Hag did."

Crane's hand gripped the phone tight at that.

"She was supposed to be number two on my list...after Isaac Koep, the last Sin-Eater. I was bein' trained up so as I could feed on her ghost from an early age. But she stuck her fool nose in the Hag's business and got herself killed."

Crane felt his heart rate build as the maniac continued to gloat.

"Everyone around here cowed to her every whim. They was more scared of her than you, but no one would've ever admitted to it. But she was an abomination. Nothin' but a hag herself!"

"You'd be wise to mind your tongue, boy..."

"You don't have no idea how much I wanted to taste her shade. How I wanted to savor her terror as I lapped her down my gullet like a bottle of cheap whiskey."

Crane's pulse throbbed, pounding away in his inner ear as he struggled to contain his rising anger.

"*She* took that away from me, but she won't take any more." The Sin-Eater was on a roll now. "She won't take Kili away from me. I don't care what she has planned for her. Kili is mine and I bet she's gonna taste as sweet as warm molasses on a pecan pie."

Crane's eyes closed. A low growl rumbled under his throat. The Raven cawed. Its wings flapped wildly with the rising beat of Crane's pulse.

"You're such a failure, Ezekiel. You put on all these airs...like yer God's gift to the world. Like yer unstoppable. All powerful. But you ain't. You ain't nothin' but one big failure. Couldn't save yer granny. Couldn't save that dumb brother of yers from bein' sucked up in one of my ghost bottles. And you ain't gonna save yer precious little red-headed tart from me neither. Let's face it... everything you touch withers and dies. You might as well put yerself...and everyone else...out of yer misery and just end it all."

CAAAAAAW! CAAAAAAW! CAAAAAAW! The Raven was going mad, screeching and squawking wildly in the room, though Crane couldn't quite pinpoint where it was. With his eyes shut tight, he could hear its accursed feathers ruffling and flapping with ecstatic glee and for the first time since he could remember, he didn't mind it. Didn't care. The Sin-Eater deserved what was coming.

"I mean look at you!" the Sin-Eater shouted into the phone. "On yer knees...unable to contain the grief of your greatest sin. Pride." There was a cough from his end of the line. "Everyone's so...so..." *Cough. Cough.* "...freakin' scared of you, but you ain't nothing. Yer friends are all gonna die. And after I kill Kili and that rich, snotty reporter, I'm gonna go after that black witch too! And I'm gonna take my time with her, let me tell ya. Gonna have me some real fun with..." *Cough.*

Crane tried to focus on the killer's words, but the only thing he could hear now was the incessant cries of the otherworldly Raven, gleefully swooping from perch to perch within the barrack rafters. And his own pulse. The steady, rhythmic pounding of his heart beating furiously against his chest. He couldn't think. He couldn't meditate. Couldn't contain the anger that boiled inside his gut. His lifelong, carefully cultivated discipline had evaporated, replaced with nothing more than hatred... unabashed, seething, and fatal enmity.

"Oh, that look on your face right..." The Sin-Eater's voice caught in a fit of coughing hacks. He wheezed for breath on the other end of the phone, before a sudden surge of gargling replaced everything else. "W-what's…" More gasping for air. "…happening?"

As the Raven continued its ecstatically macabre song, Crane was no longer aware of anything. His mind was blank with white searing rage and nothing else.

"…are you doin' to me?" The hacking gurgles only increased with each attempt at speaking. "…the death curse! The death curse! Oh, dark gods!"

Then the phone went dead. The call ended, leaving Crane alone in the barracks with the demons of his own failure.

CHAPTER
THIRTY-ONE

Tegalta Mining Camp
Underground Storm Shelter
December 21
3:56 PM

The Sin-Eater fumbled to disconnect the phone call and fell to his knees, gasping for breath. In desperation, he ripped the burlap mask from his head and tried to inhale as much air as he could between hacking coughs. Though the underground bunker he'd hidden himself in was almost completely dark—lit only by the ghostly gray illumination of the two security monitors focused on the interior of the mine's barracks—he could make out splotches of red liquid with each wet cough he made.

Blood. He was coughing up blood.

"Oh, dearie me," came a soft, grandmotherly voice from the darkness. It reminded the Sin-Eater of homemade cookies and apple pie, though he knew all too well the voice was dangerously deceptive. "You poor boy. You don't sound too good."

The Sin-Eater, his face now almost entirely disfigured by the Corruption, glared up at the old crone who kept most of herself hidden within the shadows. He tried to speak, but only coughed up more blood in the attempt.

"Bit off more than we can chew, did we?" the Willow Hag continued. She was no longer disguised in Candace Staples' Kindred body and somehow, the Sin-Eater hated her all the more for it. "I warned you 'bout pushing Ezekiel Crane too far, child. Told you I only wanted him stretched a bit...not broken. He ain't no good to me—or any of us—if he's broken."

The Sin-Eater clutched at his throat. It felt as though an invisible iron fist was now crushing down on his windpipe.

"Push Ezekiel too far and this is what you get. The death curse I laid 'pon him is a two-edged sword and ain't to be trifled with."

"P-please." the Sin-Eater gasped. "H-help me."

The Willow Hag cackled. "And why should I? You betrayed me...your own *Sponsa-Mater*. Your own mother-bride."

"Please."

"*Tsk, tsk, tsk,*" she said, shaking her wrinkled head at him. "You din't answer my question, child. Why should I? What good are ya to me if you don't follow my instructions? Bad enough you killed that rascal Thornton—a high priest of the Nameless Ones, who I've gotta answer to, mind ya—but you've gone absolutely mad with power. Yer forgettin' yer place. Yer mission. I wanted Ezekiel curious, yes. Wanted him desperate. And wanted to lead him to Bearsclaw Gully and Judith Greer. We did that. But he's gotta be strong for the Ghostfeast to work proper and you ain't helpin' none at all with you tauntin' him about Granny or Josiah or that lil' red-headed strumpet." She paused and leaned into the light so he could see the clear, ghastly lines of her bark-like face. "And get any thoughts of takin' Asherah for yerself outta yer head now. She's as off limits as Ezekiel is. I need 'em both for my plans to work."

The Sin-Eater's fingers felt cold. He glanced down at them

and gasped at their blue-tinted tips. He could only imagine his face was equally as blue. He was dying.

"I-I'm s-sorry. S-sorry, Mother-Bride. I'll behave." *Cough. Cough. Cough.* More blood dribbled down his chin. "I promise."

The Willow Hag cocked her head sideways as she looked down at him with cruel, hate-filled eyes. She then glanced over his shoulders at the monitors and smiled. He followed her gaze to see Crane finally picking himself off the floor and dusting himself off. That strange ethereal Raven that no one else seemed able to see was perched happily on the big man's shoulder. As for Crane himself, he seemed to have calmed down somewhat. He was taking slow, steady breaths. His hands were now loose at his sides and the redness of his face had begun to subside. Already, the enigmatic man was beginning to reclaim that amazing discipline that he was known for.

Despite this, however, the grip of the death curse still worked to crush the Sin-Eater's air flow. He looked back at the Hag.

"Please. H-help me."

She returned his gaze, held it for a moment, then sighed. "Very well," she said, placing a gnarled hand on top of his grotesquely malformed head. "But only 'cause I love you dearly, my *Groom-Son.*"

Since first meeting the Willow Hag more than two years ago, she'd always talked to him about her plans for him...about how she intended him to become her consort. Her mate. The one who would one day allow her to spawn an heir in case her own supernatural longevity was cut short. Since that time, she'd always lovingly referred to him as her Groom-Son. The Sin-Eater had always enjoyed those words coming from her lips—whether from the soft, supple mouth of Candace Staples or the withered, cracked ones of the Hag's true form. At this moment, the pet name offered very little comfort. As a matter of fact, the tone in which she'd used the name sounded anything but loving and for the first time since aligning himself with her, the Sin-Eater wondered if he'd made a terrible mistake in trusting such a vile creature.

Now, as she stroked the top of his head, leaning in to whisper her ancient words that had not been uttered since before the white man had stepped foot on the continent, he shuddered involuntarily. In seconds, he felt something pop inside his chest, and a flood of air rushed into his lungs once more. They inflated as he took in a breath. Then another. And a third. His body shook against her cold embrace, as it struggled to deal with the cocktail of adrenaline and other hormones released with any near-death experience.

After a moment, the Willow Hag pulled away and gave him a crooked smile.

"All better, dearie?"

His shoulders sagged as he leaned against the corrugated metal that lined the wall of the shelter, then he nodded.

"T-thank you."

"Learned your lesson about Ezekiel Crane?"

He looked into her eyes, his brows furrowing. She knew how much he despised the man. How he blamed Crane for losing everything that meant anything to him. She'd promised him vengeance against the entire Crane clan, in fact. But now...now she was asking him for what? To leave him alone? To let him carry on with his life to dish out his own brand of cruelty to whoever he deemed fit?

"I ain't askin' you to give up on your revenge, child," she said, as if reading his thoughts. "Just be a little more patient. The Ghostfeast is comin'...Ezekiel's purpose is 'bout to be fulfilled. Then, I don't much care what happens to him."

The Sin-Eater had so many questions about that. She always referred to the Ghostfeast as some event in the future, but he *was* conducting the Ghostfeast now, wasn't he? After all, she'd taught him how to catch the ghosts herself. Taught him how to subdue, prepare, and ultimately ingest them, adding their strength to his own. And why was Ezekiel Crane so necessary for the Feast? He wasn't the Sin-Eater, after all. That privilege was currently the deformed man's and his alone. He was the only one capable of performing the Feast, wasn't he?

"Hush those thoughts, Groom-Son. Everythin' will be clear as crick water soon enough." She stood up from where she'd been huddled next to him on the ground and glared down at him. "For now, do I have yer word you ain't gonna go off script again?"

Slowly, with some reservation, he nodded his head and she smiled.

"Good," she said. "Now, I got one more task for you before everything will be in place. So listen right carefully, hear? It'll be your most difficult task yet, but you're gonna have to trust your *Sponsa-Mater*." She smiled down at him with wolfish teeth. "I'll never lead ya wrong."

He nodded again and listened to her instructions with great care.

CHAPTER
THIRTY-TWO

Grand Avenue
Boone Creek, Kentucky
December 21
7:25 PM

"Geeze, Zeke, that's plum crazy," Bear Boone said as he turned his Jeep onto Grand Avenue. "So this guy is actually killin' people just to take their souls?"

Although Ezekiel Crane was thankful he'd been able to get in touch with his old friend for the drive back to town, he had hoped for a more quiet ride to meditate on the events of the day in peace. But Bear's curiosity was as massive as his physique and had been pressing Crane to share what he knew about the murders and the new Sin-Eater that was terrorizing the people of Jasper County.

"Not their souls, Bear. Not exactly anyway."

Bear's cheeks flushed crimson as he nodded. "Then what's he feastin' on, if not their souls?"

"Their shades. Those fleeting after-images that are left behind when the souls go on to their reward. They'd only be bite-sized morsels, I suspect, but enough to empower the Sin-Eater for his mission." Crane's heart was still racing from his run-in with the killer earlier that afternoon. The rage that had nearly consumed him was still burning hot in his gut. "I shudder to imagine what would happen should the Sin-Eater ever sup on a full soul. His power would be incomprehensible."

"So any idea who this feller is?"

Crane shrugged. "I have a few notions, but none I feel comfortable enough to espouse before more evidence is gathered."

"But what I don't get is…"

The sound of Crane's phone vibrating interrupted the gentle giant's train of thought. Holding up a finger to silence him, Crane retrieved the phone from his pocket. He was thankful to see a more friendly name displayed in the Caller ID: GERALD SLATE.

"Sheriff," Crane said upon answering the call. "You have news, I presume?"

"And how!" The excitement in Slate's voice was almost palpable. "We arrested the S.O.B., Crane. Caught him with a heap of pretty damning evidence to boot. Includin' the skeletal remains of two bodies."

Crane sat up in his seat. "Do tell."

"Well, the skeletons, we're pretty sure are Isaac and Gladys Koep. Of course, won't know for sure until an anthropologist looks at 'em. As for the other evidence…well, better to show than to tell," Slate said with a chuckle. "You really need to see all this. Come on down to the station and I'll fill you in."

"We're in Boone Creek. I was heading to my bookstore, but I'll be there as soon as I can."

He hung up the phone, then instructed Bear to take him to the sheriff's office in the county seat of Morriston. Thirty minutes later, they were pulling up at the corner of the government complex, and Crane stepped out of the Jeep.

"Thank you, old friend. I truly appreciate your dependability in times such as these."

Bear grinned. "Shoot, Zeke. You know I'm always there for ya. Remember that in the days ahead, okay?"

Crane slapped the roof of the vehicle with the palm of his hand and smiled back. "Thank you."

He then turned and strode into the sheriff's office, where he was instantly greeted by Alex Davenport. His eyes were wide when he saw Crane step through the doors.

"Geeze! What happened...did a piano fall on top of you or something?"

Crane unconsciously raised his hand to his face. In the flurry of activity he'd experienced that afternoon, he'd already forgotten about the injuries he'd sustained from the car crash and the rudimentary bandage Bear had applied to his lacerated scalp.

"Something like that," Crane said. "How's Ms. Kili?"

"She's fine. Still at the hospital and being looked after by one of Slate's deputies. I wouldn't have left her alone otherwise. But when the sheriff told me he had a suspect in the Sin-Eater murders, I had to check things out for myself."

"And?"

"And...I don't know. This whole thing is just weird. Weirder than the normal Boone Creek weirdness. Can't put my finger on it, but something's just not quite right."

Crane offered a subdued smile. "Actually, I know precisely what you mean. I fear that nothing in this case is adding up and smells of nothing more than manipulation and subterfuge." He sighed. "In short, to paraphrase the Bard, 'Something is rotten in the state of Denmark' and I've had just about enough of it."

Davenport nodded. "Well, Slate wanted me to take you to him once you arrived, so follow me."

They began strolling through the police station, heading toward the back of the building where the interrogation rooms were kept. The office itself was abuzz with activity; more so than normal for the small department. Uniformed deputies rushed back and forth from one cubicle to the next while an army of operators fielded calls from curious citizens and media alike. Word was spreading about the arrest and if Crane's working theory held out to be true, it spelled bad news for the sheriff.

"Is Corporal Stratton here?" Crane asked, as they approached the interrogation rooms.

Davenport shook his head. "Had to head back to Lexington. Some unexpected problem up there, from what he said."

"Undoubtedly." They came to the first room and a deputy opened the door to allow them entry. They stepped inside to a dark cinderblock room with a massive two-way mirror built into the northeast wall. On the other side of the mirror, at a metal table bolted down to the cement floor, sat Sheriff Slate and his suspect, the county EMT, Eugene Coleman. "Of course, it would be him," Crane mumbled under his breath.

"Pardon?"

"Who tipped the sheriff off about Mr. Coleman?" Crane asked Davenport, unwilling to explain his last comment.

The reporter shrugged. "Stratton. Got a phone call from an anonymous source. They said we'd find all the evidence we needed at Coleman's house and they weren't joking."

Crane inhaled, forcing himself to remain calm. His own theories were starting to strengthen with each piece of new information. It was both exhilarating and enraging simultaneously.

"...so just where did they come from, if you didn't buy them yourself, Gene?" Sheriff Slate asked Coleman from the interrogation room.

"I don't know! They wasn't there two days ago, I can tell you that. I never seen them before in my life."

Slate laughed, bent down from his chair, and came back up with a large cardboard box. He placed the box on the interrogation table and opened it. "You're telling me that you just happen to have nearly two dozen of these..." He withdrew an oddly shaped blue ghost bottle from the box and set it down in front of the EMT. "...in your basement and you ain't got no idea how they got there?"

"Exactly!" Coleman tried raising his hands in frustration, but the shackles attached to the table prevented the gesture. "I don't know how they got there, but I didn't put them there!"

The sheriff glared at his suspect in silence for several moments.

"And the bodies? You tellin' me that those skeletons just happened to wander down into yer cellar, climb into that old chest of yours, and just decompose there?"

"I'm tellin' ya the truth. I don't know where they came from. I didn't put them there!"

Slate continued his stare.

"Look, I wanna talk to..."

"A lawyer, I presume?"

Coleman paused, thinking about it, then shook his head. "Uh-uh. Like I told that reporter, I wanna talk to Ezekiel Crane."

"Crane?"

The suspect nodded. "I ain't gonna say another word 'til I talk to him neither."

Slate turned toward the mirror and stared at it a few seconds before offering a shrug. "Don't know if he's here yet, but if he is...sure, why not?"

He got up, then walked out of the interrogation room. A moment later, he entered the observation room.

"Glad you made it," he said to Crane, reaching out a hand. Crane shook it without a word. "You heard all that?"

"Most of it," Crane said. "You really believe Eugene Coleman is our guy?"

"It's all adding up. First, he had a...*ahem*...special relationship with our last victim." The sheriff began ticking his points off on his fingers. "Second, he's been at every single crime scene, making our jobs a livin' hell. Third, we found a ton of those crazy ghost bottles boxed up in his basement. And fourth...and here's the doozy...our tip informed us that Coleman was pegged to replace Isaac Koep as the next Sin-Eater. He'd been trained up by the man. Was supposed to be initiated by him right 'round the time when they went missing. Which is why we think the bones we found belong to the Koeps."

Crane nodded. "You mean, this anonymous tip that conveniently spoke only with Corporal Stratton, I take it?"

Slate glowered at Davenport. "I see you've been briefed."

"Enough for the moment, yes. But I'm curious...given that both of them are from Bearsclaw Gully, what does our esteemed Kentucky State Trooper think about our suspect?"

"Oh, would you give that a rest, Crane? Whatever personal issues you two have with one another, Stratton has nothin' to do with this Sin-Eater business."

Crane moved over to the glass and peered into the interrogation room. "And neither, Sheriff..." Crane said as he strode out of the observation room. "...does your suspect."

CHAPTER
THIRTY-THREE

Jasper County Sheriff's Office
Morriston, Kentucky
December 21
8:20 PM

E zekiel Crane stepped into the interrogation room, shut the door, and took a seat at the table without a word. He glared at Coleman with cruel, ice-cold eyes, and pursed his lips as he leaned back in the uncomfortable metal chair. The suspect shifted in his seat, averting Crane's dark gaze while his fingers fidgeted with the chains around his wrists.

After several long minutes, Coleman cleared his throat. "Um...yeah. So, I tried to talk to you at Sam's place earlier this morning, but I couldn't. T-too many eyes watching." He glanced up at the mirror, then back to Crane. "But I need...um, your help."

Crane raised an eyebrow, but said nothing in response.

"Look, I know you and me ain't gotten along much lately..."

"Until recently," Crane said, "I didn't even know you existed."

Coleman blushed at this. "Yeah, well, point is...you're the only one honest enough to help me. The only one I can trust right now, no matter what else I might think of you and that cursed family of yers." He paused, taking a series of nervous breaths before continuing. "Look, I ain't the Sin-Eater. At least... not no more. I ain't got nothin' to do with these other murders."

"Not the Sin-Eater anymore?" Crane asked, the back of his neck beginning to tingle. So, the 'anonymous tip' had at least been truthful with that.

Somewhere, down one of the hallways of the sheriff's office, he could hear the Raven crying out for him.

The EMT clenched his eyes shut, bringing his fingers up to the bridge of his nose, then sighing. "Okay. I'll admit that. I was Isaac Koep's chosen replacement. Had gone through all the trainin' and was about to be initiated when..."

"When?"

Coleman glanced over at the two-way mirror, then back at Ezekiel Crane. "When *she* chose me."

Crane leaned forward in his chair, face hardened with frustration and still burning with the rage from earlier that day. "Mr. Coleman, you really are going to have to be a little more precise in your tale. I really haven't got all evening while you hem and haw around."

"Candace Staples!" He shouted. "Candace Staples happened. Look, every weekend, Candace comes by Bailey's and chooses one of the guys there for..." The tough-guy skinhead actually blushed. "...ya know."

"Sex, Mr. Coleman. You can say it. We're not children around here."

"Okay. Yeah. Sex. It's the highlight of most of our weeks and it's dog-eat-dog to get an invitation. People have even gotten stabbed to get picked by her."

Though he wouldn't allow himself to show it, Crane was intrigued by this. The Willow Hag cared nothing for such mundane notions as sex. Her motivations were always more devious than that. For her to be nurturing these contests of testosterone at Bailey's on a weekly basis could not be as simple as sensual delights.

"So one *lucky* weekend, she chose you."

Coleman nodded. "But not just one weekend. Every weekend for a whole month. It was the most amazing month of my life, I gotta admit."

"And your girlfriend, Samantha Reardon? How did she take it?"

He bit his lip in response. "Well, she wasn't exactly my girlfriend. Just someone I'd hook up with every now and then." He paused, then his eyes widened. "But don't get me wrong. I cared about her. I really did. It just wasn't like what everyone's saying. We were basically just friends with benefits. That kind of thing. We were both allowed to see other people."

"Fine. Proceed with your account, Mr. Coleman. How did these sexual rendezvous lead to what happened with Isaac Koep and your initiation as the next Sin-Eater?"

Coleman fidgeted some more, looking back and forth from the mirror to Crane, then to the exit. "I, uh..."

"If you want my help, you'll tell me what you know." Crane's voice was soft, but stern.

"This has gotta be off the record." He glanced up at the corner of the room where a red LED flashed on top of a video camera. "I got a family to worry about and she's already threatened me about tellin' you anything. The last time we were in this room, as a matter of fact."

Crane didn't take his eyes off the suspect. "Tell me what I want to know and we'll deal with the dangers to your mother and sister. Don't tell me, and I'll be sure to talk about our chat with Candace next time we see each other."

"You wouldn't..."

"Mr. Coleman, by your own mouth in this interview, you've

already confessed to murdering at least one of our victims. Don't think for one moment that I have any sympathy for you or that I would hesitate to play dirty if the need was there to stop these killings from continuing."

The EMT exploded from his seat. "I never said I killed the Koeps! Just that he chose me to be the next Sin-Eater."

Crane offered a cool smile before nodding toward the man's chair. "Take your seat, Mr. Coleman. In fact, in the same sentence that you told me you were a Sin-Eater, you told me you committed at least one of the murders. It was as plain as day, in fact."

Coleman blinked. His mouth gaped as if his brain worked at rewinding their entire conversation. Then, he dropped back into his seat in defeat.

"Yes. That's right," Crane said. "Your own words: 'I ain't got nothin' to do with these *other* murders.' Notice the emphasis on the word 'other', Mr. Coleman. I figure you are responsible for Mr. Koep's murder. And by default, Gladys's as well. After that, I'm not so certain. So pray tell...why should I believe you're not our current serial killer? Tell me about your rendezvous with Candace Staples. How did that change the direction of your calling as a Sin-Eater?"

Tears were streaking the man's face now. His nose nearly glowed red with congestion as he sniffed back the tears. He leaned forward conspiratorially. "First of all, she ain't *really* Candace Staples."

Crane remained silent, inwardly commanding his heart to quiet its own pounding. Of course, he already knew this, but no one else in Boone Creek believed him. For the first time since the Dirge and the rise of the Kindred, he finally had another soul to corroborate his claims.

"I don't think she's even human. Something else entirely, if you ask me."

Crane waved the comments away. "Fine, but this doesn't explain how she is responsible for you murdering the Koeps."

"That's easy. She asked me to."

"She...asked you to? And you just did it?"

Coleman nodded, wiping away a tear. "Oh, there was more to it than that. We spent a lot of time during those weekends doin' more than partyin'. We did a lot of talkin' too. She was fascinated with the whole Sin-Eater thing. Don't know how she knew I was bein' groomed for it, but she did somehow. Just figured it must have slipped while she and Mrs. Koep chatted at the store or something. But she kept asking me all sorts of questions about it. Then, she started tellin' me about things I didn't know. Things that Isaac never told me. Things about how a feller can gain power by feedin' on the spirits of people whose sins weren't cleansed. She made it sound amazin'...the things I was supposed to be able to do with that kind of power. She even gave me a bunch of old books about it...ancient books with words written with weird letters. Weird thing is, I was able to read them even though I'd never learned them."

"And so, she asked you to take what she had taught you and kill the last Sin-Eater."

He nodded. "I figured ol' Isaac was as good as dead anyway. He was on his very last leg, after all. I mean, was it really murder?" Coleman held up a hand to stop Crane before he replied. "I know it is now, but at the time...it just made so much sense. Then Mrs. Koep walked in and I ended up killin' her too. At that point, the whole 'he was gonna die anyway' thing really didn't much matter." He sighed. "Thing is, I didn't care. It was a thrill I ain't never experienced before. The takin' of a life. Made me feel more alive than anything I'd ever done."

Crane stared at the man, processing everything he'd just been told. "And yet, you're telling me that you stopped after Mrs. Koep."

"Oh yeah. Definitely."

Crane cocked his head to one side. "It's funny. Most who describe the sensation of murder the way you just did find it extremely difficult to give up. Most of the time, it actually escalates."

Coleman shrugged. "I can't explain it. A few days later, it all seemed like a dream. Like it never happened. The thrill just sort of died away. After a while, I just sorta forgot I even did it."

"And the Koeps' shades? Did you feed on them?"

"Oh, heck no! I went back to where I hid their bodies...and those blue bottle things that Candace gave me...but they was all gone. After a while, I started thinking I really did dream it all. That it had all just been made up in my head or something."

"And Candace was the one to supply you with the ghost bottles?" He'd already suspected as much, but wanted confirmation.

"Only the ones I used for the Koeps'. I honestly have no idea where the ones in my basement came from."

Crane turned to look into the mirror, then back to Coleman. "The answer there is obvious. Candace wanted you to take the fall for these murders. She's been the one pulling the strings all along. But why leave you alone all this time, only to set you up for the murders now?"

Coleman's head turtlenecked down into his shoulders as Crane asked the question.

"What?" He asked. "What aren't you telling me?"

The EMT clamped down on his tongue.

"Change of topic for a moment." Crane decided to return to the first question in a moment. For now, something else was bothering him. "Why exactly did you come to me at Samantha Reardon's house this morning? Why ask for me now? You had to know I would have very little sympathy for you. It's true, I already knew you weren't the serial killer. I wasn't going to allow them to charge you with these other murders. But why ask for me specifically? Especially knowing how much you despise me."

"Because *she* asked me to." Coleman's hand shot up to his mouth as his eyes widened. "I don't know why I just said that."

"Well, did she or didn't she?"

He shrugged. "I...I don't rightly know. I don't remember her tellin' me. But..."

"But you felt compelled to do so nonetheless."

Coleman gave a slow nod.

"So back to my original question. What has happened recently to get her to try to frame you for the Sin-Eater murders?"

"I...well..." He glanced around the room once more with nervous sweeps of his eyes. "...well, after I killed Mr. and Mrs. Koep, Candace...she stopped seein' me. Wouldn't even look at me. I got upset. Started goin' to her house at all hours, just tryin' to get her to take me back." Coleman cleared his throat, then nodded toward the mirror. "That state trooper ain't back there is he?"

Crane's blood ran cold. "No. Why?"

He cleared his throat again, then tried to wipe a stream of sweat from his brow with the sleeve of his orange jumpsuit. "Well, one night, I went by there and some feller was walkin' out the door. Didn't recognize him at first. It was too dark out. But the way he skipped outta her house, he looked happy enough. Knew he must have been the lucky winner for the evenin'. Only, it wasn't a weekend. It was a Tuesday night. Figured the feller must have been really special or something to get that kind of attention.

"Then I saw him again. This time at the Thornton murder two nights ago. Recognized the arrogant strut instantly then."

Crane sat up in his chair. "Stratton."

Coleman nodded again. "I saw Candace last night. Told her

what I seen. Demanded she give me one more chance to be with her and…"

Suddenly, there was a pounding against the mirror. Coleman let out a ghastly shriek before cringing in his seat. Crane turned to the glass, stood, then walked out of the door to be greeted instantly by Alex Davenport.

"We've got to get to the hospital!" the reporter shouted.

"Why?"

"Earlier this morning—like around two-thirty or so—Corporal Stratton came by Kili's room. He was doing something…whispering in her ear or something…when I walked in on him. He made some excuse about praying over her or something. Said he was just checking on her to make sure she was okay, but I never felt right about it and…"

Before he could finish the thought, Crane was already sprinting down the hallway of the station, waving Davenport to follow. Slate yelled after them, but the two ignored him before slipping through the front doors and climbing into Davenport's sports car.

CHAPTER
THIRTY-FOUR

Jasper Community Medical Center
Morriston, Kentucky
December 21
10:05 PM

E zekiel Crane had already hopped out of the car before Alex had come to a complete stop at the turnabout in front of the hospital. The reporter watched as the tall mountain man dashed through the spinning doorway and made straight for the bank of elevators directly opposite the information desk. Fortunately, no one seemed to be manning the desk, so there was no one to reprimand Crane for his brash behavior.

With a grumble, Alex parked the car and caught up to Crane just before the elevator door opened.

"I don't like this," Crane said quietly as they stepped inside and pressed the button for Kili's floor.

"What? That Stratton might be the Sin-Eater and that he's after Kili?"

"No. I don't think Stratton is the killer. Yes. I do believe she's in danger...whether by Stratton or the Sin-Eater. But that's not what I'm uncomfortable about." He checked his watch as the elevator began its crawl up to the fourth floor. "It's just after ten in the evening. There should have been someone at the desk. Should have been security guards there, at least."

"But surely this guy couldn't get rid of all the staff. Not without making some major noise and alerting the police anyway. I mean, even with a skeleton crew, a hospital this size should have enough people to..."

The elevator dinged and the door slid open to a scene so ghastly Alex could find no words to describe it. The florescent ceiling lights flickered on and off, the hospital's battery backup system struggling to power the floor. Blood coated the walls and floor directly outside the elevator's doors. A security guard lay face down in a crimson pool, two circular holes dotting the back of his shirt.

"Dear Lord."

Crane gasped, then dropped to one knee before rolling the guard over. Though his face was smeared with blood, the guard looked to be young. No more than twenty or so. Seeing this, Crane eased back into the elevator with a sigh.

"Thank God," he said.

Alex's eyes widened at the comment, but Crane shook his head. "I mourn this one's loss, to be sure, Mr. Davenport. But I was concerned it might be a dear friend of mine. Of course, even as we speak, Mason Ellis might be in a similar state. I managed to glimpse around the corridor as I checked on our dead guard here. Things look equally as grim at the nurses' station, I'm afraid."

Considering Crane's words, Alex bent down and pulled up his right pant's leg, revealing a leather holster containing a Smith & Wesson .38. He pulled it from its case and cocked the hammer.

Crane raised an eyebrow as he appraised the weapon.

"Look," Alex said. "After everything I've been through... between your crazy cousin in New York and those Leechers a few months back, I've learned my lesson. I never go anywhere feeling helpless anymore. From now on, I'm packing."

Crane offered him an approving nod. "This is Kentucky, Mr. Davenport. People carrying sidearms isn't the scandal it might be in other parts of the country. Keep the gun handy. We may well need it."

With that, Crane edged toward the corner of the elevator and peered around. Then, quietly, he gestured for Alex to follow and dashed off down the corridor. Keeping the gun pointed to the ground, Alex quickly followed, struggling to keep from slipping on the blood-slick floors of the hospital. Within seconds, the two were huddled down beside the nurses' station, and looking around the corner toward Kili's room.

A nurse, her light blue scrubs now almost purple with wet blood, lay unmoving in the hallway. The deputy who'd been assigned to guard Kili's hospital room lay on top of the nurse, as if trying to shield her with his own body.

"My question is, where are all the patients?" Alex asked. "Surely they've heard what's going on. They've got phones in their rooms. Family members visiting. Why isn't anyone calling 911?"

"An excellent question," Crane whispered, poking his head up over the nurses' desk before bringing it back down to look at Alex. "But I suspect some sort of magic is at play here. The nurse on the other side of this desk appears uninjured. Yet, she is staring off into space like a corpse. I can see her breathing, but there appears to be no motor activity in her limbs. Could be some paralytic, but I conjure that the Willow Hag is behind this to some degree. I've seen something similar to this before." He paused. Cleared his throat. "In Somerset. The night Granny died."

Alex recalled his account of that night. How everyone in the special rehabilitation ward seemed to be in a dreamlike state. The story had sent chills down his spine at the time. Now, living it for himself, he felt utterly overwhelmed. Magic. Monsters. Serial killers that fed on ghosts. It was so far beyond his experiences. So far beyond what he believed to be real...notions he would have scoffed at a little over a year ago. Before he'd met Obadiah Jackson. Before he'd met Ezekiel Crane.

"...Alex?"

"Sorry. Just thinking."

Crane nodded. His face was about as grim as Alex had ever seen it. "I asked if you were ready. We need to get to Ms. Kili's room."

At the sound of the redhead's name, Alex gripped the gun tighter in his hand and jerked his head in a determined nod.

"Good. Then, keep your eyes open for an ambush and let's go."

The overhead lights flickered again as the two rushed to Kili Brennan's room and thrust open the door. The room was dark, lit only by the soft blue green glow of hospital monitors. They stood in the doorway, letting their eyes adjust before proceeding. But before they could do anything, a massive hand shot out from the dark, grabbing hold of Alex's wrist and flinging him forward. He tumbled end over end; his gun flung from his grasp to clatter somewhere across the room. Before he knew it, Alex crashed against the A/C wall unit with a blinding smack to the head. Remembering the danger they were in, the reporter sought to right himself. He twisted around and came up to his feet in a boxer's stance, only to be greeted by the barrel of a .40 caliber Glock pointed directly at his face.

CHAPTER
THIRTY-FIVE

Crane stared slack-jawed in the entrance of the hospital room, his eyes adjusting to the darkness faster than most. He watched as Alex twisted across the floor, striking his head against the air conditioner and coming up ready to fight. Of course, it was a moot point. The Sin-Eater stood between the two of them, training twin firearms at both of them simultaneously.

There were three things Ezekiel Crane knew within the first three seconds of entering the room. First, Kili wasn't there. Her bed was empty. The equipment that should have been monitoring her vitals were flat-lining across the screen, their wires dangling uselessly off the side of the bed.

The second thing he knew was that the gun-toting madman before them was not, in fact, Corporal Cody Stratton of the Kentucky State Troopers. Though the burlap sack with skull-like paint across the front prohibited identifying the killer, he was far too short to be the trooper. Not just short, but stocky too. His clothes practically bulged with muscles...oddly malformed, asymmetrical muscles. Muscles similar to something he'd seen before...someone he'd seen before.

One-Eyed Jack.

The third thing he knew—confirmation to what he'd already suspected really—was the identity of the killer and it tore at his heart like a dull, rusty blade. The sorrow was doubly so when Crane thought about the fury he'd unleashed earlier that day.

"Jimmy," he said quietly. "You need to stop this."

The Sin-Eater's head whipped around to look at Crane with baleful eyes beneath his cowl, though he didn't respond. The hand that held the gun on Crane trembled, betraying his fear.

"Jimmy?" Davenport asked, prompting the killer to re-acquire his aim at the reporter. "You mean, the kid?"

"Indeed. I recognize the deformities of the One-Eyed Jack spores. The last time I saw her, I remarked to the Willow Hag the changes we'd all noticed in the boy. The rapid aging. The rash. Certain muscular abnormalities. She went so far as to admit that she'd been feeding the spores to the boy to help him grow faster. I thought at the time that it was no doubt to expedite maturity so she would have a sire for her heir." He looked at the Sin-Eater with sad eyes. "I realize now just how wrong my assumption had been. It was to prepare him for this." His eyes froze on the Sin-Eater. "When Cian Brennan was infected by One-Eyed Jack, it not only affected his stature...physically changing him into a monster. It also warped his mind. Drove him insane. The Willow Hag knew this. It was her purpose all along. With the use of the spores, she was preparing him for the role of the Sin-Eater and this parody of the Ghostfeast."

"Parody?" the Sin-Eater spat. "You've seen what I can do, Ezekiel. You've seen the power I've got! You think it's a big joke, do you?"

Crane held up his hands and shook his head. "It's anything but a joke, Jimmy. In fact, it may be the grimmest of all tragedies. You've been sent on a fool's errand by the one who looks like your mother."

"You mean, my Mother-Bride? The one that's chose me to be her mate?"

"Eeew," Davenport said. "Dude, that's your mom."

"Alex, hush!" Crane said. "The Willow Hag has no intention of being in the Kindred body of Candace Staples when it comes time to conceive. She's chosen…another for that."

"Kili," Davenport said as if realizing it for the first time.

"Precisely." Crane turned his attention back to the Sin-Eater. "Which is why I don't believe you are here to kill her." He pointed to the empty bed. "So where is she, Jimmy? Where's Kili?"

The Sin-Eater laughed as he pulled the cowl from his head. Crane heard Davenport gasp at the sight. Jimmy was no longer recognizable. Although his countenance was easily that of an eighteen year old man, the shape of his skull was warped. The left side swelled with mere bits of hair hanging onto the scalp in rough patches. His left eye had swollen nearly shut with the mass of skin and tissue that had grown so rapidly over the last few days. His mouth sagged at one corner, showing brittle and chipped yellow teeth underneath the lips.

Crane's own eyes widened at the sight. He'd been completely unprepared for the child's visage and he felt his rage begin the boil again. This time, however, it wasn't directed at Jimmy Staples, but rather at the creature that had caused this on an eleven year old child. "Oh, Jimmy," he said.

"Don't!" The Sin-Eater stiffened. "Don't feel sorry for me. My Mother-Bride gave me the power to do what I've dreamed about since my mama died. Gave me the power to destroy you. You ain't nothin', Ezekiel Crane. You might've got the upper hand on me earlier today…unleashin' that devil curse on me like that…"

"You did what?" Davenport asked, but both Crane and the Sin-Eater ignored him.

"…but I'm prepared for ya now. And I ain't scared of you no more. Because of you, my mama is dead. It's your fault and it's Mrs. Crane's fault. I can't do nothin' against her now…she's outta my reach, but I sure can make you suffer the way I have."

"Seriously," Davenport continued. "Will someone explain to me what's going on? Since when did the kid start hating you? You guys took him in when his mom was killed by One-Eyed Jack. You guys were close. You all were set on adopting him... until those Kindred showed up."

"You forget, Mr. Davenport, that during his time with us, he was closer still to Granny's apprentice, Delores McCrary," Crane explained, his hands still up submissively. "Who turned out to be possessed by the Willow Hag. The Hag has had quite a while to poison Jimmy against the Crane clan, as well as teach him forbidden arts such as those he's using for his ghost feeding rituals." Crane looked back to Jimmy. "Which begs the question...if you're so hell-bent on killing me, why am I not dead yet? You have me at a grave disadvantage with those pistols of yours. Why not just pull the trigger?"

"Don't think I won't!"

"Actually, that's precisely what I think. Or rather, I think you can't. I don't think the Willow Hag will allow you to do it."

Jimmy sneered at this; his twisted lip stretching at an impossible angle across his deformed face. "I can do whatever I want. My Mother-Bride doesn't control me."

"Like she controlled poor Eugene Coleman? Spinning her magic against him. Possessing him in much the same way she did Delores to have him kill the last Sin-Eater and his wife?"

"So that's what happened?"

"Alex, please...remain quiet."

"Sorry."

"Are you sure she's not doing the same with you even as we speak, Jimmy?"

The boy laughed. It was a deep-throated bellow of a laugh. "Wow. Ezekiel Crane, the 'genius'. The cursed man who seems to know everyone's deepest thoughts and can stare into everyone's souls. What a joke you are."

Crane's eyes narrowed. "No, it wasn't her that controlled Mr.

Coleman. It was you. Somehow, you've learned the Hag's secret to inhabiting another person and you murdered the Koeps through his hands."

"And that whore, Samantha Reardon. Oh, I was there all right. Guiding and directing the conversation. Playing with her small little mind. But it really was Gene's hands what drew the knife across her throat. Oh, that one was actually quite a lot of fun lookin' back on it." A small growl slipped out from Jimmy's throat. "Actually, it was doubly so usin' that creep to do the killin' too…after what he did to my mama. After he defiled her like that."

Crane clenched his jaw tight, his mind racing through thousands of variables in the course of a second.

"And who else have you used like this, Jimmy? Who else defiled Candace during her regular weekend trysts?"

"Oh, you'll find out soon enough," he laughed. "Like you said, I ain't allowed to kill ya. But I sure as hell can destroy you." Giggling, he raised his guns up into the air, then carefully lowered them to the floor before backing away. "That's why I'm doin' this. That's why I'm givin' myself up." More giggles. "'Cause it's all set in motion now. I got one more ghost to feast on and it's gonna tear you up inside."

Davenport's eyes widened. "Kili!"

"Jimmy, where's Kili now?" Crane said, moving over to the boy and grabbing him by the slimmer of his two wrists. But Jimmy merely continued to laugh as he fell backwards into Kili's hospital bed, moving his unnaturally augmented arms and legs up and down the way children do to make angels in the snow.

"For me to know and you to find out," he said after a minute, continuing to make his imaginary snow angel. "For me to know and you to find out. For me to know and you to find out. For me to know and you to find out…" He continued repeating the phrase over and over until Sheriff Slate and a squad of deputies arrived and took him back to the police station to be booked.

CHAPTER
THIRTY-SIX

Crane Homestead
December 23
4:56 PM

E zekiel Crane dropped into his chair in the living room of his ancestral home, pinching his nose to stave off the headache he could feel coming on. It had been almost two days since Jimmy's arrest and Kili was still missing. Sheriff Slate and his deputies were no longer optimistic about their chances to find the former FBI analyst alive and were about to give up the search. Jimmy had not been cooperative, continuing to chant the childish gibberish he began inside Kili's hospital room.

"It's for me to know and you to find out. It's for me to know and you to find out. It's for me to know and you to find out."

For all the sympathy Crane tried to muster for the child—corrupted as he was by the Willow Hag—he was having more and more difficulty feeling anything but ire for Jimmy Staples. The very thought of it made him cringe. *Granny would smack me silly for that, Crane. She had no end of love and mercy to show even the most vile of creatures.*

Still, despite knowing that, it didn't make things any easier. At the moment, deputies were loading Jimmy up to transport him to the Jasper County Mental Health facility for psychological evaluation. Crane's sister, Jael, was on her way down to Morriston to conduct her own tests on the boy since she was now the world's foremost expert in the effects of the One-Eyed Jack spores. The hope was that she'd be able to re-discover the cure Granny had concocted to treat Crane's and Kili's own exposure when confronting Cian Brennan at the Devil's Teeth a while back.

There'd been no word from Candace Staples either. Whether she was aware that Jimmy had been arrested or not, she was nowhere to be found and hadn't bothered to try to see him during his incarceration. Cody Stratton was still M.I.A. as well. Numerous calls to his superiors in Lexington and Frankfort had been useless. They'd been unaware of his activities these last few weeks and had no idea he was even in Boone Creek. He'd already been suspended for failing to show up for his patrol shifts and the troopers were now conducting a statewide search for him.

As for Crane himself, he'd exhausted every trick in his considerable tool belt to try to locate Kili. Even dousing had been unsuccessful. It was as if she'd simply fallen off the face of the earth.

So, Crane had been busying himself with preparing for what he knew was coming. He'd gone to Bearsclaw Gully to visit Judith Greer one more time about the Feast and asking her for a particularly unusual favor.

He'd sent Davenport off on a fool's errand, in hopes of keeping him out of harm's way until this affair was finally over. He would need the reporter's skills later. Much better to keep him out of the Willow Hag's crosshairs for now.

And finally, he'd gone to Noah McGuffin's compound to confront Asherah about her role in the Willow Hag's scheme.

He'd been met with considerable apprehension by the Caribbean witch. Things had not ended that encounter on a positive note, but he thought, in the end, she'd finally come around. Only time would tell in that regard.

So now, there was very little to do, but sit here. Rest a bit. And wait.

With a sigh, Crane reached over to the end table next to his chair and picked up the ghost bottle containing the spirit of his brother.

"Then there's you," he spoke to the bottle. "I finally get you back after all these years, only to lose you to that witch again." He shook his head. "Brother, I have no idea what to do to help you. For the first time in memory, I'm truly at a loss."

Granny, of course, would have known precisely what to do. He could even imagine some of her responses to this crisis. First, she would never have allowed him to wallow in his own self-pity as he had through much of this investigation. She would have grabbed Crane by the ear and dragged him outside, not allowing him to return until Kili was found. She definitely wouldn't approve of the plan he'd finally concocted that should set everything right.

"But I don't even know where to start," he said to the bottle again.

"How about at the beginning," came a soft feminine voice from behind him. He didn't even need to turn around to know it was Asherah.

So she's here earlier than expected. This might not bode well.

"You obviously know the way into my home," he said. "Therefore, you know the way back out as well."

"Not quite yet, my love. We didn't exactly finish our conversation yesterday. We still have much to discuss."

He sat unmoving in his chair, keeping his gaze fixed straight ahead and refusing to acknowledge her presence with even the slightest of glances. After a moment, he gestured toward the couch. She accepted the offer and glided into view.

"There are some things I need to tell you, Ezekiel," she said, as she took a seat. "Things you need to understand before anything else happens."

"Like why you were at Bearsclaw Gully the other day."

She froze, then offered a slight nod.

"No need. I already know."

She let out a soft, nervous laugh. "I highly doubt..."

"You were there in preparation for the Ghostfeast. The *real* Ghostfeast."

Asherah visibly tensed.

"Not the facade the Hag sent Jimmy Staples on to garner my attention."

She swallowed. "Then you know..."

Crane nodded. "What I don't understand is why you're helping her with it. You, of all people, know what she's capable of...know exactly what she is."

"I'm helping her because of my love for you, Ezekiel. It's the only way to..."

"I'm fully aware," he said, rising from his chair. "But you have no right. Too many people have died because of this. And Kili is out there right now...I don't know if she's alive or dead... but she's out there and it's because of me. It's because of this blasted Ghostfeast. And I'm not going to stand for it any longer." He walked over and pointed down at her. "So are you going to tell me where Kili Brennan is or am I going to have to tear the Gully apart piece by piece until I find her?"

From somewhere off in the distance, a raven cawed.

Asherah blinked at the sound.

"Ezekiel, you wouldn't..."

"Try me. My death curse almost consumed Jimmy just the other day. I'm losing control of it and I think you know there's a very good reason for that. My time is running short. The curse has an expiration date and with it, so do I." He paused, waiting until Asherah nodded her understanding. "Ms. Kili has been an innocent pawn for far too long. The Hag's already started the ritual of Corruption on her...preparing her to be her permanent vessel."

"And what makes you think she has her? She gave Jimmy explicit orders to leave her alone. She only wanted to up the ante for you to catch the Sin-Eater. It was Jimmy who went after Kili...of his own accord...against the *Mater-Matris*'s express wishes."

Crane sneered. "So we're still calling her that, are we?"

"Whether you believe me or not, I'm doing all of this for you."

"Then prove it. Tell me where I can find Ms. Kili. You and I both know she doesn't need to be part of this."

Asherah sighed. "Please, Ezekiel. Don't make me do this. Don't ask me to be the Judas here."

"Aren't you playing that role already, Ash? I know that's why you came here tonight. Tonight of all other nights. I know that's why the Willow Hag sent you to me. I believe you're here to offer me an invitation."

"This is a no-win situation, Ezekiel. It cannot end well for you."

Crane hefted the ghost bottle in his hand and showed it to Asherah. "Maybe not. But then, there are more important things in the world than me."

"Not to me!" This time, Asherah shot up from her seat to meet Crane's stare. "The entire world can wither and die for all I care. You're the only thing that matters to me."

Crane's face softened as he watched the tears trickle down Asherah's caramel-colored cheeks. He reached up, brushing them away with his thumb while cupping her face in the palm of his hand.

"It's fine, Ash. Everything has been leading up to this. It's why the Willow Hag chose me to begin with." He smiled at her. "One final confrontation with her and it'll all be over. Who knows? Maybe then we can finally..." He trailed off, unable to finish the sentence. "So tell me, Asherah. Where can I find Ms. Kili."

The Caribbean woman's emerald green eyes looked up into his, glistening with the tears she seemed unable to stop. She rose up on her toes, gently placing a kiss on his lips before pulling back.

"I'm sorry, Ezekiel," she said quietly, looking past his left shoulder. "But you're right. I am playing the role of Judas...even now. And I betray you with a kiss."

Before Crane could react, a powerful set of arms wrapped tight around Crane's neck, forcing him down to his knees.

"Good to see ya again, Zeke," laughed a high-pitched male voice in his ear. "I'd love to say this wasn't personal, but ya know...it kind of is." Crane twisted his head to see the smiling face of Corporal Cody Stratton. Thick, wet strands of saliva oozed from his twisted grin as the trooper applied more pressure to Crane's neck. "This is for what ya did to my daddy."

The trooper slammed a fist against Crane's kidney.

"And this is for nearly ruinin' my life with those accusations you made about that whore of a sister of yours."

Another kidney punch. Crane heaved for breath.

"Cody!" Asherah shouted. "Enough!"

"Just know this, Crane," Stratton whispered in his ear. "This time tomorrow, you'll be little more than a memory and that pretty lil' sister of yours? Well, let's just say I aim to pay her a visit or two. You know...to console her as she mourns your loss."

He laughed at this while sending a third punch into Crane's back.

"Cody...beware of..."

But before Crane could finish his warning, he felt the prick of a long needle entering the base of his neck. He struggled against the trooper's surprisingly strong arms, trying to free himself, but it was no use. With each beat of his heart, the drug now pumping through his system took a stronger hold on him and he felt the world around him fading fast.

The last thing he heard before passing out completely was the sound of Asherah's steady breathing beside his ear, then, "I'm so sorry, my love."

CHAPTER
THIRTY-SEVEN

December 23
The Hour of Yule

The first thing Crane was aware of when he began to regain consciousness was a weight on his abdomen and chest. The second thing was that neither his arms or legs could move. The cold bite of metal caressed his wrists and ankles telling him he was currently in some sort of shackles or chains. Handcuffs, maybe.

As awareness increased, so did an understanding of his surroundings. Though he knew his eyes were open, he could see nothing. His eyelashes brushed against some sort of fabric, telling him he was blindfolded. He could see a warm glow through the material however, and the acrid tang of smoke filled his nostrils, so he assumed he was near a bonfire of some sort. The air around him was frigid. Tiny flecks of something wet smacked haphazardly against his exposed skin, telling him he was outdoors and that it was still snowing.

And finally, he could hear the random rustle of clothing, the occasional cough, and a chorus of whispers around him, informing Crane that he was surrounded on all sides by a large group of people and all their attention seemed to be directed at him.

Though his head felt sluggish from the sedative he'd been dosed with, he managed to find his voice. "I believe," he said, deep and commanding, "that you can now take the blindfold off. I'm quite aware of where I now lie."

"Oh, sweet Ezekiel," cooed a soft silky voice in his ear. "But I rather like you all bound up and helpless like this. No tellin' what a gal might wanna do with a gift like this."

"Be that as it may, Hag, you and I both know the blindfold and chains are not allowed."

"Oh, poo," she said. He felt her fingers working at the knot around the kerchief acting as the blindfold. "You never were any fun, Ezekiel Crane."

A moment later, the blindfold was off and Crane blinked back the tears as his eyes adjusted to the trio of large bonfires surrounding them. As his vision began to clear, he discovered his assumption had been correct and he was indeed in the fire pit town center of Bearsclaw Gully. A large group of onlookers, adorned in dark robes and hoods, encircled the stone slab he now rested on—no doubt the entire roster of citizens of the settlement. Finally, he looked up to see Candace Staple's grinning face hovering only a few inches from his own. Her body straddled his at the waist. She, too, wore a silk robe—blood red and opened completely down the front to reveal that she was wearing nothing underneath.

Her grin broadened when she realized he had noticed and she leaned forward and kissed him deep on the mouth.

"Oh, Ezekiel, I've waited so long for this night," she said when she pulled away from his lips.

"If you recall, I denounced your claim on me almost two decades ago. It's the reason you cursed me. So, if you don't mind..." He nodded to the shackled chains around his wrists.

"You never have truly understood our bargain, have you? Even after all these years...you never understood exactly what I had planned for you."

Though he'd recently surmised the answer to this accusation, for now, he thought it best to play dumb.

"Simple. You wanted me to sire your heir. The same as you were grooming Jimmy for."

Her face twisted in an irritated scowl. "That little runt was nothin' but a pawn. I would have never soiled myself with his inbred seed."

Crane turned his attention back to the crowd, his eyes scanning the shadows underneath each of the hoods until he came to the face he was looking for...Cody Stratton.

"So that's why he's part of this. The closest thing to aristocracy as you can get in the New World. The last heir to a long bloodline from the old country. He's your new consort."

Her smile returned. "When...or rather *if*...the need arises, yes. You were always so clever."

Crane found himself getting bored with the conversation. It was time to move things forward. Time to end this once and for all.

"So tell me...*Hag*...what have you done with Kili Brennan? I assume Cody removed her from the hospital room before your little monster could get to her."

Candace pursed her lips in a pout. "Oh, you are such a grouch. It's always Kili this and Kili that. If you and the negress didn't have such a history together, I'd swear you were in love with the red-headed tart."

He refused to take the bait. "Show me Kili or kill me now," he said. "We're just wasting valuable time otherwise." He motioned up to the sky with his eyes. "Tick-tock, Candace. Tick-tock. Yule won't be around much longer."

In response, she rolled her eyes and climbed off of Crane before looking over at Stratton. "Release him."

"But Candy!"

"I said release him. He's right. We can't do this with him chained up. He's gotta be free."

Stratton scowled, before moving over to the stone altar, withdrawing a set of keys from his pockets, and unlocking Crane's shackles. Before he could move, however, the state trooper placed a hand on Crane's chest, holding him down on the slab. "Don't try none of your tricks, Zeke. Candy may need you alive for this, but she don't need you necessarily in one piece."

Crane grabbed hold of the trooper's wrist with his index finger and thumb carefully placed on a nerve cluster near the joint. Stratton's mouth stretched wide as a bolt of searing pain shot up his arm to just below his shoulder. Crane smiled up at him.

"I don't need the death curse to deal with the likes of you, Mr. Stratton," he said, pressing down tighter on the nerve cluster. "Touch me again, and you'll never use this arm again."

The younger man stumbled back, grasping at his arm in obvious agony. Crane sat up on the stone altar, then stepped down and straightened his clothes before looking up at Candace. "Now, take me to Kili or kill me. But without my friend, you'll get nothing from me."

Candace offered the slightest of curtsies. "As you wish, child. As you wish."

She turned and began making her way to the closest row of hovels, gesturing for him to follow. As they walked, Candace began to talk.

"The thing is, Ezekiel, tonight is what it's all been about." She glanced over at him. Her face appeared serene. Serious. Perhaps even the slightest trace of regret, as well. "Our deal. The curse. It's all been leading up to this moment."

"So I gather. I also assume that Judith Greer left out one little tidbit concerning the rules of the Ghostfeast. The part that states that the voluntary sacrifice must be a seventh son of a seventh son?"

They turned a corner and started heading in the direction of Mrs. Greer's wood-shrouded home.

"So you *have* figured it out. Once again, perhaps I've underestimated you."

Crane let out a quiet laugh. "You underestimate nothing, Hag. I daresay you anticipate almost everything an adversary might do in any given situation. Please don't attempt to flatter me with false praise."

The two reached the wood line encircling the house. With a swipe of Candace's hand, the trees and bramble began to shift and sway until they parted, making an easy path to the home. With her attention on creating the path, Crane slipped his hand in his coat pocket and smiled. They'd apparently not searched him very well before chaining him to the slab.

Good.

"After you, dear boy," Candace said, gesturing for Crane to take the path she'd created.

He complied and a moment later, the two were standing at the door of the immaculately maintained residence of the only person in the world capable of performing the Ghostfeast ritual. Without knocking, the door opened to reveal the small sweet-looking frame of Judith Greer. She was looking up at Crane, a warm smile across her face.

"Come in, Mr. Crane," she said. "Bless my heart, come in. You'll catch yer death of cold standin' out there in the winter chill like dat."

"We certainly wouldn't want that, now would we Mrs. Greer," Crane said, smirking at the Willow Hag as he stepped inside.

For her part, the thing living inside Candace Staples made no attempt to follow. Instead, she stood there at the doorway, looking with an impatient glare at the old black woman. After a moment, she spoke, "Well?"

"Well, what?" Mrs. Greer replied.

Candace rolled her eyes. "Are you going to invite me in or not?"

Judith glanced over at Crane, who nodded his approval. "Unfortunately, it's a necessary evil. She can't come in without an invitation and we really need to get this over with."

The black woman sighed. "Very well. But not that abomination of a body. The real Willow Hag may freely come inside."

Instantly, Candace Staples dropped to the cold earth, her eyes staring passively up into the dark, overcast night sky. A moment later, a flicker of a shadow, followed close by a gust of death cold air, swept past the threshold and into the home. A moment later, a vaguely humanoid form materialized in a cluster of shadows on the other side of the room.

"If you two are conspirin' against me," came the sound of an ancient grandmotherly voice, "you better think twice."

Judith Greer closed the door and turned to face the shadow thing across the room.

"You ain't got no choice in this, old woman," the Hag continued. "It's as much yer destiny as it is his. You can't turn yer back on the Feast and you know it."

"Don't reckon I have much aim to," Mrs. Greer said. She straightened up her bent frame and patted Ezekiel Crane on the shoulder. "But it don't mean I have to like it none. I'd much rather perform the ritual on you, truth be told."

Crane held up a hand. "Ladies," he said. "Time wanes. The Yule has nearly passed. We should proceed with all due haste." He looked over at the shadow. "You were going to show me Ms. Kili, I believe."

Without waiting for the Willow Hag to respond, the black woman took Crane by the hand. "Come dear. I'll show you to them. Just come with me."

Them? What did she mean by...

They rounded a corner to enter a small bedroom with two twin beds sitting side by side. Asherah Richardson sat in a wooden chair between the two beds, placing a wet washcloth on the sweat-beaded forehead of Kili Brennan. Ash looked up at Crane, giving him a sad nod, before returning to her ministrations on the redhead.

From what he could see, Kili slept soundly in the bed closest to the door. The strange rash and boils were already beginning to dissipate. She looked peaceful. At ease with her environment.

But when he saw who occupied the bed next to her, Crane's blood began to boil.

It was his brother, Josiah.

CHAPTER
THIRTY-EIGHT

Judith Greer's Home
Bearsclaw Gully
December 23
The Yule Hour

E zekiel Crane wheeled around in rage, searching for the shadowy specter of the Willow Hag.

"WITCH!" he shouted. "Where are you, woman?"

His pulse pounded hard against the temple of his skull, the anticipated effect of his death curse preparing to unleash its fury on the subject of Crane's wrath. Only here, within the confines of Judith's home, the curse had no power. He'd been disconnected from it the moment he'd stepped foot through the threshold.

This, no doubt, was why the Willow Hag had chosen this place for their final show down. Crane wasn't sure whether the death curse could work on a spiritual being such as the Hag. Chances were, she didn't either, and wanted to be prepared just in case.

"What is my brother doing here?"

He turned to Ms. Greer.

"I'm truly sorry, Mr. Crane," Judith said. From the frown lines running across her face, she was sincere. "I din't have no choice in da matter. Da Willow Hag's goons brought him inside just minutes before you woke up. But he's fine. I promise you that. He's safer here than anywhere else on God's green earth."

"Hag! Speak to me!" He turned back around to face the home's living room. "Why is Josiah here?"

There was a dull-throated chuckle from somewhere in the room ahead. "He's added incentive, dearie," the Willow Hag's grandmotherly voice said. "Look on the nightstand beside him."

Crane looked back into the bedroom and peered at the nightstand. The ghost bottle, containing his brother's soul, rested safely on top of the marble top of the stand.

"See? I aim to make things right, Ezekiel," the Hag continued. "All the harm I did to yer family. Yer brother. All of it...in one fell swoop...I aim to fix it all."

"Ezekiel, please," Asherah said in a hushed tone. "Hear her out. You know as well as I that you don't have much time."

He looked back at the living room. The Willow Hag's shadow had solidified more in the few minutes she'd been invited into Judith Greer's house. She was gathering her power. Becoming more substantial. Yet, still, she hadn't moved from her original spot.

Curious.

He made a quick visual search of the place and quickly understood why. The hallway leading to the bedroom was protected by numerous Kongonese wards carved into the wood paneling of the hall entrance.

"Your brother and friend are quite safe from her," Judith said, noticing his reaction upon seeing the wards. "She can't enter their room unless I allow it."

"Thank you," he said to the black woman before turning his attention back to the Hag. "All right, witch. You obviously have a deal to make. State it."

"It's simple, child," the Hag said. Her voice was calm. Confident. Unemotional. "You're dying. As Asherah pointed out, you ain't got much time left. It's why you lost control of the curse the other day with Jimmy. It's why even now, you struggle to keep it in check. The death curse I placed on you had a time limit. Yuletide. Today. That's when it matures. When it comes to its fruition." She looked over at the grandfather clock tick-tocking away in the corner of the living room. Eleventy-fifty. "At midnight, you'll be dead. Or…"

"Or…" He sighed. Resignation evident in his voice. "I volunteer to be the sacrifice in the Ghostfeast."

"Precisely." The Hag raised her spectral arms in victory. "But take heart! Yer sacrifice will save this ol' world from the Nameless Ones…forever! After you, there won't be no more need for Ghostfeasts. After they feed on yer soul, that death curse I placed on you will transfer to them…they'll waste away to nothin' and I…and the rest of the world…will finally be free of them vermin once and for all."

"Da rules of the Ghostfeast are very specific, Mr. Crane," Judith Greer interrupted. "The soul must voluntarily and knowingly sacrifice himself to the Feast. He can't be tricked or forced to do it. His soul can't be forcibly taken from him, lest the sacrifice be for nought. The soul must be contained in a ghost bottle specifically crafted to the sacrifice's own essence, too."

"Which is why I worked so hard to lure you to Bearsclaw Gully," the Hag added. "So Mrs. Greer here could size you up for yer own bottle."

The black woman glared at the Willow Hag's shadow and continued. "The Ghostfeast must take place on the Winter Solstice…Yule. And finally, as you guessed…and I'm sorry for keepin' this from you, Mr. Crane…but yes, the sacrifice must be the seventh son of a seventh son." She paused, then offered the slightest trace of a smile. "But here's the thing…the sacrifice must have at least one living male sibling to carry on his name.

Without the remembrance of that name, the sacrifice is wasted."

"And my name can't continue as long as Josiah is trapped in that bottle or in a coma."

"Exactly."

Both Crane and Judith turned to stare at the Willow Hag.

"Fine. Yes!" She let out a low wolfen growl. "Be the sacrifice and I'll free your brother."

"Not just of the bottle...free his mind and soul as well. He awakens. In his own body. Whole and healthy."

The Hag hesitated, then shrugged. "Fine. He'll be his own man once more."

"And Kili."

"Never!" If a ghostly vision was capable of spitting, the Willow Hag's spirit essence would have come close to doing it. "She's mine! I've marked her. She's my property. And you know as well as I do...the choice is now hers, Ezekiel Crane. Ain't nothin' I can do about that now. She has to decide."

Crane looked from the Hag to Kili, then back to the Hag, before turning and stepping into the bedroom and walking over to his friend's bed. He took a knee on the opposite side from where Asherah continued her healing rituals and leaned in to whisper in Kili's ear.

"I'm sorry, Ms. Kili. For everything I've put you through." He took her hand and squeezed it. "But my time is comin' to an end. You're going to have to make do on your own. At least, for the time being. You and my brother...you've got to work together. The time will come when you'll understand what I've done and I'll need you to be strong until that day comes."

He reached into his coat pocket and withdrew a tattered piece of fur and bone—the length of a yard stick—and placed it in her hand.

"Wait! What is that?" the Hag shouted from the living room. "What did you just give her."

Crane ignored the question. "Listen to the Taily-po, Kili. When the time comes to choose, I've a feeling he won't lead you astray."

"The Taily-po?" the Hag screamed. "No fair! You can't pass that on…"

"That's the one thing I most definitely can do, witch." Crane retorted without turning his eyes from Kili. "The tail rightfully belonged to Granny. I stole it to fight off the Leechers. It found Kili in the midst of all that. She's the rightful heir to the tail now and so is the Taily-po."

"Trickery! Deceit!" the Willow Hag shouted.

Crane smiled, leaning in and kissing his unconscious friend on the cheek before standing up and facing Judith Greer. "All right, Mrs. Greer. I offer myself in exchange for my brother and the safe returning of Kili to consciousness so that she can make her choice when the time is right."

The old woman grinned.

"Good," she said. "Then follow me down into the basement and we'll begin."

CHAPTER
THIRTY-NINE

Judith Greer's House
Bearsclaw Gully
January 23
11:59 PM

Asherah Richardson sat quietly in the bedroom, tears streaming down her cheeks. Her limbs felt numb. Her temples throbbed from crying. She still couldn't believe he'd gone through with it. She'd warned him. Begged him to leave things well enough alone...to leave town. But he wouldn't listen.

She wasn't entirely sure that he could have run far enough away to stave off the Willow Hag's death curse. He was destined to die tonight...no matter what. Unless, by some miracle, he could have the curse removed. Unless the curse was somehow rendered useless. Then, the Ghostfeast sacrifice wouldn't work the way the Willow Hag intended. Her machinations against the Nameless Ones would be exposed and they would undoubtedly make her pay dearly for her treachery.

Of course, she could dream of such a thing in a perfect world. But the here and now was hardly perfect.

A sudden male scream ripped through the house, echoing violently through the hallway into the guest bedroom. Then, everything was silent.

Asherah no longer attempted to stop the flow of tears. She let them flow freely as she grieved for her love.

She wasn't sure how much time had passed since the anguished cry of Ezekiel Crane lashed out at her soul like a cat-o'-nine tails. But when she heard a throat clearing at the hallway entrance, she startled awake and looked up to see the Willow Hag's shadow standing defiantly close to the wards.

"It's done, child," the Hag said. Surprisingly, her voice sounded sad as well. "Ezekiel's body is in the cellar. Do with it what you will."

"And Josiah? Kili? Like you promised?"

"They'll be along any minute now, dearie."

With that, the shadow turned and disappeared from view, leaving Asherah with two unconscious patients and an empty void torn straight from her soul.

"Oh, Ezekiel...what have you done?"

Deciding she needed to keep busy or risk falling into a malaise in which she might never recover, she dipped the washcloth into the bucket of water next to her feet, and swabbed at Kili's forehead.

"It's all because of you," she whispered into the redhead's ear. "Everything was fine until you came along."

Asherah, of course, knew that was a lie. Crane's problems began long before Ms. Brennan stepped foot in Boone Creek in search of her missing brother. The truth of the matter was, if anyone was to blame, it was Asherah herself. It had been her, after all, that had encouraged Ezekiel to seek out the Willow Hag...to grovel at her feet in a bid to bring his dead family back to life. When it was all said and done, she was to blame for the death of the only man she'd ever truly loved. Worse, the only man she could ever possibly respect.

"Why so sad, child?" came a voice at the doorway.

Asherah turned to find Judith Greer standing there, holding a strangely glowing blue bottle in her hand.

"Is that...is that...?"

Mrs. Greer gave a sad nod, then looked over at the two sleeping soundly in the twin beds.

"How's our patients?"

"What difference does it make? Ezekiel's gone. I don't even know why I'm still here."

"Didn't he come to your house yesterday in the dead of night? And while there, didn't he ask you to stay behind to look after his loved ones when he was gone? To look after his brother and Kili until they woke up?"

Asherah nodded.

"And why, do you suppose, Ezekiel would ask that of you... knowing how you'd feel?"

"Because..." She wiped a tear from her eyes, pulled her hand away, and unconsciously began studying the salty water on the top of her finger. "...that's just the way Ezekiel was."

The old woman smiled a broad, warm smile.

"And you don't think there was another reason for it?"

Asherah looked up from her hand. "What are you getting at?"

A groan came in the direction of Kili's bed as she began to stir, rustling the blankets that covered her.

"She's waking up," Judith Greer said happily. "It's almost time!"

There was a rattle of glass on marble and Asherah turned toward the nightstand next to Josiah's bed. The ghost bottle began to shake violently, shimmying across the stand's surface until it tipped over and crashed to the floor.

"Almost time indeed!" the black woman cackled.

Asherah stood up, glancing from Kili to Josiah as both began to stir in their beds. Her heart pounded. Something was happening...they were indeed awakening. But that was to be expected. The Willow Hag had given her word they would. So why was Judith so excited about it.

Suddenly, both Kili and Josiah bolted upright in their beds. "We've got to save Ezekiel!" they shouted simultaneously.

The old woman cackled again, clapping her hands together with joy. "Oh, sweet things...you will. You will."

Asherah's head whipped around, her brows furrowed at her.

"Speak woman! What are you tiptoeing around?" she yelled.

"Ezekiel Crane, my dear. He came to see me last night, after he finished with you." Judith Greer could hardly contain herself. She seemed about to explode from holding back what she knew. "He's got a plan, dear girl...and he needs the three of you to set him free!"

With that, the old blind woman laughed some more, turned around, and skipped down the hall carrying the bottle that imprisoned the soul of Ezekiel Crane.

9 781088 291924